THE CURVE AND THE TUSK

STUART CLOETE achieved world fame as the author of such best-selling novels as *Turning Wheels, Rags of Glory* and *How Young They Died*.

Of South African descent, he spent his childhood in the sparkling Paris of the early twentieth century, attended public school in England, then went straight into the army as one of the youngest commissioned officers of World War I.

After the war he lived for a time in France but in the 1920s, drawn increasingly by the land of his forebears, he went out to the Transvaal as a farmer.

He began to write in the 1930s and his first novel *Turning Wheels*, an instant success in both England America, launched him on a distinguished writing career. By the time of his death in 1976 he had published fifteen novels and seven volumes of short stories, as well as two volumes of autobiography.

STUART CLOETE

The Curve and the Tusk

FONTANA/Collins

First published in 1953 by William Collins Sons & Co Ltd
First issued in Fontana Books 1957
Second Impression March 1972
Third Impression February 1978

Made and printed in Great Britain by
William Collins Sons & Co Ltd Glasgow

*Dedicated to my wife, Rehna, who went elephant
hunting with me and endured without complaint the
dangers and hardships we encountered*

CONTENTS

AUTHOR'S NOTE

In the world there are four great classes of men upon whom we all live and without whom we should die. Those who reap the harvest of the soil, cultivating crops on its surface and burrowing beneath it for its hidden minerals: the farmers and the miners. Those who seek the harvest of the sea: the fisher people. And finally, those who reap the forest. The lumbermen, the foresters, and the hunters who seek meat, ivory, and skins. They are the pathfinders who precede the plough.

This is the story of one of these classes—of the hunters; and of elephants, the second greatest mammal on the face of the earth, the leviathan of the forest; of ivory and of love.

It is the life story of two elephants; some natives— Thongas, who with the other Africans of the coastal belt of Moçambique are loosely described as Shangaans by the Europeans; and some white men and women. Ethnologically, I have stayed close to the Ronga group or clan of the Thonga tribe, for it was with them we hunted. But I have added, for the sake of drama, certain Bantu customs common to the Swazis and Zulus, both of whom border and to some extent merge into the Shangaans. The very name 'Shangaan' coming from their Zulu conqueror Tshangaan. That being one of the surnames of Manukosi, the chief who subjugated them in the time of T'Chaka.

If some of their customs appear shocking to us, especially their sexual customs, we can console ourselves with the thought that ours, if they knew them, would probably shock the Bantu.

Some exception may be taken to the use of the word 'Kaffir' when describing Africans. This word is artistically more attractive than 'native' or 'African.' It was also current usage until relatively recent times, and would certainly have been employed by the old hunter Carew.

To obtain the material for this novel, months were spent in the bush, on elephant trails, in native kraals, in trekking from one place to another, from one water hole to another even less good. For weeks we watched elephants. We saw them making love, we saw baby elephants drinking from their mothers, we watched others playing, and tiny ones, not much bigger than a big dog, following their mothers, holding on to the switch of their tails with tiny trunks. We saw great, solitary bulls and were impressed by their magnificence.

We saw witch doctors and talked to hunters about the wild animals of Africa and the natives who were, till the white man came, their co-possessors of the continent. And out of all this the tale was born.

A tusk is measured along the outer curve. Its diameter is measured, and its circumference. But none of these measures, which are, like everything scientific, only a matter of measurement, tells anything of the elephant, any more than the rings in the section of a tree trunk give more than its age. In good years the distance between the ring is wider than in the bad, and on this statisticians, the meteorologists, and the botanists base their premises. But they cannot tell of the men who have rested in its shade, of the wild beasts that have sharpened their claws, or rubbed their backs against it; of the fires and storms that it has survived. A great tree is a monument in the world of vegetable matter. A great elephant a monument in the world of mammals, the greatest mammal on the face of the land, the leviathan of the forest. But no man knows the story of the dents and chips on its living ivory. The tale of its fights with other monsters, of dead men—its victims, carried like cordwood across them—of other elephants, old or wounded, supported by them as a man supports a fainting friend.

A man can say 'I have a daughter. She is fifteen years old. She is five foot three inches tall. She weighs a hundred and twelve pounds.' These are facts, scientific and calculable, but when he says 'I love her,' it means nothing to science. Yet that immeasurable love is the vital thing in their relationship.

The weights, lengths, circumferences and diameters of record tusks tell nothing of the elephants. The elephants that carried them, that have fought and loved as men fight and love, and have been killed in conflict with men, as men are killed in conflict with men.

The curve is one thing, calculable and without mystery.

8

The tusk is another—living matter, the sheath of a nerve greater in size than a man's arm, incalculable, pregnant with history. There must be no confusion between the word, the name and the thing itself. Nothing, not even a pencil can be fully described. The word, the name, are only approximations that carry associated ideas.

The book may please some people as a story; some it may interest as an easy-to-read study of natives and animals. But this is not its primary purpose. That purpose is to clarify to some extent the black African's outlook, to explain his great problem, which is the white problem, and to break down, if possible, the notion that he is a kind of half-baboon, incapable of love or sacrifice, to whom nothing is pure or sacred. He is, until spoilt by civilisation, a simple, stone- and iron-age man whose reactions are in no way comparable to those of the American Negro. In this simplicity lies the danger. He must either become more than he is—a civilised man—or become less than he is—a dangerous animal in human form. Which he becomes depends less on himself than on us.

From him we can learn something of our own dilemma. For in this new world that science has thrust upon us we are only children, unequipped to deal with the phenomena that surround us. As unequipped as Mashupa was when he was torn between the old ways and the new. As unequipped as a boy brought up in a good Christian home, thrust into the 'dog eat dog' of modern competitive business.

All around us voices call to us. The voice of the film, the voice of the radio, of television, of the press, and advertising, and none of it makes sense. There is no picture. There is only confusion, and crushed between the upper millstone of a collapsing economy and the lower of escape mechanisms, of an amusement industry that has arisen out of man's desperate desire to flee from himself into fantasy, the human spirit is being ground into dust.

We fear life, we fear death. We seek only comfort that is no more than a cushion between man and reality. We have no beliefs. Both God and the devil are now regarded as myths. With them has gone even the idea of good and evil. Living in cities of steel and concrete, eating processed foods, we have attempted to rise above nature, regarding ourselves as in some way superior to the laws that govern life. A man is no more alive and no less than a potted geranium on the window sill, or an elephant in the forests of Africa.

It was because of this, because I felt myself becoming divorced from reality, that I returned to the wilds. I chose Moçambique because there the paradox is most apparent. That is the place where one of the more obvious and convenient holes is pierced in time.

What I went to seek was a fresh perspective in a life where, though the new was easily obtainable, it was also easily avoided, and the primeval began only a few short hours away.

This book is an attempt to bring the past nearer, and to clarify our own tensions by dealing with the problems of relatively uncomplicated African natives. Like them our culture and our sanctions have broken down. Our morality, our home and business life, utterly changed by the theories that now govern our behaviour, by the labour-saving inventions which took women out of the home, by their emancipation and subsequent entry into business—even into such businesses as war. Looking at native problems, we can see in them a simpler microcosm of our own. Seeing this will not help us, except that before a thing can be dealt with it must be recognised.

Wherever else the system of *laissez faire* may operate, it fails in human relations, and can only lead to anarchy, and finally to communism, that is born of misery.

I feel that the religion of life goes beyond pantheism and hedonism, into a mystic worship of ecology, the balances of nature, where the worst crime would appear to be a breach of those subtle relationships which bind man first to woman, his mother and his wife; then to children, the result of union between a man and a woman; then to his fellowmen of all kinds; and then, going beyond them, into the animal, vegetable, and mineral kingdom where all things are seen to be linked, part and parcel of each other, merging imperceptibly into each other so that at various points there is even some question as to where the organic begins and the inorganic ends.

The basis of every great religion is a respect and love for life, and to love life is to be religious, again in the widest sense; to such, death has few terrors, for it is not an end, only a new beginning.

God of some sort must be found again. Right must be established as an ideal, for the Graeco-Jewish tradition, which we describe as Western culture, is based on the idea of God, of good and justice.

There is no justice in the forest. To live without justice as we do is to turn our cities into jungles.

Chapter One

A MAN WITH A MAID

'Where does a story begin?' Mashupa said. 'A story is part of life, and life has neither a beginning nor an end. You say, "Why did I follow you?" "To speak with you," I answer. You say, "Why, when I am a stranger to you?" I answer, "Because you are beautiful and have driven a spear into my heart." '

'Aa'u,' the girl said.

The young man pointed with his bare foot to a native dog lying in the sun on the pavement. 'And the dog, if he could talk, would say: "Why does this young man disturb me, walking so quickly that I must move?" And to the dog I would say, "I disturb you, dog, because a maiden has disturbed me, thrusting an assegai into my heart," and the dog would understand. Are you less intelligent than a dog? Are you a child who casts his spear into a pool at random and spears a fish, or a woman of a bad kind whose look invites all men who pass her by? No,' he said, 'you are neither of these, but a maiden of our nation, and in your heart you know why I am here.'

'Eh,' she said, 'I know.'

'My name is Mashupa,' he said.

'I know,' she said, and laughed.

And he laughed and said, 'You knew it was not the first time?'

She said, 'I knew.'

'And you asked about my name—you said, "What is the name of that handsome young man who follows me at a distance?" '

'I asked,' she said, and laughed.

And he laughed—and they were both suddenly very happy, for the spell was upon them. They were young and strong, they knew each other, and had many days before them.

'Now,' she said, 'you must go, because my Senhora does not like strange men in her yard.'

'I will go,' he said.

'Stay softly, N'Tembi,' he said.

'You know my name,' she said.

'I know it,' he said.

'You inquired,' she said.

'I asked,' he said. 'I said, "What is the name of the beautiful young girl who lives in this house?" and they told me.'

'Go sweetly, Mashupa,' she said.

'Stay softly, N'Tembi,' he said again.

He put out his hand. She took it. Their soft, pink palms met in the double handclasp of the Shangaans. He held her hand as white people do in meeting or in parting. Then their hands slipped upwards, palm to palm, so that they held each other's thumbs. In them both something stirred. Life stirred, as it had in their fathers and mothers before them. In their fathers and mothers, who were the beads that joined them to their ancestors strung on the thread of time. Joined them to their ancestors who had ruled the land before the Portuguese came and had fought the Portuguese, and been defeated by them. Their fathers and mothers, that joined and separated them from their ancestors.

They parted, the girl going into the house to finish ironing her mistress's silken underwear, the boy going up the street again into the sun, whistling softly as he went. He was going nowhere because it was his afternoon off. But there was no need for him to go anywhere, for he had arrived. A man whose heart is pierced by a woman's glance has arrived. If he cannot go to the woman, there is nowhere else to go. He can only dream and wait.

So they parted, but something was begun.

The grey hunting dog lying on the hot pavement knew something was begun. N'Tembi and Mashupa knew something was begun. But the white man sitting in the shade of a flat-branched flamboyant did not know. He had looked at them and seen nothing. Kaffirs were invisible to him. He only had an impression of a maidservant wasting her time with some man in a back yard. Just as he had a vague idea of one day, when it was not so hot, doing something about the kaffir dog that was always lying about on the pavement near his house. He did not know that it was an Egyptian greyhound, a descendant of dogs brought to East Africa by traders a thousand years ago. To him, it was the

13

kind of dog that natives kept, a kaffir dog, and ought to be destroyed.

A mile away, on the stoep of an old house built of corrugated iron, sandwiched between modern villas, two men were talking. They were hunters and one of them was very old, over eighty, a great age for this place, where white men die young of boredom, or drink, or fever. He was very small and slight. His skin was burnt brown and crinkled like the skin of a grenadilla. There was no life in it. Only his blue unfaded eyes showed life.

He said, 'He had a white tail and the biggest tusks I ever saw. Ten feet long and thick and blunt. That elephant was the father of all elephants. He must have been a hundred and fifty years old or two hundred. There's no knowing how long elephants live. Nobody knows,' he said. 'I shot him but he got away. I had fever. Never shoot with fever, but I had to. It was die of fever or die of starvation for me. That was in 1870. I was nineteen then.'

The other man—he was a Portuguese—said, 'Yes, Senhor. What you say is true. No man, not even men like us, knows the full story of nos amijos elefantes. Their age, their history, their habits. Each of us has his ideas, each has learnt from others who went before him. but, mixed with what we know, as water is mixed with wine, is superstition, is hearsay, is myth. That is why, when I heard that Senhor Carew was back, I took the liberty of calling upon the Senhor, the old hunter whose fame will never die.'

'Die,' the old man said. His brain caught at the word and held it, weakly, as an old dog would hold a struggling bird in toothless jaws, lacking either the strength to kill or to carry it; not clear about the motive that prompted it to snap, regretting the impulse, but holding the bird still. 'Die,' he said again. 'That is why I came back,' he said, 'to die.'

'That is what I heard,' the other said. 'They said Senhor Carew has come back to die.'

'It takes a long time,' the old man said. 'I am very strong.'

'The Senhor has been away a long time.'

'Twenty years,' the old man said. 'But now I am back to end my days where my happiness began. To die where it died, when she died, in the same room, so that I shall not be alone. Neither when I die, for she will come to me, nor when I am buried, for they will put me to sleep beside her again. It is twenty years since I slept beside her,

Senhor. It is a long time,' he said. 'It takes a strong man a long time to die.'

Maniero said nothing. He was a hunter and could wait.

The old man said, 'So he's still alive.'

'He's alive,' Maniero said, 'and he's killed six men. That is to say, we know of six but there may be more. He travels far.'

'Kaffirs,' Carew said.

'Yes, Kaffirs.'

'And they say I'm responsible for their deaths, that because of me he's become a rogue. Pretorius wounded him before I did. But that is so long ago that no one remembers. He killed Pretorius.'

'No one blames you, Senhor. Many men have been after him. I have been after him. They say he is bewitched.'

'I had fever,' the old man said. Then he said, 'Have you got a bit of paper on you? An envelope or something?'

'Yes, Senhor.'

'And a pencil?'

Maniero gave them to him.

The old man put the envelope on his knee, drew something on the back of it and passed the envelope to the Portuguese. 'Was his spoor like that?' he said. He had drawn a circle and overlapping the circle was an ellipse, but it did not overlap it neatly, it leant outwards. It was twisted.

'That is the spoor of the lame one,' Maniero said.

'That is the way it was when I shot him,' Carew said. 'Pretorius wounded him in the fifties. Manie Pretorius, the Boer hunter, and he killed Manie.'

'I did not know he had killed a white man.'

'It was in the fifties,' Carew said again, 'a long time ago. Before I was born, and stories get lost.'

'I have heard of Manie Pretorius the Boer hunter,' Maniero said, 'and I knew he had been killed by an elephant, but I did not know it was the lame one.'

'I had Manie's tracker,' Carew said, 'and he told me the tale.'

'Tell me,' Maniero said

'I will tell you. It was like this. In those days, as you know, elephants were not as they are now. They fed in the daytime and lived in open country, so that you could hunt them in comfort from a horse.'

15

'Yes,' Maniero said. 'That is the way Selous hunted, and Cummins, and the others in the old days.'

'It's the way I hunted, until my horses died,' Carew said.

'Yes,' Maniero said.

'Well, Pretorius had wounded him; he was the biggest elephant he had ever seen, he hit him with his four-pounder in the near thigh.'

'Yes,' Maniero said, 'in the left thigh.'

'He was trying for a shot into the liver, but the elephant moved as he fired and then charged. Manie swung his horse and galloped away. That's what we always did, but the horse fell and the elephant was on him. He hit him with his trunk. Broke the horse's back, then he knelt on him. On them both, the man and the horse. He knelt on them several times and as he knelt, he trumpeted. Then he stood up with bloody knees and chest and went to wash himself. All this my tracker saw. He washed for a long time in a pan nearby, filling his trunk and squirting water over himself. Then he came back and looked at the dead man and horse. He walked round and round them for a long time and then he pulled some branches from a fever tree and covered them up and went away. That is what my tracker saw from where he was hiding behind an antheap.'

'And then?' Maniero asked. 'That was the end?'

'No,' Carew said, 'then they buried Manie Pretorius. The tracker, and the other boys, by the big fever trees where he had been killed. While they buried him, the vultures came down and ate the horse. But that is still not the end because, when I saw the place, and that was twenty years later, the fever trees were broken down. An elephant had eaten them. And the spoor of that elephant was the one I have drawn for you. It was there that I picked it up and followed it. Every twenty years, the Kaffirs told me, he comes back to eat the trees round the grave. To eat Manie Pretorius as it were, for the flesh and blood that was Manie had gone into the ground, and into the roots of the yellow fever trees, and into the leaves thereof, and into the belly of the elephant that he shot.

'So that is why they say he is bewitched?'

'Perhaps that is why, and now, my friend, I have told you the story, leave me and come back another day because talking of the past leaves me tired. I am alone to-day, the friends I had are dead, my servants are dead, my dogs and

16

horses are dead, my wagons consumed as firewood.'

Maniero had heard what he had hoped to hear. News of the lame one. Carew had not only seen him. He had wounded him sixty-odd years ago.

Lower down in the town nearer to the docks, Ferdinando, the mechanic, was greasing Maniero's truck. After a trip in the forest, there was much to do. Nuts to be tightened, bolts replaced. Oil changed and ignition checked. Ferdinando often wondered about the hard life of a hunter. Near the car, walking about among the parts of motors that litter every garage, was a little brown kaffir hen. She had been bought to eat, but had not been eaten because she had laid an egg. While they waited for more eggs, she lived, because as Ferdinando said, 'A dead hen lays no eggs.' Then he had become attached to her. She was so small and there would not be much meat on her, and besides, how could you eat a hen that took food from your hand?

The hen stood near the truck because when they cleaned its bed, bits of meat often fell out on the ground. Fragments of what had been elephants. Little slivers of rotten meat, also crumbs of bread and the like. The little brown hen knew the truck and always waited beside it when Maniero brought it in. Perhaps she knew Maniero.

Next to the garage was the house of prostitution. It had a garden filled with poinsettias as big as small trees. The women lived on the second story and had a veranda that was closed in with torn mosquito-netting. Outside the veranda was the pipe that protected the wire which brought electricity to the red lamp that shone like a bull's eye in the night. Out of their slit window the prostitutes looked into the garage, looked down at Maniero's car. But they knew nothing of ivory or of elephants. The only facts of natural history they knew concerned meh.

In an Indian store not far from the garage, two men were waiting to see Karagee. One, because he was black, was waiting outside the office, in the shop, standing among the bright coloured tablecloths the capalanas that the native women wear to cover their nakedness, to carry their babies in, and to spread over their mats of split bamboo when they sleep. Inside the waiting room, a white man, a Spaniard, an agent of the Government, sat on an overstuffed American arm-chair smiling to himself. Karagee was the biggest dealer in ivory, both licit and illicit, in the town. In the small, dirty toilet behind the store, the illicit, the cow tusks, that weighed less than five kilos, were stacked, waiting for the carver in ivory who would collect them and turn them into little religious figures. Madonnas, images of our Lord hanging on the cross, and winged angels. Who could question the virtue of a religious figure, or know the size of the tusk from which it had been cut?

In the passage that led to the toilet were the legal tusks, the bigger ones, wrapped in hessian and marked with their weights in indelible pencil—forty-five kilos, fifteen kilos, twenty-two kilos.

Karagee was a stout Indian from Goa. He had been educated in Lisbon, and had worked as waiter in an Indian restaurant in London to learn English. He was, according to his lights, an honest man and did much to help his people both in Portuguese East Africa where they needed little help and in India where they needed much. He was dressed in the Western style, in a grey business suit. He sat on a swivel chair behind a roll-top desk. He said to the clerk who was waiting for his orders, 'Show Senhor Ortega in.'

Senhor Ortega heard his name and came in before the clerk could fetch him.

'Good morning,' he said.

'Good morning, Senhor Ortega,' Karagee said. 'And what can I do for you?'

'I want ivory,' the white man said.

'You have come to the right place.'

'I have seen what you have in the passage, but nothing there is big enough.'

'You want a big tusk?'

Senhor Ortega made a gesture.

'There are no tusks like that any more,' the Indian said.

'But if one comes in?'

'If one comes in, I will keep it for you.'

'I will pay well,' Ortega said. 'What is the price of ivory to-day?'

'A hundred escudos a kilo.'

'I will pay two hundred.'

'And ask four?' the Indian said.

'It is for the church,' Ortega said. 'It is to carve a figure of our Lord, for a great crucifix, as a gift to the Holy

Father in Rome.'

'You shall have it when I get it, but it will not be to-morrow,' the Indian said. They shook hands and the white man left.

When he left the black man was shown in. He also was dressed in Western style: he wore a navy blue suit and brown shoes and carried a grey felt hat in his hands.

'What is it you want?' Karagee asked. 'Mouti,' the man said. 'I want hair from the tails of elephants, bristles from the tips of their trunks, eyelashes, dried livers and hearts, and the matter that seeps from their tusks where they join the skull.'

'Where will you sell these things?' the Indian asked.

'In Zululand, to the witch doctors.'

'You shall have them,' Karagee said, and told the clerk to get out the things he wanted from a locked box in the outside store, where such things were kept because they stank.

When he had gone, Karagee meditated upon the strange superstitions of other races, on their religions, and habits. Karagee was a reasonable and educated man. He had recently married a new wife who had just turned twelve, would have died before she ate meat, and would allow a toothless cow to starve to death in her old age rather than kill her.

Four hundred miles away in the north, two great bull elephants stood side by side with their trunks entwined. They were companions and loved each other. One had tusks so big and so heavy that he stood with them resting on the branches of a chamfuta tree. The other was tuskless, and out of the foliage came his trunk to hold the trunk of his friend. Perhaps he was suffering, perhaps his great teeth ached, perhaps the weight of them, that had been upon him for so many years, had at last become too much for him. The tuskless elephant let go and plucked a branch from the tree. With the branch, he wiped his back, driving away the flies that bit him in the cracks that veined his skin. Then he flicked the branch over his friend's back and then he moved forward away from the tusked elephant. When he had gone twenty yards, the tusked elephant followed him, looking at the ground and putting his feet precisely into the spoor of the tuskless elephant. When they moved, their great haunches and tails were visible. The hairs that had once been long were now short and thick, like white bailing wire.

After they had disappeared, soundlessly into the bush, anyone coming across the spoor would have said that only one elephant had passed. A great elephant, the greatest ever seen by man. And he would have remarked upon the spoor, upon the way the near hind leg was crippled so that, instead of merely overlapping the round spoor of the forefoot, the ellipse of the left one cut into it and leaned outwards. If he had been a native, he would have covered his mouth with his hand, and turned back. He would have said, 'A'au, this is the spoor of the lame one, the bewitched one, the great one inhabited by the spirit of Moselekatse and T'Chaka. The kind elephant, inhabited by the spirits of the Kings, who sometimes is one and sometimes two.'

This is the scene. These are some of the heroes, the protagonists and, as each must have an end, each must also have a beginning. The beginning of one being sometimes the end of another. The trees die that the elephant may live, the elephant dies that the hunter may live, and God, varying the pattern upon occasion, sometimes lets the man die terribly, so that the elephant may live. But always in the end, He feeds the soil with the blood of the leviathan so that the grass and trees of the forests obtain again the sustenance that was reft from them by the elephant while it lived. And always, endlessly, life renews itself from death equally from the death of an elephant that has lived a hundred years or a butterfly that has lived a day.

Chapter Two

GRAND HOTEL

An event—assuming that an event can be separated from the causes that lead up to it as an effect, which leads to new causes—must be set in time, as we know time; and in a place, as we know places. The time was nineteen thirty-seven. The place, Lourenço Marques, the capital city of the Portuguese colony of Moçambique.

Lourenço Marques is, perhaps, the most beautiful miniature town in the world. Twenty-five thousand white people live there in new little houses that are surrounded by gardens. If they do not paint up their houses, they are fined. The wide streets are lined with flowering trees—blue jacarandas and the red flamboyants that they call *Acacia rubra*. Masses of bougainvillaea pour in scarlet, cherry-red and purple floods over white walls; over the great plumes of bamboo into which they have climbed. Golden Shower, a bignonia, covers arbours; frangipani, the shrub of a thousand phalli, perfumes the air. And it is hot.

To some people, Lourenço Marques is the end of civilisation, the last place on the road, with nothing north of it till you come to Nairobi, unless you count Beira. To others —those from the north of the colony—it is not merely the beginning of civilisation; it is the hub of their universe, the centre of all trade and culture with only one place surpassing it in all the world—Lisbon, the sun round which the Portuguese mind revolves. For the Portuguese, now immune to greatness—having proved long centuries ago that they could be great—are resigned to a static culture that permits the world to pass them by; and it passes, leaving them ignorant of what they have missed, ignorant but in peace with their hours of siesta, their wine, their dances, their music, and their loves. The Portuguese are great lovers.

The social life of Lourenço Marques is dominated by the Polana—the great hotel. Here, in the winter, come the rich from the Union of South Africa with their women. They come by car through Komati Poort where the customs examine their luggage, they pass Moamba where the British Empire Cotton Estate established its colossal failure. They come through the town of Lourenço Marques and climb the hill on to the bluff, which, like the Berea of Durban, overlooks the bay, and catches the fugitive breezes, the life-giving zephyrs that assuage the torment of the summer heat. In summer there are few visitors and the residents have the Polana to themselves.

At this moment of time, in this pinprick of space, a group of visitors from the Rand was watching an Indian snake charmer squatting on the wide red stoep of the hotel. They sat well back from him because, though they held whisky, distilled in Scotland, in their hands, they had a fear of snakes in their hearts. The women feared the snakes more

21

than the men because of the snake that had tempted the first woman in Eden. The men feared, without knowing it, the women, for the gift of power that they had had from the snake on that day, the power of their beauty and what it could do to men. And the men and the women sipped their whisky, tinkling the ice in their glasses, to quiet their fears and give them confidence.

The Indian piped his little pipe, and the snakes writhed and rose up. The cobra extended his hood, the sluggish puff adder crawled, the long black mole snake undulated about him. He picked up the mole snake and put it about his neck. About his neck it was dry and cool, like a jewel, like the articulated gold necklace that one of the women wore. But she did not know that a snake felt like that. She did not know that the ancient artists, who first made jewels of this kind, simulated snakes; she did not know of the double-snake crown of the Pharaohs, or even that the two rubies in the clasp of her golden necklace were derived from the eyes of a snake, or that, in taking it from the man who had given it to her, she was an Eve herself, and had tempted him, with desire for the knowledge that only she could give him. She did not know that the big black mole snake was harmless.

These people were rich and divorced from the land. Divorced from the grain that had made their liquor potent, and the water of the mountain burns that was its base. They did not know that for a thousand years there had been snake charmers on this coast—Indians who came to entertain the Arab masters of the country on the winds of the monsoon. They did not know of the significance of the snake, of how the art of the humble snake charmer was derived from an ancient Phallic snake worship, or that the bull fighter was an acolyte of the mithraic cult, though neither the charmer nor the matador is any more aware of it than those who sit watching them in pleasurable fear.

These people were rich and civilised. They knew about money and clothes, food, houses, motor cars, radios and refrigerators. Of the sources of these things, they knew nothing, not even of the source of the gold that they spent, nor of the black miners who sweated so that they should be cool. To them the Indian was just another Sammie, like the man who came to their suburban villas on Tuesdays and Fridays with vegetables in a cart drawn by a starving horse.

The women were young and beautiful, gowned in expensive white; the men, at once their masters and their servants, were dressed in beige, in palm beach suits of sharkskin. Looking out beyond the snake charmer, across the bay, they could see the opposite side. Its low hills, forest, and swamps lay in a pearl-grey mist along the skyline. The bay itself was calm, dull, mud-coloured. It looked like a sheet of old zinc polished in patches to a mirror-like clearness. In one of these patches, a big coastal schooner was moving slowly with the aid of her engines. There was barely enough breeze to fill the sails that were reflected under her, so that she seemed to have masts springing, not only out of her deck, but out of her keel as well.

Over there, on the other side of the bay, was Maputo. There were elephants there—wild elephants. It was a reserve, but there were other elephants nearer still that were being hunted while they sat drinking. At this moment there were elephant hunters less than sixty miles away. Here was a hole in time. Beyond the town, only a few miles into the forest, was the past.

The people who watched the snake charmer had flown over the reserve in an aeroplane and had laughed to see the fear of the elephants as they swooped on them. They had laughed at the little calves, no bigger than big dogs, that had galloped on clumsy legs after their great mothers, and the bulls that stood as if to fight, and then made off too.

When the snake charmer had done, he put down his pipe, picked up his snakes, and put them, as if they were great skeins of silk, into a little basket that was like a woman's sewing basket. And the people who had watched him practise his art, threw escudos on to the red granolithic floor of the stoep. The notes were crumpled and dirty because the Portuguese use their notes till they wear out. To the Indian they were money, the source of life. But to the givers of the notes, escudos were not money. Only pounds sterling and dollars were money; not escudos, that went a hundred to the pound sterling, and were dirty. The pound notes at home were not dirty, though they might be stained with sweat and blood.

Below the hotel, among the palms on the dark sands of the Indian Ocean, were the banana-campers, so called by the Portuguese because they brought their own food with them and bought nothing but bananas. They were Boers—

farmers who came each year, as their fathers had done before them, from their farms in the low veld, from beyond the Lebombo Mountains, for a month at the sea. They camped, and they talked, and they held religious services— the nagmaals of their fathers. They courted and made love, they begat children and they had them, and then they struck their tents and went away again, back to the lonely farms whence they had come.

The people who had watched the snake charmer came from Johannesburg. To-morrow they were going back to their city of gold, of hope and disappointment. Their cars were clean, shiny with polish, filled with gas, the treads of their white-walled tyres, knife-sharp. To-morrow they would be back in their homes, fine houses set in gardens that blazed with flowers like jewels, but barred like prisons against the Kaffirs who served them and whom they feared. As they sat in their houses, the steel bars in their windows came between them and the panorama of the high veld, which, even within the memory of man, had been the playground of countless herds of game, of springbuck and wildebeeste, of lions, of buffalo, of eland, and in the wooded ridges, of kudu. But all were gone now, replaced by the sludge of the mines, the grassless kopjes of dead pulverised rock—rock crushed beyond recognition and poisoned with the cyanide of extraction.

The aim of these people and their like was luxury, was comfort, which is the cushion that comes between man and reality. Comfort, the great divorcer of man from his universe and his maker. These people had been here a month. While they lived here, Mashupa had begun his courtship of N'Tembi, old Carew had told Maniero his hunting stories. Elephants had been killed within a few miles of where they sat, and in Europe the devil's brew was almost on the boil. They are without importance except to underline the time, the place, and the situation. They are part of the back-drop, the curtain, the mise en scène. Having significance, but no value.

Chapter Three

MANIERO THE HUNTER

Guido Maniero, the hunter whom the natives called 'the Bull' because of his strength, was thirty-five, the son of a customs official and a peasant girl from Portugal. She was a postcard wife. That is to say, as often happens in the colony, where women are fewer than the men, her marriage had been arranged by relatives at home; by the exchange of letters between the couple, and by photos—static studio photographs printed upon postcards and sent through the mail. The situation, character, and financial stability of Maniero's family had been guaranteed by his father's superiors in the customs house. The virtue and capacity for hard work, that so distinguished his mother, had been guaranteed by the village mayor and priest, and their marriage was more of a success than many that are due only to the passions of youth which, in the end, often prove less reliable than the opinion of a senior customs-house official and the word of a priest.

It was his mother's peasant love of the soil that first drew Maniero to it. But there he found things, beauties, that she did not see. Small creatures that were to her only destroyers of vegetables were to him subjects of the greatest interest. From the garden he progressed to the zoo, where he went holding his father's hand, and which became his Sunday treat. From the zoo he moved to the lands surrounding the town where the forest is tame, its will broken by plough and fire; and from there, as he grew older, to the greater forest where, for the first time, he found happiness. In the forest he found that which usually only comes to a man through a woman. In the forest he found peace.

There are no worries in the forest. Worry is a matter of communication and once beyond letters, beyond the telephone and telegraph, there are only anxieties, dangers, which to a resourceful man are no more than problems to which he must find an immediate solution. Perhaps the difference between these difficulties and the worries of the town is that they demand action. The answer to them must come from a bold heart, must be instinctive, and is therefore a natural reaction to circumstances. In the forest a man, like an animal, must fight, run, or remain frozen, immobile, waiting for danger to pass, crouched like a buck in its form in the long grass. Above all, win or lose, the choice is his own. He owes nothing to any man, to any circumstance, save those that he has created, and his life is in the hands of God.

Maniero was short, thickset, with the barrel chest more common among the Portuguese than other peoples. By some accident of good fortune, he found himself to be relatively immune to fever. He got it, but he got it less severely than most men, and the bouts left him more quickly, and when they were over, he was less affected by weakness.

He lived with his widowed mother in a small house situated a mile away from the Polana Hotel. It was on the high ground, but of course it had no view of the sea. The villas with a view of the sea belonged to the rich, and a hunter's life, whatever its other compensations, did not lead to riches.

In the house were hung his trophies of the chase. Tusks and horns, native weapons and musical instruments. On the floors and on the backs of the chairs were the skins of lion and leopard, of cheetah, kudu, and nyala. He had a collection of skulls that were as white as the walls. He cleaned them with lye, and would show them with pride. Lion and leopard skulls, the skulls of wild cats, monkeys, and baboons, He would show the dog-like fangs of the baboons, ask you to feel the razor-edge at the back of the great teeth, and explain how a baboon fought, biting and then gripping its enemy with arms as strong as those of a man, first drawing him towards him, and then forcing him away so that the knife-sharp edge of his canines sheared through the flesh and sinew.

His friends laughed at him, and said, 'Guido, when you marry, you will have to get rid of the horns!' For among the Portuguese, when a man is a cuckold, they say he 'has horns,' which is why you see trophies in no houses except those of bachelors and foreigners. And he would laugh back at his friends and say, 'I am married, amigos, I am married to the forest,' and then they would all laugh together and drink the good wine of Portugal, and he would tell them of his love of the forest, and the wild beasts that

26

were in it. And they would tell of their loves—the dark-haired, ivory senhoritas of the Colony. For the Portuguese see no shame in love, which they regard as an art and a pleasure.

But always after a month, or sometimes after so little as a week at home, Maniero left town again, and went back into the forest, to the wild animals and people that he loved and understood. Called there by the profound silence of the bush, the green sea of forest that separated the mountains of the interior from the ocean, blending into it with mangrove swamps, and climbing back again into the kloofs and valleys of the hills—the low veld that was his real home.

He often wondered at the paradox that caused him to love animals and yet live by killing them. Sometimes, when he was sad, he had said, 'I am just a butcher without a shop,' but those times were over for him now. He had felt like that when he hunted meat for the great coastal sugar plantations. Killing buffaloes by the thousand; and elephants, rhinos, and hippos. For the Kaffirs that sweated in the cane fields must have meat, and white hunters were employed on contract to get it. A man contracted to produce so many tons of bleeding meat a week, so many pounds a day, for even though many natives like their meat rotten, it will not keep forever. Once even the army was fed on wild meat; it was butchered on the roadsides, even machine-gunned, and loaded into trucks from the barracks. It is a curious fact of natural history that the warriors of any nation, white or black, must have meat. The meat of the ox and the elephant, the sheep and the antelope.

Only the slaves and peasants eat grain and the pulse crops. This is the food of the docile. In war there must be anger, and anger is found in the flesh of beasts that have died under the knife, the axe, the arrow, the spear, and the bullet. And in their hearts the Kaffirs were still warriors and craved flesh.

Maniero was not a great meat eater, nor a drinker of alcohol. Some wine and a glass or two of Madeira was all he ever took. The solitary life of a hunter, he held, should be abstemious. He did not even smoke, for smoking tended to affect the nerves and sense of smell. He ate Kaffir corn and maize, that in Africa is called mealies, and maas, the sour thickened milk of the indigenous people. He ate of native food, among them, from their pots with his hands, and drank curdled milk from their calabashes. Only when there was no grain did he eat meat, and then he ate it as a lion eats it, preferring the viscera, the guts, where the source of life and increase is.

Maniero was not a butcher and the work had irked him. Now he was an ivory hunter, a hunter of the great pachyderms, and a collector for museums all over the world. At heart he was a naturalist, a lover of the wild, more by nature a game ranger than a killer, and what he saw going on about him depressed him. For the history of Africa was the tale of the rape of a beautiful woman, of a land that might have been soft and tender with men who had loved her; who gave, and did not only take. As gentle as a native woman whose skin was like brown silk and whose hands were petal-soft upon her child. But the white man had come upon her unawares and had thrown her down and taken her, and was now beginning to pay the price.

For one Maniero, who understood the land, where the pace of the ox is swift enough, and time flows by like a wide slow river, there were a thousand who must goad the ox and harness the stream into turbulence and profit. Who saw wild animals only as meat and hides, and men only as labour to till their fields and work in their mines and houses.

Maniero, at this time, was in Lourenço Marques because of Carew. He saw him almost daily. Carew was a master and he was a pupil, following in his footsteps. Carew had known Africa in the old days, known it before the black man was finally subdued by the Portuguese in these parts, before the English had smashed the Matabele, piling them up in black plumed heaps before their rifles. Carew had known Lobengula, the king of the Matabele, and Doctor Jim, as they called Jameson, and Wilson, who had died in the fighting, and Matabele Thompson, who had survived, and Frederic Courtney Selous, and the other old-timers. And the water of every river, pan, and vlei in the land that lay between the sea and Angola he had boiled for tea in his kettle.

It was for this that Maniero went to see Carew, to hear tales from him, for the old man was a great storyteller. He told of white men crawling on their bellies before black kings because they wanted concessions from them, because they wanted young black girls to wrap in their karosses, and tusks of ivory and gold. He told of the slave trade which had still existed, though forbidden by law, in his time; and of the half-caste mulatto brigands, robbers, poachers, and hunters of beasts and men, who had lived in the half world of the undefined border country. As he spoke of the past, the eyes of the old hunter grew bright and the blood came back into his sallow face. His hands grew strong as he pounded the table in anger at some of the things he had seen. The cruelties, the abominations of the native police in Matabeleland which led up to the rebellion, the maimings and thrashings of the Congo rubber trade, the breaking of the Herero people, and other things which only men as old as he could remember.

And Carew talked as much of men killing men as of game. He talked of T'Chaka who killed thousands when his mother died so that the whole nation should mourn with him. Of Moselekatse who had devastated the north, of the white men who had hunted the little yellow Bushmen as vermin.

He talked of the old long-barrelled elephant guns that fired bullets the size of a small egg, that were called four-pounders, because they went four to the pound. He talked of bullet-moulds, and of how he had made his own bullets and had cut them out of the animals he shot, to melt down again. He talked of the chiefs he had known, of indunas long dead, of black captains and kings dressed in kilts of monkey and leopard tails. It was his conversation that held Maniero in Lourenço Marques longer than he ever remembered remaining there before, because, when this old man died, his tales would die with him, and to listen to him was to hear stories of a world that had gone. He spoke with the voice of the dead. Maniero felt no haste to return to the forest, for Carew carried it with him. Carew carried the forest and its denizens in the pocket of his mind. And, woven through the warp and woof of his memories, was the thread of the lame one. How he had seen his spoor here, or heard of him there.

This elephant had for many years been of paramount interest to Maniero for he was the greatest mystery of the forest—a spook elephant, a ghost. A ghost that sometimes left a double spoor. That sometimes had been glimpsed with mammoth tusks, and that sometimes was tuskless. That had been seen as both at once, a giant tusked and a tuskless elephant, as two elephants. If there were two elephants, which he doubted but could not entirely disbelieve, the tuskless one would be the more dangerous. Tuskless elephants had better sight. They carried their heads higher, and even in the herd they held their own because, by some form of compensation, the strength that should have gone into the tusks went into the trunk and made it stronger and bigger. A tuskless elephant could smash the tusk of an adversary with a blow as if it were a matchstick.

It is possible too, that Theresa Ferreira held him to the town by the invisible cords of her desire. The silken threads which she, the wife of his friend, had spread to snare him. Wise in the ways of the forest, Maniero was still unaware that the forest, untamable and savage, exists in the heart of every woman.

At any rate he remained, and Carew was the reason that his mind gave to his heart. For he was also unaware that the heart can betray the mind. Maniero the hunter was a simple man. He knew only a widow whom he visited with much discretion, and women that were paid with gold. Who only wanted gold. He knew knothing of the vampire women who want blood, or the Circes.

Chapter Four

THE BARREL

Charles Carew had come to Africa with his father to trade when he was fifteen. A year later his father had died, and having no relations for whom he cared in England, the boy had remained. That was in eighteen-sixty-seven.

He had attached himself to a transport rider carrying goods from Pretoria to Delagoa Bay by ox wagon, and then had gone trading and hunting on his own with more than ordinary success. When he was twenty-two he had met a missionary new to the country and had guided him into the interior and helped him to establish his mission there. It is doubtful if he would have spent as long as he did on this enterprise—a full year it had taken—had the missionary not been accompanied by his wife and daughter. The girl, Esther by name, was a fine young woman, red-headed and lively, and to her the young hunter was like something out of a book of adventure stories, while to him she seemed like a fairy-tale princess. They were much together and she took to the life in the wilds much better than her parents, which was why, when Carew proposed marriage to her, though he could offer her no better home than a tended wagon, she accepted him, and after being married by her father, the two left the mission station and returned to his old business of hunting and trading. Esther loved the life, the peace and freedom of the forest, the chase and its hazards, and the natives with whom they came into daily contact. As they became older, the hunting grew less and the trading more, so that they finally owned posts in many parts of the country.

These they visited at intervals, and the rest of the time, when Carew was not hunting for pleasure, they spent in the small corrugated-iron house that they had built in Lourenço Marques. This was their home, the centre from which they started on their expeditions and to which they returned when they were done. It was here, in this house, that she had died twenty years ago, and it was now, just as it had been then. No changes had been made and his agent had kept it in order, having it kept clean and treating the poles on which it stood and other woodwork against the ravages of termites.

Carew had returned to die. He had left Johannesburg, where he had established himself after his wife's death, for this purpose. But Maniero had disturbed him. Maniero's talk of the bush and his own memories, as he revived them in talking to Maniero, were proving a deterrent to his plan. Before Maniero's coming all had been going well. Death had been approaching comfortably on the wings of bore-dom. But now he was no longer bored, and death came no nearer. Instead, it seemed further away, and a mad idea had entered his head.

The mad idea was a last hunt, or safari, as they called it now. The idea kept recurring, and growing stronger each time it came back. Maniero had begun it, but he had carried on himself from there, and then his old hunters had come back to him. Lunda who was older than he was, with his grandson who, he said, was as good a tracker as he had ever been, and Matissa who said, 'Come to our land, Lord, we are hungry, and the elephants are many. They destroy our gardens and we need meat.' How often had he supplied these people with meat in the past, and now they wanted him to come again. But suppose he died up there? What would happen to his plan about lying beside Esther when he died? He thought of his age, and the hardships of hunting and then he made nothing of the hardships. What were they now? Why, to-day he could hunt with a car. He need not walk thirty or forty kilometres a day as he had done when he was young and Matissa had said, 'We will carry you, Lord, we will carry you in a machila, a hammock, to the vicinity of the elephants and carry you back when you have killed.' But still there was the question of his promise to Esther to lie beside her. But at last he had solved it. All problems could be solved if one really thought about them. He looked at the great cask in the corner of the room, and then he looked out of the window and at his watch. Mackenzie, his agent, should be here any time now. A good man, Mackenzie, a very punctual man. And, as he put his watch back into his pocket, Mackenzie came.

'Ah, Mackenzie,' he said, 'I am glad you came.'

Mackenzie said, 'What madness are you planning now? I thought you had come here to peg out!'

'So I have,' Carew said.

'Then why don't you pop off nicely in your sleep and we'll give you a slap-up funeral?' This was his way of angering the old man. He was fond of him and he knew if he could keep him angry, 'the old bastard 'ud never die.' With Carew dead, something else interesting would have gone from the world. They did not breed his like to-day.

'See that?' Carew said.

'See what?'

'The barrel, you fool.'

'Of course I see it. What's in it? Brandy?'

'Yes, brandy.'

'Are you going to drink yourself to death?'

'No, but it's poisoned, or going to be.'

'What's it for then?'

'To pickle me in,' Carew said. 'That's all that stopped me from hunting. I said to myself. 'Suppose you die up there. You wouldn't keep, not even in the cold weather.' So I had to make a plan. I'll take it with me,' he said.

'Take what?' Mackenzie asked.

'The pickle barrel, you bloody fool, and if I die, or get killed, they'll bring it back to you, and you can bury me with Esther. That's why I'm going to poison it, so no one drinks it,' he said.

'And I'm to bury you, hey? Brandy and all? In a barrel! Think Esther'd like that? Think she'll like it when the last trump sounds and the dead rise up and you come out of your barrel pickled, and drunk as a lord?'

'I'll keep that way,' Carew said, 'and besides, you can pour it out when you get me.'

'You'll be the wrong shape,' Mackenzie said. 'You'll be all curled up like a baby in its mother's belly.'

'Then uncurl me,' Carew said, 'or bury me barrel and all. Anyway what you do is your business, but you've got to do it.'

'Well, it's your funeral,' Mackenzie said.

'I know,' Carew said, 'and see that it's a good one!'

'So you're going?'

'Yes, now that this business is fixed up, I'm going. But I'll wait a bit yet. There's no hurry, I just wanted to get it planned. I like to think about it,' he said. 'I like to sit and think about it.'

Mackenzie leaned over and took his hand.

'I know,' he said. 'And I'll bury you.'

'Thanks,' Carew said. And then he said, 'You know, it was a mistake to leave her, to go so far away from her and the forest. The forest belonged to us in a way, and I'd like to be able to give her news of it when I get there. I'd like to be able to say, "It's the same, Esther. The big baobab we made love under when we first married is still there, nothing is different, even our names that we carved like tourists, are still there." That's what we all are,' he said, 'tourists in the forest, strangers in the land of the trees, the bush, and the animals. That's what we all are in life, Mackenzie, tourists. Dust is what we are. Earth matter, and then, for a while, we are tourists on the face of the earth, crawling about on her, as a baby crawls about the body of its mother on a bed, and then we go back to her. I'm nearly back,' he said, 'and I understand at last.'

When Mackenzie had gone, Carew thought about that love-making under the great cream of tartar tree. He thought about his big furry fruits that were like goose eggs covered in green plush. He could remember very little about it because the making of love cannot be remembered. These acts in a man's life are out of time. They are instants in which he is one with the past, with life itself in which there is no time. All he could remember was the happiness of it, and their great contentment with each other. It was the first time, and they had chosen the tree without a word, in preference to the wagon that was their home. They had lain down and made love upon the ground, as Kaffirs did, and had hoped that a child would come, blessed, somehow, by the great and ancient tree. A tree that already had been thousands of years old when Christ had walked the hot sands of Galilee. But nothing had come of it but love itself, and nothing had come of the other times, the many thousands of times, but greater love and understanding. He thought of the thousands of times that men make love in their lives, and of the women, though in his own life, there had been but one. Esther, who had been the light of his life, and the light of life had been extinguished with her death, so that all the world was dark and dull with her passing, and only beginning to brighten again, now that he was near her, and getting nearer every day.

There had been bees in the tree. Even in the dusk when they had made love, there had been a great buzzing inside the tree, which, like all such trees was hollow. But the bees had done nothing to the lovers, save to play on their wings an accompaniment to their love, and add to their murmurings their own, their mystery, to the mystery of a man and a woman making love. Often, later, they had camped by the tree for a night or two. Esther had said, 'We will come back, Charlie. We must come back whenever we can.' And they had. That was why they had left the two flat cooking stones there, ready for the next fire, the next time. He remembered the stones well, though it was years since he had thought of them. That had been a trick of his —to carry a few flat stones in the wagon to hold the pot and kettle and to make cooking easier. The stones were one of the comforts of the forest which was stoneless.

Their love was also a death tree; it stood less than three

hundred metres from the pan where Pretorius had been killed, and he had shown her the name of Pretorius that someone had carved on the tree to commemorate his death. There had been other names too. He could not remember them now. All he could remember was that some had been indecipherable. He had carved their own initials in the soft bark—C. & E. C.—and surrounded them with a deep-cut heart.

Now this was the end of a love, the last petal clinging frailly to the stem of life. A single petal trembling where once there had been a bud, a bloom, a throbbing perfume that had filled two hearts. Now, the scent was the scent of age, faintly mouldy, and the colour had gone from the flower of passion. Those who would have remembered it were also dead, or had their faculties so impaired by age that the name of Esther meant nothing to them, for their minds were busy with the memories of their own childhood and youth, and of the women they had known when they were strong. He was like them himself, and knew it. He thought of nothing but Esther, and could remember none other clearly, nor could he remember her as she had been when she died, but only as she was when he first knew her. Slim as a spear, red-headed and quick to both laughter and anger. He could remember her body as he held it in his hands, and the parts of her, and the warm feel of her flesh, as he looked at his old hands and wondered at them. Wondered that their caresses should have made her happy. Wondered at the way he had been able to touch her firmly and calm her, as one calmed a frightened horse, wondered at what there was between a man and a woman, and woman and man, which made them one flesh, and one mind and one heart. Wondered at two becoming one, and then at the one becoming a half. Something much less than he had ever been before, when she had been taken from him. A blind man could live on. The sun warmed him, but he did not know it was the sun. It was not bright for him any more, and the leaping flames of the fire were without colour. That was the way it was with him, and the others like him who had lived too long. They could still see, but the light and the glory had been taken from them. The light, he thought—the door. You entered life as if it were a room, from between your mother's thighs. All your life you lived in that room which slowly grew darker, and then you perceived another door. You saw light coming through it from the other side. This door was called death. It was ajar now, and every day it opened a little more. Soon it would be wide enough for him to go through into the last room. The immense room of the dead where Esther was waiting for him. Esther, and his friends.

Chapter Five

THE HOLE IN TIME

Once beyond Lourenço Marques, once beyond the asphalt, tree-lined roads that lead for a short distance out of it, you fall through time as if it were water, causing a ripple of interest among the natives as you pass them, a ripple that subsides when you have passed them, and into the beyond where time has stood still for centuries, into the land of giant baobabs; of livid yellow fever trees and of grey-trunked hardekools. Into the land of the elephant—the land of fever, sleeping sickness, and nagana.

Here civilisation falls like a cloak to the ground, leaving man naked, the law fades into mere rumours of law, and order is the nature of order, of fang and tusk, of bow and arrow, of high velocity shell, of water holes; of quinine as a specific against the most dangerous animal in Africa— the anopheles mosquito, which has, until to-day, kept so much of the interior inviolate. Malaria, the curse of man and the saviour of wild animals, and the tsetse fly, their twin protectors.

Here, beyond the Pongola, beyond Bella Vista, the seat of local government, beyond Sala Manga which means, *it is still a lie*, and is the place where once again the white man broke his word to the black; beyond the sandy roads, that are only tracks and lead deviously towards the lakes and marshes of the coast, lay the kraal of Shibiti, the old induna who was the father, by his youngest wife, of the girl N'Tembi, a house servant in the home of a white woman in Lourenço Marques. Of her life in Lourenço Marques he knew nothing, save that she sent him money in letters that he could not read, which came to him passed from hand to hand, through a country where the people were notoriously honest, from the store nearly thirty miles away. Eventually that money found its way back to the store, and the storekeeper, an Indian, benefited most from the work of N'Tembi, more than her father, for the profit he took was exorbitant.

Shibiti considered that the priests and the sisters of the mission had stolen his daughter from him, tempting her, telling her to cover her childish breasts, and, for covering them, rewarding her with the wherewithal to cover them, and a knowledge of reading and writing, simple arithmetic and sewing. In his eyes, for he was one of the old ones who had fought the Portuguese in the nineties, nothing that the priests and the nuns did was good, even though much that they did was good. More had been lost, in his opinion, than the land and the right to carry spears; of course men still carried them when they went abroad because of the wild beasts, but it was against the law. And the women carried them in their periods, when they were unclean, because they believed that the baboons, knowing it, would rape them, though in the memory of the eldest none had been so raped. But the right to carry arms was the right of a free man, and to have that right questioned was not to be free. Nor could a man, who could be sent far from his kraal and his garden to make the white man's roads, the 'corvee' as it was called, consider himself free. Nor was it right that man should have to work even for himself for six months of the year with the spade, the hoe, and the mattock, which were the tools of women. A man's business was war and hunting; and the care of the cattle that were his heritage, whose mystic increase was a compliment to the spirits of his ancestors, and the only safeguard, with the children of his loins, of his own future, after death had caught up with him in the race for life. All life was a race with death. True, the white man had removed some of the odds by checking slave raids and wars, and reducing the numbers of dangerous beasts that surrounded him, but the price paid in liberty for this security was too great, and, with such safety, much interest had gone from the world of the forest.

N'Tembi had written to him of a young man who had

come into her life, but he could not read what she wrote, nor could any other in his kraal, and he would have died before he asked the missionaries, who had stolen her from him with the promise of this new knowledge, to read her letter to him, nor did he wish to show it to the Indian store-keeper. So this letter went with her others, into a basket that hung from the cross-beams of his sleeping hut. It lay there with his things of value, the mouti—the medicines and specifics against disaster and disease which had, at intervals through life, been bought from the witch doctors, and had been saved by him against a repetition of emergency. Besides, he knew about a man without knowing—his daughter was a young woman, and there came a season when desire fell like a wave upon a woman, overwhelming her, causing her to bloom like a flower after the rains, and gave her a beauty and a perfume which drew men to her inevitably, as bees were drawn to honey. This was the law of life. He also knew that, since she had given up the old ways and taken to the new, he would not get lobola for her. That she would give her body without the security of cattle. She might even give herself to a man who was cattle-less, a wanderer, a man detribalised and shameless. All this he knew and his heart was sore. True he had other daughters but it was between the horns of the lobola cattle that the true happiness of a woman lay cradled. They were not lightly paid, and a clear mind as well as a hot heart must go into the paying.

In another kraal, this time to the north, across the Limpopo, which in the middle is called the Crocodile, and in one of its beginnings the Magalaqueen—beyond even the great Zambesi, on the mountainous borders of Nyasaland—lived M'Queni. He was a chief and the father of a multitude. Among this multitude bred from many wives was Mashupa, the boy who had gone to the white man's town to seek his fortune and his manhood. For, among the Kaffirs, among the Thongas, the Swazis, the Zulus, to work in a town, or go to the mines, was the equivalent of going to war; a substitute for it since now there are no wars. A man who went and returned was a warrior—a bold man. And it was a bold man who dared to walk alone through hundreds of miles of lion-infested country with nothing but a spear in his hand to seek work and adventure. To him the women gave themselves. To those who did not go they gave nothing, even exposing their bodies naked before them, as they did before other women, bending to wash in the river pools as if they were not there, or as if they were women, for a woman does not fear to expose her nakedness to a woman, and they were as women. And since a woman will not sleep with a woman, they got no wives. All they got was the sight of the women's nakedness, by which the women sought to shame them into being men, the nakedness they exposed for the honour of their tribe and clan, serving to turn cowards into men, by the force of their desire.

M'Queni was of the old time too, and had fought with spear and bow, kerrie and short sword, against the white man and, like the others to the south, had suffered defeat and humiliation. But because his land was rich, he had built himself up again, and his tribe had built itself up. His clan and totem were strong. Their arms were strong, and their loins, and the bellies of their women, and the land was fat, so that the women's breasts and the cow's udders flowed with milk. The babies were sleek and shiny, and they wore little white beads in their woolly hair to show that their teeth had come at the appointed time.

M'Queni's land was happy, for his people were strong and many, but not too many for the land, and his cattle were fat and many, and not too many for the land. And the soil was rich for the tillage of the women who, fat and strong, were eager to till the rich land; there was game in great numbers and the water from the mountains was cool and plentiful. The bees were many and there was always honey to be had, and under the dung of his kraals were great sealed pits of buried grain, guarded by the spirits of his fathers who were in the cattle, and by the strong horns of his bulls that were trained in the old fashion, so that they could run with the young men in battle and gore any stranger to death. The cattle were gentle with their own people, so that the small shining boys could ride upon them and race them, guiding them with a string made from the fibre of the cream of tartar trees that ran through a hole pierced in the membrane of their noses. One fear alone had M'Queni. That Mashupa, the apple of his eye, would abandon the old ways and marry a woman of the new kind without lobola. It was in his heart to honour the wife that his son chose, with cattle. The cattle to be paid for her were already picked in his mind. They were among the best he had, for was she not going to be the bride of his son? The mother of his son's sons, in whose blood his own would flow? The blood of M'Queni whom even the Portuguese had once called, 'the Lion of the North.'

Nothing was missing in this beautiful land, all was there to be had for the taking. Poles, saplings, and grass for the huts, fibre to bind them, wood for pillows and spoons and basins, trees that could be made into bows; strong reeds to make arrows fletched with vultures' pinions; clay for the pots, wild bamboos to split for sleeping mats, skins for warmth and clothing; ostrich eggs and tortoise shells for receptacles, gourds from the gardens in which to ripen and turn sour, the milk of the cows. Everything was here. Everything that man could desire. Wild animals to hunt, maidens to love, swift waters to bathe in; fish to spear, musical instruments to play, wood to burn on the fires; grain and cane with which to brew beer. All was here and all came from the forest where, in the morning and evening, the birds sang, where the crested guinea fowl cried out and the turtledove cooed. This was a land that was still untouched. Nothing of the white man's was here; even the iron they used for their spear blades and arrow points, hoes, swords, and axes, they smelted themselves in fires made of charcoal and cow dung, blown with bellows that looked like bagpipes made from the whole skin of a goat.

To the west, on the borders of the land of the Mashonas, whom the Matabele had once called 'dogs' and hunted, and which is now Rhodesia, was another kraal—the kraal of Tembula the wizard. He was a man well known throughout the land for his wisdom. He knew the lore of the plants and the trees, and of the animals that ate them, and the men that ate the animals. He knew them in this order, which is the order of creation, for it is earth, the great mother, that nourishes all green things, and upon them live the grass eaters, the bush and fruit eaters; and upon these live the eaters of flesh, both cooked and uncooked. He knew that the pathway to the heart of a child is a dog, and the pathway to the heart of a woman is a child, and the pathway to the heart of a man is a woman. These are things that give them happiness, and, to all, warmth and a full belly. Men along the coastal plain said, 'Wisdom lies in the path of the setting sun,' and they looked towards it, towards the kraal of Tembula, the wizard, the rain maker, the medicine man. They looked at the sun as it went down in the west.

In Moçambique, the sun went down in Mashonaland; and in the land of the Mashonas, it went down in Angola; and in Angola, it went down in the dark green sea. Everywhere wisdom is beyond man, no matter how he stretches forth his arms to reach it, or his mind to acquire it, or his hands to grasp it. Tembula knew this because he had wisdom, the wisdom to know that what he had was but a small part of all wisdom. He knew, because of his heritage, and his training, and because he was old. He also knew that his wisdom was like a small child compared to the greater wisdom, which was like an elephant, or the wisdom of the dead, who, because they were dead, knew all things. So, when people looked to the west, to Tembula's kraal as the sun went down, in the hour that the Kaffirs call, 'the time when all things are beautiful,' they wondered at his knowledge. To them, Tembula held the answer to all their questions, and because of this simplicity, Tembula was rich with great herds and many wives, some of them young girls, and from them both, the cows and the bulls of his herds and their calves, and the young women in his kraal, he got pleasure.

In the east the men said, 'Wisdom lies in the west.' In the west men, also looking towards Tembula's kraal, said, 'Wisdom lies in the east, in the land of the rising sun.' Tembula loved no man and hated no man. Only the white men, whom he did not regard as men. The white men and all their ways and everything that came from them, and their occupation of the land.

Once, and that not so long ago, within the memory of man the land had been free and the men free, to come and go, as the buck and lions came and went. Men who were hunters and men who were the hunted. The young men's spears had drunk blood and their loins had tasted the honey of the captive women. Enemies had been killed or sold into slavery and there had been none to say nay to the strong, nor succour the weak. None to check the doctors in their smelling out. None till the white man had thrown his net over the land and drawn it tight. So he hated the

41

white man. But kept his hatred secret for they were strong, stronger even than the wizards. Still sometimes he got a chance to hurt them. To act invisibly as became a wizard, to work as a worm works in the bowels of a lion, living with it, within it, and finally bringing it down.

Chapter Six

LE CHEF DE POSTE

Raimundo da Silva was the Chef de Poste at the district of Querida. He was for God and Salazar. A picture of Salazar hung in his office opposite the big desk where he sat in judgment. It was surrounded by a pattern of native weapons and curios—bows, arrows, clubs, assegais, and musical instruments were arranged with great precision. He had no pictures of the Almighty, but in his bedroom there was a picture of the Virgin Mary, and an ebony cross with the Lord Jesus in ivory, nailed with silver nails upon it. And a second picture, a smaller duplicate of the first, of Salazar. So that the walls of both his home and his office proclaimed his faith, his belief in God and Salazar. Communists he hated, but said that he feared that 'the world would eventually go Communist!' 'Why do I say that, Senhor?' he would ask. And then, answering himself, say, 'It is a matter of food. A Communist is a man who has been hungry too long, and the hungry in the world to-day outnumber the well-fed by a thousand to one!' By hunger, he meant the hunger of the belly, and also, though it came second, like Salazar after God, the hunger of the spirit for an ideal. The Communists had an ideal, an idea, and though they never lived up to their promises, it remained an ideal and an idea. It sufficed to fool the hungry and the foolish. And that meant the masses of Mankind. 'Where,' he would say, 'is our idea? Our ideal? What have we put in the place that was once occupied by religion and by God?' Only in America did he maintain that there was no danger of Communism, because they had food and the films. He had great faith in films. 'In America,' he said, 'the people's bellies do not rumble with hunger, and the blank spaces of their minds are filled with dream pictures, with ideals of comfort that could be achieved by the simple fact of having money.' And in this money they saw the symbol that would, if they had more of it, give them their hearts' desire. It was, therefore, only a matter of degree, only a matter of making more, to achieve the happiness that they pursued. This pursuit, even if it was vain, occupied all their lives and when it failed them, as it must for most of them, they were too old for revolution. It had been suggested by some that Da Silva was a cynic. This was untrue because a cynic is without beliefs. Da Silva believed in God, Salazar, America and money.

His first wife, a Portuguese lady of gentle birth, had died some years before. She had died of boredom, of the abominable climate and from bearing too many children, who had also died and were buried, in a long row of little mounds, beside her in the official graveyard, with the other white servants of Portugal who had come to this land in hope and had died in despair. But before she died she had begun a garden which each year became more beautiful. Sometimes he thought she must look down upon it from heaven, and see in it her achievement upon earth, a garden that was a consolation to many, where now her successor, a girl of peasant extraction, sat making garments for her own children, who, owing to their hardier blood, did not die. This, of course, might nullify Octavia's pride in the garden, but that was a question he had never tried to answer, regarding it as academic.

In both the garden and the house, the work was done by murderers because, as everyone concerned with justice knows, such men are not criminals. They are simply men who in anger have struck too hard. There is never any question in the mind of an intelligent man about the integrity and honour of a murderer. His crime is the result of an emotional error, of some unfortunate concatenation of circumstances, of an accident of time and place. And nowhere in the world were there a nicer or more contented set of murderers than at Querida. The poisoner naturally does not come under this category and has nothing to recommend him.

Da Silva's work of administration was not difficult, and he had assistants. But, nevertheless, he had his worries, and among the greatest of these were elephants. They devastated the gardens of the natives in his district. They attracted poachers, among whom were many unprincipled men, who armed the natives with guns though it was contrary to the law, and sent them against the elephants. And although the government continually questioned him about the 'found ivory' that should have come in from his district, he never had more than a cow tusk or two to report as being brought into his office. As he pointed out to the authorities, it was not reasonable to expect a man to bring a heavy tusk many miles on his back and then obtain no reward. But governments are not composed of reasonable men, it is not a profession that appeals to them, and the complaints continued to come in. 'Found ivory' was the property of the government, and so why, when there was so much hunting in his district, and so many elephants were known to have perished of their wounds, was more ivory not brought in?

What happened, as he well knew, was that the 'found ivory' was hidden till a white hunter or a trader came to the vicinity. Then its owner went to the man and said, 'Will you buy a tusk?' 'Is it big?' the man would ask. 'Yes, it is big, too big. And heavy too.' 'How heavy?' 'Very heavy.' 'Is it fresh.' 'Oh yes, it is fresh. It is an elephant that I killed, or one that I followed till it died and was still warm when I chopped the tusks from its mouth.' 'Then bring it,' the man says, 'and I will buy.'

The native then goes to where it is hidden in a cave, or in the grass roof of his hut, and brings it in the night. And the hunter smells the nerve hole and finds that it stinks. 'This is not fresh ivory,' he says, 'the nerve was not withdrawn from this tusk, it has turned putrid within it.'

'Not putrid,' the native says, 'but perhaps it was not quite as fresh as I thought it was.' He smells the nerve hole and says, 'You are right, Lord, I can detect a faint odour.' This, when the air is polluted with the stench. Nevertheless the white man buys at a cheap price, for the solid part of the tusk will be good unless it has been exposed too long to weather and the bacteria of the soil, which can eat into it and destroy it. When the tusk has been bought it is well cleaned, mixed with those of his own hunting, and finally finds its way into the hands of the Indian storekeepers in town who hold a monopoly on the ivory trade, as the Arabs did before them.

Da Silva knew the natives well, the Thongas and other peoples of the east coast—the Zulus. Lalla peoples, and Swazis. He had no fear of the Africans. The feral smell of their bodies was not revolting to him, and their songs and dances, their crafts and habits were familiar to him. More familiar now than the customs of his almost forgotten homeland which, when he visited it, became ever more strange, distant, and alien from the land which was now his home.

To Da Silva, the blood of all men was red, and the hearts of all men were human, but whether this was to justify his own views, or the result of his philosophical and biological studies, it is probable that no one, not even Da Silva himself, could ever be certain. But one thing he did know, that in the heart of a black man, or his liver, if you cut it out of his body, there was no trace of pigmentation.

So Da Silva is defined. A capable administrator of an area the size of Portugal itself. A philosopher, a hater of elephants, because they caused him so much trouble by ruining the gardens of his people, and pushing over the telephone poles which were his source of communication with authority. A hater of them, but no hunter of them. That he left to other men—madmen, in his opinion. He was also a husband and father, a collector of native curios, and an ardent philatelist. His stamp collection was probably the finest in Moçambique, and his greatest anxiety, after the health of his family, was the fear that white ants would get into, and consume, his collection.

He was a medium-sized, rather fat man of immense resistance to both disease and work. A good-tempered man who enjoyed his pleasures—the simple pleasures of matrimony, of stamp collecting, and sitting with a cigarette and a glass of wine in the evenings in the garden that his first wife, Octavia, had made. No difficulty in his work was too great for him to surmount, no problem insoluble except the elephant problem and, like the poor elsewhere, the elephants were always here, in lesser or greater numbers. But what he hated most was the tagati elephant, the spook that was known as the Lame One, who came into his area every few years. This beast no one could shoot, and while he was about, there was no peace in the land. Not only was he physically dangerous, having killed several men, but he was politically dangerous. The idea of a politically dangerous elephant appeared to scandalise His Excellency the Governor General in Lourenço Marques, and to amuse the highest authorities in Lisbon, who were, the more he reported of his doings, coming to the conclusion that he, Raimundo da Silva, was mad (which was unthinkable) and ought to be removed (which was even worse than unthinkable).

Yet how else, except in these terms, could he explain the unrest that came over his docile subjects when this elephant's presence was reported? Immediately, the spirit of insubordination and revolt grew among them. They said, 'The "great one" is here. The Zulu kings have returned to us in the guise of the King of the Elephants. That he kills some of us is a sign, for the old kings killed too, by the hundred and the thousand, for a whim.' So they said, 'What is the death of a man or two in these days, compared to the sign that is given to us by the departed spirits of dead chiefs and kings?' And while with his native police and a handful of white men he sweated to deal with the trouble, Lisbon laughed. 'The elephant revolt,' they said. 'Here's another of those periodic elephant revolts reported by our poor friend Da Silva!'

Sometimes, he thought, this elephant was the only fly in the ointment of his content. But, after all, an elephant was a great fly and the pot of his ointment was small, so small that it was something most men would not ever have had enough imagination to see. For to be content at Querida, one must be an uxorious philosopher, a philatelist, and as strong and patient as an ox.

Chapter Seven

THE BOY

Now the heart of Mashupa was divided between the old ways and the new. The new ways meant N'Tembi and the town, the clothes and things of the town, the white man's things, the magical things that one day he hoped to possess. The three great magical things were a bicycle, a sewing machine, and a gramophone. But all these ideas were only four years old. Behind these four years were sixteen summers of the old ways, the years of his upbringing in the traditions of his people, and behind them, the thousand years that had brought about that tradition. Behind that again was the black, spawning womb of Central Africa whence all had issued, that had split off the people who became the Bantu. For the Bantu came from the north and rolled south—a black snowball picking up volume as it ran, picking up men and women, picking up the blood that refined its features and the customs that changed its habits. And all the varied bloods that were blended in Mashupa called to the past, and were not at peace with the present in his heart. He was happy. Never in his life had he been so happy. But there was in his heart a sense of unreality about it all, even about his happiness. It was like a dream within a dream that had come true.

Perhaps our ancestors in the forests of Europe knew what was in his heart, and felt it when the Romans came, bringing their culture with them. But the Romans absorbed the people they conquered, as the white man has not done. It was not impossible for a barbarian to become a free man and a Roman citizen. This is seldom possible for a Bantu, for his black skin differentiates him and his sons from his masters, and none will accept him, so that in many parts, the best hope of a Kaffir is that of a dog. His best hope, that he may find a good white master. And his heart is bitter, for the old way is destroyed, and there is no new way that can fully fill the void of his aspirations. So far he can go, but no farther. So much can he own, but no more. He is tied to his inferiority by his brown skin, and the hearts of the indigenous people of Africa are torn two ways, are split between a nostalgia for their brutal past and a desire for the ways of the white man. Frustrated at being able to achieve neither, they turn inward in sullen introspection, or outwards into revolt. As the white man's problem is the black man, so is the black man's problem the white.

When Mashupa had been born at the back of his mother's hut, mats had been hung to give her, and the midwives who helped his entry into the world, more privacy. While they helped her, Mislani leaned against a great wooden mortar, and the place where he was born, the arrangement of mats and the mortar, was called busaken, meaning the nest. Over them, shading them, were the branches of a big tree.

There was no gentleness in the women as they kneaded Mislani's belly. When the child came forth, the midwives tied the cord of his navel and anointed it with fat. The afterbirth, which is called the 'house of the child,' was buried under the floor of the hut, lest the dogs dig it up and eat it, and the child was washed with water which was thrown away, being polluted with blood.

On the day following his birth, Mashupa got his baby name which was Nkulu, because the tree behind the hut had been of this species, which the Portuguese call the mafueira. This time, the first week of his life, was called busahana and was the week of confinement for both mother and child. His mother had to eat special food and was unclean. The food, mabele, kaffir corn mixed with medicines, was eaten with a special spoon, for there might still be particles of blood upon her hands. It was cooked in a special pot. A cock was killed because the child was a boy. The broth was drunk with medicines by his mother, and his father ate the flesh. This was the nearest that his father came to them, for he was not allowed to enter the hut. Young girls were welcome, but they were not allowed to touch the baby because he was not firm yet. He was, as they said, only water.

There came the great day when the shrivelled remains of the navel cord fell off. Immediately the hut was cleansed by his mother and its floor smeared with mud, after which her husband, and any others who wished, could enter it. Then came the rite of the broken pot. The doctor took a shard of pottery and put into it pieces of the skin of all the animals of the forest. The skin of the elephant, of bucks,

48

wild cats, leopards, cheetahs, civets, rats, and snakes. These he roasted till they burnt and, when they burnt, he held the child in the smoke till he coughed and choked and cried out. Then, with what was left, he made an ointment and, mixing the ashes with fat, rubbed the child all over, paying particular attention to the joints. By this means Nkulu was protected against the animals of the forest—safe from the lion and the snake, and enabled to cross the footprints of all wild beasts without danger.

In a measure, this ceremonial does give security, for the knowledge that he has been doctored as a child makes the hunter fearless, which, in turn, reduces his danger. It is an established fact that a man who expects danger is likely to get it. The man who fears elephants is more likely to be charged than the one who does not. In some way not yet understood, animals appear to be able to sense the hunter's state of mind. Just as when being stalked, if they feel the hunter's eye upon them, they sense danger and become uneasy. Which is why the wise hunter, once he has located the game, ignores it and seeks only a suitable position from which to fire.

After this ceremony, amid much joy, for the birth of a child is good, the people all smeared themselves with fat and ochre—his mother, father, and all the village. A goat was killed. And they feasted with much meat and beer.

After the feast everyone, except his mother, washed off the ochre. She continued to smear herself for three years, till Nkulu was weaned. And during this time his father could go to his wife but have no full intercourse with her, lest she become with child again. For, until a child is weaned, it is not regarded as fully alive, so great is its danger of dying.

Nkulu could now be taken outside into the outer air and sunshine. He was carried on his mother's back in the softened skin of a goat which had been prepared by his father, M'Queni, when he was born. To have prepared it before his birth, would have been to break a 'taboo.' Nor could the cradle skin be that of a sheep. It had to be that of a goat, a duiker, or an impala. The forelegs of the animal went round his mother's neck and the hind were bound around her waist. In this leather sling Nkulu sat, his head bobbing as she walked. It was comfortable for him and he was happy, with his belly against her warm back. As he grew older, he learnt to peer out of his skin or, if shy and afraid, hide his head, like a little kangaroo in its mother's pouch. When he was hungry, he cried and his mother gave him her breasts, first one and then the other, swinging the leather cradle forwards so that his little clutching hands could reach her. When he had drunk, he slept and was content, and his mother, relieved of her milk, was content also.

There is the possibility that this prolonged and intimate contact between mother and child is responsible for the resistance to disease and physical damage exhibited by the natives. The long continued flow of milk and tenderness producing a sense of security unknown to the white man, and all the other advantages of breast feeding, which the privileged classes deny their children. The fact that a raw native, as he is termed, can be taken from the forest and thrust down to work in the mines, in the bowels of the earth a mile below sea level, without going mad, requires more explanation than it generally receives.

The next ceremony to take place in his life, and the life of an African is filled with ceremonies, was that of being shown the moon. At the first new moon, after her periods had begun again, some three months after his birth, his mother, Mislani, washed her clothes to purify them and prepared to give her son his moon, for, without it, he would never become intelligent. On the appointed night, when the new moon was a silver half ring in the dark blue sky, she took a burning brand from the fire, and, followed by the child's grandmother who carried him, went to the ash heap behind her hut and there threw the brand towards the sickle moon while his grandmother tossed him in the air saying—'Nkulu, this is your moon.' Then she put him down on the ashes, and his mother caught him up and gave him suck.

After this there were changes in Nkulu's life though he was unaware of them. He could, for instance, now be pushed gently by the elbows, his father could pick him up in his arms, and, if he cried, he could be consoled by songs, all of which had been 'taboo' before his presentation to the moon.

When his body had become a 'little firm,' as they put it, his mother began her work again—cooking and hoeing in the fields. When she did this, she made a small nest in the earth for him, scooping it out in a circle and setting him in it. At three months, he could already sit up, and to relieve herself of the continuous watching a small baby required, she got her niece, the child of her sister, as a nurse-maid for him. She was eight years old, and played with him as if he were a big living doll, carrying him around on her back.

As soon as he could crawl, there came the ceremony of tying the cotton string. Before this could take place, his father and mother had to have intercourse, but in such a manner that his mother did not become pregnant. The sperm and mucus of this union was smeared on a cotton string which was tied about his waist, where it remained till it fell off. Now Nkulu was considered a grown-up child. He assumed a measure of reality, and should he die, could now be buried in dry soil. Had he died before this, he would have been buried in wet ground near the river. By the act of the cotton string, he had entered the family, before this he was scarcely considered a human being. Now his parents could again have intercourse though it was still 'taboo' for his mother to conceive till she had weaned him. And he could be carried on the shoulders without the cradle skin.

When he was a year old, his mother cut his hair for the first time. Before beginning she sprinkled some of her milk on his forehead and above his eyes. Then, cutting his hair, she threw it away in the thick grass. Her own hair she cut too, but left a lock on each side of her head for him to play with. When he bit her while nursing, she scratched his head as a punishment and he soon learnt to be careful. As soon as he began to get his teeth his mother took a white bead and tied it in his hair, above his forehead, which she believed would help them to come in without pain.

As soon as his teeth were in, the bead was thrown into the tala—the ash heap behind the house. His milk teeth were called tinyo-menyo, which means, 'a grain of pounded corn—that which is white.' Nor would he be allowed, when he lost them, to drop them just anywhere. He would have to take the tooth to the ash heap, say—'Kokwa, Kokwa ndji hwe hobe,' meaning, 'Grandfather, Grandfather, give me a grain of maize,' and throw it over his shoulder and go away without looking backwards.

Of much of this Nkulu had little memory. He vaguely

remembered playing with his cousin, the little nurse girl, being carried by his mother into the fields, and being pushed away from the fire when, attracted by its flames, he had crawled too near it. Because he was not weaned till he was almost three, he could remember his mother's breasts, and standing beside her to drink from them. It is only the swiftly weaned white child that cannot remember, even if it has had the comfort of the breast, for its time there is too short. Or, perhaps, when it is bottle-fed, it does remember, and turns back to the bottle again as soon as it can. To the Coca-Cola bottle and the beer bottle which, in its hands, have the same feel as the mother substitute on which it was raised. Nor is this all; the abstract love of the bottle may continue in such children so that everything that comes out of a bottle is good, whisky and gin, vitamins and sauces, soft drinks, and poisons. So the bottle on which they began their lives, being contrary to the law of nature, may end them in alcoholic graves, or in death from an overdose of veronal. For the truth is, that for babe or man, there is no warmth or security to be found in a bottle. There is only one thing to do with it, and that is to empty it. It cannot be toyed with, caressed or stroked. It is not warm or soft. A bottle is a stone, is sand fused and processed into a vaguely breastlike shape for the holding of liquids, but to an infant it is a mockery.

One thing is certain, there is no abstract breast, nor can there be any substitute for long feeding there, or for the food provided by the Creator for all young things, or for the security given to Nkulu by the feel of his mother's naked skin against his belly, and his introduction to the strangeness of the world, its work, and its wonders, from the cradle skin upon her back.

His weaning he remembered well. When he knew the names of things, could fetch them and could perform small useful tasks perfectly, his parents said, 'Behold, the time is come,' though his mother, delighted by his intelligence, was sad at the thought of breaking the tie that held him so intimately to her.

His father now went into the forest and found the wild custard tree which the Thongas call ntjopfa. It has a long tap root and its juice is supposed to make people forget. His mother cooked the root in a pot with kaffir corn and gave it to him to eat. And the Witch Doctor came to perform the necessary magic. He killed a fowl and offered sacrifice. He prayed to the spirits to bless the little one, and tied the beak of the hen, one claw, and one feather, about Nkulu's neck. Then, laying him on a mat, he smeared him with medicine mixed with grease. Meanwhile, his father had found the nest of a special kind of ant, which makes a large hole in the ground, and his mother went at night to this hole, and thrust a ball of medicine into it in such a manner that the ants must take it into the nest. When she had done this, she returned home without looking back, which was taboo.

And now the great moment of parting was about to come. For, on the day of its weaning the child must leave its parents and go to its grandparents. If it is the first-born, it goes to its mother's parents. And Nkulu was the first child of his mother who was a new wife to his father. And so, to her parents he was taken in the night. His mother made a little bundle of his things—a tiny mat on which to sleep and a little skin to cover him. He had no clothes. The walk through the night astride his mother's hip, he remembered. He remembered the moon, and his grandparents squatting by the fire as they waited to receive him. He remembered his mother's embrace and the hot taste on his lips from the biri-biri she had smeared on her nipples to prevent him from clinging to them. But somehow, the wild custard failed to make him forget and those first days were sad for him and he was at a great loss in a strange kraal among dogs and chickens he did not know.

Though he was unaware of it his mother came each day, for a week, to peer at him through the bushes that surrounded her parents' kraal. With a sad heart she watched him walk over the beaten earth where she had played as a small child. The act of weaning was called lumula, and comes from 'luma,' to bite. And when they said it of Nkulu, people smiled, becaue of the relation of this act to the intercourse of his parents, for as soon as Mislani's milk was fully dry, they were free of all restraint, and his mother was soon pregnant again. She had nursed him for three ploughing seasons, three summers or 'three hoes' as it is sometimes called. Now his place was to be taken by another.

Nkulu got used to the separation. He grew. Till he was eleven, he herded goats with other naked little boys. The

Thongas have many goats, goats and kaffir corn having been with them from the beginning of time, maize and cattle being relatively new among them. Then he was promoted to the cattle herd. All this time he ran wild and nearly naked on the veld. He passed his time playing little trumpets made of a buck's horn, bone, or reed. He hunted mice and rats and small birds. He learnt to throw a stick so that he could hit a partridge on the wing. He trapped other game in snares. He stole pumpkins by creeping into the fields, cutting the stems, attaching long strings to them, and dragging them to the boundary. He did these things because he was hungry, as are all the little herd boys. For their bellies are only filled at night and the hunger of the day must be met by herbs and game, by wild fruits and honey. The boys had many games and secret passwords. If he emitted a sound from the rectum, they said 'Fakisa,' and he answered, 'Cita munyakana goben,' which means, 'I have done it.' This secret formula came from the Zulus and should he not have replied, the other boys would have set upon him and beaten him.

He learnt the ways of the veld and of the wild things. He ate caterpillars and beetles, and locusts, and the eggs of birds, whether they had young in them or not. He played games with the boys and the girls. They had battles with the wasps, cutting branches and then attacking the nests, killing them, and ignoring the stings. Sometimes they fought with herders from other kraals. Sometimes they set their bulls upon strange bulls. They rode oxen and cows, guiding them with string through the membrane of the nose, even racing them. They did the milking in the kraals, letting the calf out to its mother and competing with it, for a native cow will not milk without her calf. So when the milk is coming down nicely, and the calf is pushing into its mother's udder, the herd boy forces it away, takes her milk into his calabash, and then lets the calf drink again. And so it goes until the cow is empty.

All this was the life of Nkulu as he lived it with the other boys of his village. He was one of a group, and his mind was part of a group mind. He was like a bee, part of a swarm, living the life prescribed by the customs of his people. And his mind, active in gaining information within this framework, was as yet unstirred and unawakened,

Having been a child he was now a boy. The great leap into manhood was still to come and he awaited its coming. Then, after the formalities and ceremonies necessary to his new state, he would be adult. He would have, as they say, 'drunk the nkanye,' and have entered into the age of puberty.'

This happened when he was fourteen. It happened in the night. He was excited but not perturbed. It was born of a dream—a miracle, though he knew nothing of miracles.

In his dream there had been a girl, like no girl he had ever seen, so beautiful was she, but also she was like all the girls he had ever seen. She was a lovely, red-brown colour, with big eyes like a buck, and she stepped like a nyala, daintily. Upon her head was a great kaffir pot and with it she went to the water. This water was like all the running waters he had ever seen, but also like no running waters. It was more clear, more swift. It appeared to him alive. And the girl, who wore only two small aprons, one before and one behind, put down the pot by the river, removed her aprons and stood naked, poised like a slim arrow beside the waters, before she stepped into them. This was the first time he saw this girl in the night, but he was to see her many times and finally one day, to find her, but he did not know that then. All he knew was that a wonder had happened and that, by it, he was changed. That he was what he had not been and could not now go back. His childhood was gone, and he could no more get it back than he could get the seeds of white corn that had been his milk teeth, which he had thrown away over his shoulder at the tala. But he was not frightened by the event for he had known it would come upon him, as it had to the other older boys. As it had to his father, and his father's father, and each had acted as he must now act.

There was precedent. There was the law. He went and bathed in the river as soon as it was dawn. Then he informed his grandfather of the event, and the Witch Doctor was called to make medicine.

The medicine consisted of the flesh and small pieces of the skin of all the animals of the veld, mixed with a handful of half-digested foliage taken from the stomach of a goat and roasted in a broken pot. This he had to eat and rub into his joints. It would strengthen him when he went with girls and prevent him from being overcome by their charms.

He was now promoted to clothes. The shifado, or 'thing with which one closes.' And his ears were pierced with a knife. The Witch Doctor cut his ears and put a reed into the hole. Each day he did this, washing the wound and stretching it. Till the wounds were healed, it was taboo for him to eat porridge in other kraals because the food might have been prepared by a woman who had had intercouse with her husband. This would do him great harm. Also he had to avoid the company of girls. But when it was over, a pretty bone disc replaced the reed, and he could now choose a man's name. He took the name of Mashupa—a warrior of his people long dead, hoping to renew his fame —and was free to go where he willed.

The old circumcision rites had been abandoned and he was now, with no further formality, a man and at liberty to practise gangisa. Which means, 'to choose a lover.'

He went to a pretty girl called Landa and said, 'Choose me.' She agreed without further ado because she had always wanted him to be her lover. He gave her the customary present of a piece of blue and white checked print, and they began the games that are customary among young people, playing at being married, building a little house together, walking, talking and singing and laughing, because it was the springtime of their lives and their blood leapt within them.

Mashupa lived with the other unmarried boys in a large hut. And Landa lived in another hut with the unmarried girls. Both huts were situated at the entrance of the village and so, though they behaved decorously by day, the nights were secret and nothing but pregnancy was forbidden by custom to the young.

This, then, was Mashupa's life. The simple, prescribed life of a tribal native—hunting game, making love, feasting and listening to the stories of his elders. It was a happy life and one which, because the country was rich in fruit and game, was without hardship. But one day something happened to change it.

A stranger, on his way still farther north, came to sit by their fire. He was dressed in a blue suit. He had a blue shirt, a blue tie, and a blue felt hat. He had entered the village carrying his brown shoes slung by their laces round his neck. In one hand he had a blue imitation leather suit-case. In the other he carried a spear. When he reached the kraal, he sat down on the ground and put on his shoes. He wore no socks. His name he said, was Sansao—Samson—because of his strength. He had worked on the mines of the Rand and he told stories of the wonders he had seen.

That night Mashupa did not sleep and in the morning he went to his father.

'My father,' he said, 'I am a man and I must go.'

'Go?' his father said. 'Go where?'

Mashupa pointed to the south. 'To the world that Sansao spoke of. If to-day was yesterday,' he said, 'I would be a warrior and go to war.'

'Aai,' his father said. 'That is what I did in my youth.'

'But now there is no war,' Mashupa said, 'so I must go to the white man's town and see the world, or the girls will laugh at me and say I am not a man!'

'That is what all the young men say to-day,' his father said. 'But many go and few return. Or they return and are filled with the sickness that they catch from the bad women in the white man's town. Before the coming of the white man there was no such sickness and a man could take any woman who was willing without fear.'

'Yet I must go,' Mashupa said.

'Yes, you must go,' his father said. 'But you must come back. Remember, there are cattle in the kraal with which to pay lobola for a wife when you are ready. You must go,' his father said, 'but my heart is sore at your going and your mother will weep for many days.'

'You have other sons,' Mashupa said.

'I have other sons,' his father said, putting his hand on his arm. 'And in the sky,' he pointed upwards, 'there are many stars, yet should one go out, its going would be noticed and there would be an empty place in the firmament. My sons are not as numerous as the stars, and my kraal not so great as the heavens.

So Mashupa talked more to the stranger, Sansao, and heard more tales. At last, able to bear it no longer, he left his father, and his mother, and his lover. Taking his spears, his mat, and a blanket to cover himself, he set his face towards the south, and began to walk.

Johannesburg was his final objective. The south, the white man's land, his immediate aim. He wished to see for himself, to learn, but he wanted to do it gradually. He did not want to be recruited by the labour agents, the black-birders of the twentieth century, and go straight from the bush to the bowels of the earth. Sansao had warned him of this. 'Go slowly,' he had said. 'Work for this man and for that at once—a raw Kaffir—as they will call you? If you will do as I say, you will not need to go to the mines at all. You will find work in a house or a garden, or in a garage washing cars. First you must learn the white man's language, and his ways, and then, when you have worked for a while, you can come back with honour and riches and lead the life of a sensible man. This is what I have done,' said Sansao. 'I have saved the money that they paid me and have bought wives to work for me. Each year I have re-turned to beget children and to rest in my kraal. Now I am coming back for good. I have wives. I have children, cattle, sheep, and goats. Now it is all done and I can live as a man should, in freedom.'

'My father would buy me wives,' Mashupa said, 'with cattle from his herds.'

'Aai,' the man said. 'He will buy them. But what of the women? You will not get the best. For the best want men who have travelled, who are mature and can manage them. My advice to a young man in the bush kraals is, "Go, learn, and then when you have seen everything, return." Why,' he said, 'you have never even seen a motor car, or a train; a road, or a bridge. You have never seen a big house or the appurtenances thereof. All the nonsense things that the white men use. Cups and plates and forks and spoons without number, every time they eat. You have never seen a horse, or a white man or woman, for that matter.'

'I have seen the Chef de Poste and his wife,' said Mashupa.

'They do not count,' Sansao said, 'for they are the ser-vants of the Government. To see white people,' he said, 'you must see them in great herds, in hundreds, in thou-sands, like ants in their great kraals that are called towns. See them swarming like bees out to gather honey in the morning and returning like bees, exhausted, in the evening. Why,' he said, 'you have never seen the lights that they make at night, just by going like that!' He snapped his fingers.

'No,' said Mashupa, 'none of these things have I seen.'

'Then go to see,' Sansao said. 'Go and come back rich, and a hero to the women.'

It took Mashupa nearly a year to reach Lourenço Marques. A year during which he saw much and ate at many strange kraals, giving each the news from those he had passed through on the way. He had permits from the Chef de Poste and the police. He was an honest boy, going from the bush to the city to find work. He was one among the many who went each year. And as he went forward, the past fell behind him, the historic past of his nation. He was a black man, leaving the blacks, leaving history, and advancing into the unknown.

So, as the young white man goes to seek his fortune among the dark peoples of the earth and hopes to return rich and a hero to his homeland, the young black goes adventuring among the whites. Thousands go each year from the kraals of the bush. Some die on the lonely way, are eaten by lions without anyone being the wiser, or die of fever, or snake bite. Others go and never come back. But many finally return to their land to sit in the shade of the great trees that are the guardians of their kraals and tell tales of the wonders they have seen.

As he walked, Mashupa met them. Home-coming boys, dressed in white man's clothes—in lounge suits and felt hats, walking through the bush with assegais in their hands, followed by people they had hired to carry on their heads their suitcases that were made of brown and blue imitation leather. Suitcases filled with the trinkets they had bought to astonish their simple relatives. Some had things they had stolen. Very little they had was useful. Its purpose was prestige, a passport to the councils of the men and the beds of the women. The equivalent of our jewelled cuff links, onyx waistcoat buttons and gold cigarette lighters. Conversation and temptation pieces.

In the kraals Mashupa met men, all but naked, wearing proudly, like medals, the helmets that are worn underground on the mines of the Rand, as a sign of where they had been, and of what they had done.

He passed through white men's settlements that seemed great towns to him. He reached the coast and saw the sea. He followed the coast. He passed through Macanda, Maxumanana, Incanine, Ville Louisa, and at last he reached

Lourenço Marques. By this time he was tired. And here was a really great place. The greatest in the Colony.

He worked for one man and then another till he found a master who suited him, and then he met N'Tembi. She was the beautiful girl whom in his dream he had seen go down to the living waters and strip herself to bathe. It was she who was to become all life to him. The one in whom all meaning was vested. The one in whom, as he buried the past, the future sprang up like a golden flower. Till he had loved N'Tembi, he had not lived, and without her, there could be no life.

The girl Landa, and the others who had been instrumental in his going, for their talk was of men they would marry—men who had seen the world, men who had worked on the mines, men who had been to Jo'burg, and who were men, warriors—became as nothing. The ferment in his own daring spirit, to which had been added the heat of the stranger's tales, that had created his resolution, was forgotten.

Meeting N'Tembi changed his plans. When he saw her, he knew he had gone far enough, for what is there beyond the heart's desire?

Chapter Eight

THE GIRL

The early life of N'Tembi had been much like that of Mashupa save that her father, Shibiti, was not a chief and was poor, whereas Mashupa's father was rich and a king, and that the south, where she came from, was dry and infertile so that the women of that country must work harder and reap less for their work.

But like Mashupa, when she was born she was nothing. For a child, boy or girl, is nothing till it becomes a person. Before that, should it die, it is not mourned, since it is considered scarcely to have lived. A girl remains a girl till she is a woman, and a woman as long as she can bear children, after which her functions are social and political rather than biological, and the taboos of her nubility cease to be of any importance. She can then, for instance, eat monkey or porcupine. Both these foods are forbidden in her youth, for what man would wed a girl with the face of a monkey or embrace a porcupine? The idea of giving birth to a porcupine being enough to keep women from eating them, and their pride in the beauty of their children, saved the monkey's flesh for men, and the women who had passed the age of child-bearing. She learned that at no time might a woman eat the hoof of an ox, because if she did, she might run a great distance looking for a husband or a lover, and never be at home. Nor could a woman drink cooked ox blood, or, if married, eat the stomach, because it would cause the child in her belly to be spoilt. Nor the testicles, which were the perquisite of the uterine nephew of the owner of the slaughtered beast, nor of the underlip of any animal. The rectum was also taboo for women and children as it might cause them to make unseemly noises.

From her birth, N'Tembi was governed by custom and taboo, and underwent all the rites that necessarily separate the infant from the child, and the child from the girl. The final rites that divide women from girls N'Tembi did not undergo, because the mission school, that was set up in her area, took her under its white cotton wings and educated her, much to her father's annoyance. But since in bad times he received help from the sisters, he had to agree to what he privately considered the theft of his child by the white people. Yet he accepted the corn and other help that they gave him with more philosophy than a younger man might have, for food to-day was worth more to an old man than the wedding price of a daughter that he might not live to receive in the future. Besides, if he was lucky, he might get both. If she met the right kind of man—a man of honour. A man who still believed that the old ways were best. And if not—well, if not, he had other daughters, and besides, when he did get cattle, most of them died of one thing or another. His kraal was on the edge of a small fly belt, there were terrible droughts, and wild animals took the calves if they wore not carefully watched.

What he did not understand was why N'Tembi was one of the few children favoured by the missionaries. That she was smart and bright meant nothing to him. That she might grow up strong and pretty meant more, but the only thing that really mattered was that she would be a woman, a mother, and in this she was no better and no worse than any other girl. It was in this light that his people saw girls, as little women, as little mothers, as miniature wombs—small cups, one day to be filled with the seed of men. They thought of them as they thought of their cows, some even using the same word, ntumbi, to express both ideas—the girl idea and cow idea, so neatly were the principles of birth and increase welded into one in their minds.

The cattle could not be divorced from the people. Many cattle meant many people, and few cattle few people. A small clan with many cattle, stolen or captured, could soon increase its strength by exchanging them for women, several to each man, and thus breed up its strength. The new strength being used to obtain more cattle by capture, and more women. These were the simple economics of the past which still exist, vestigially, to-day.

But the changes that have come are many. Lobola can now, for instance, be paid in cash instead of cattle, can be paid on the instalment plan, can even be paid in goats and other animals which have not the same symbolic meaning as the horned stock into which the spirits of the departed can enter.

Nor is the lobola idea wholly bad. By no other means can a man be certain of having his wife's parents on his side in the event of a minor quarrel. For should the wife decide to leave her husband, for such causes as we describe as mental cruelty, her parents would have to return the beasts that were given to them in compensation for her loss to the family when she left home. The African rule being that you cannot have both your bride-price, cattle, and your daughter.

In N'Tembi's mind was the knowledge of all this. She had heard nothing else spoken of in her childhood. Custom and taboo, the law, and the dire effects of its breach. Then had come the good sisters who had superimposed on this youthful knowledge a new knowledge and a new set of laws and new gods. A great God who was like a great Chief, and his Son, and his Son's mother, and a spirit who was everywhere—all separate and yet, at the same time, one. This did not confuse her since it was no more remarkable than the tales to which she had, since babyhood, been accustomed to listen. Were there not lion-men, wolf-men and leopard-men who could change their form at will? Were not virgin births, and all-powerful spirits, generally accepted by her people? All this new knowledge was, therefore, grafted in to the old in her heart, superimposed upon it, as a superior form of magic was imposed upon a lesser, older, and simpler form.

She learnt too of love. The white man's form of it. And, absorbed with her lessons in fine needlework was the knowledge that man and woman were created for each other, and that lobola, which the white man considered the selling of a woman's body, ignoring the psychic and social factors that governed it, was a barbaric and despicable custom. Her duty to her father ended with sending him a portion of the wages she earned. The tribe she was divorced from by her education. And when Mashupa came into her life, everything became clear to her. Love, marriage, a Christian life in which she, one of the newly emancipated women, would be an example and a shining light to her people. In her heart there was no war with the past. In her heart there was only love and joy. It was full to the point of overflowing. It overflowed in the songs that leapt to her throat when she worked, in her hips that she swung as she walked, into her eyes which became soft as those of a buck when she looked upon her lover.

The past meant little to her. She was a woman. She was heredity itself. She was life itself, a part of the never-ending stream of its guardians and containers. A black pearl, born of a pearl, whose destiny it was to bear more pearls. Human beings to be threaded by God on to the infinite string of time.

Chapter Nine

THE WILL OF THE MASTERS

Senhora Ferreira, N'Tembi's mistress, was a beautiful woman. Last week she had been thirty. It had come to her as a shock, almost as a surprise that she was no longer in her twenties, though for ten years she had been thinking of being thirty, of being old, of losing the beauty that was her joy, her pride, and her consolation. She had no children, for which she blamed her otherwise blameless husband. Had she had the chance, she would have taken a lover, but so far she had no chance. Lourenço Marques was too small, her life too guarded. Maniero was the man she fancied because she could not understand him. It was not as if he liked native women. That kept some men from the white. since it appeared that once such a taste was acquired, white women were without piquancy and seemed dull and tame. Yet how a man could mate with an animal was beyond her, and natives, even her maid who was so civilised, she regarded as animals. But no breath of scandal ever seeped back from the kraals of the interior about Maniero as it did about so many others. The man was an original, perhaps even a virgin. That was unlikely, but the thought excited her. One day, she thought, one day.

Sitting at the mirror, she put her hands up to her hair. The movement raised her breasts. Her red, painted nails smoothed the thick, black widow's peak on her forehead. Her eyes gazed into the dark eyes and scarlet mouth in the glass. Her lips parted in a smile of appreciation showing even white teeth, divided from each other by faint pink lines of gum. Her lips and mouth were perfect. Those of a young girl, she thought. Beauty, Mother of God, she had it yet. As much now as last week before she was thirty, more even, now in the fullness of her womanhood, than when she was twenty. She rubbed her neck and chin. There was a slight fullness there that she must watch. Everything was all right, but she had come to the time of watching, of taking more care, of using more preparations, and greater hygiene. She applied a deodorant with a little brush. She touched a long fingernail with a file. She moved some of the pots on her dressing-table, putting the cold cream jar on the right of the astringent and then moving it back again. She was getting into a temper. A mood she called it. That damned girl. Always it was the same—as soon as you got a girl, it started. Men in the yard, men on the back stoep, men in the kitchen, men in bed. Only yesterday she had caught N'Tembi in the arms of a big nigger. They were all the same. All harlots with the morals of lascivious cats. Animals, black animals. How she wished for the old days of slavery that one read about. Soon there would be a baby.

These girls had a baby if a man so much as looked at them. Like animals, she thought again, and her own childlessness gave her, for an instant, a sense of superiority. And such a good laundress too. No one had ever done her lingerie so well. Now she would have to get another girl and the sisters would blame her. Blame, she thought. You might just as well blame me because the cat has kittens four times a year! She thought of her wasted beauty, of losing N'Tembi, and slammed shut the drawer of her dressing-table.

Maria Theresa Ferreira was neither a good nor a bad woman. She was a bored woman who felt her potentialities had been wasted. That Maniero, she thought. That Maniero —how I hate him! Smug, self-satisfied fool, and apparently so stupid as to be happy. If he became her lover, she would soon cure that!

And N'Tembi singing all over the house. What was there for anyone to be happy about? After thirty there was no time for happiness. Now there must be haste. Haste to make hay while the sun still shone. To make love while beauty lasted. How she hated the smug and happy!

The love of N'Tembi and Mashupa depended upon the will of their masters, upon the whim of Senhora Ferreira who was served by N'Tembi, and of Senhor Abraham Abrahams, who was served by Mashupa. Both were good masters and pleased with their servants and kind to them, but nevertheless, their love depended upon their masters, and the time that they gave to love. If, for instance, Senhor Ferreira said—'N'Tembi, this is your afternoon off, but people are coming and you must stay,' then an afternoon of love was lost, for Mashupa had arranged his affairs with his master for this afternoon, and there could be no change.

Nevertheless, their love proceeded and took shape, as the loves of the birds take shape and form, in displays, in nuptial flights, in sitting bill to bill. And would continue to the nest where the small beginnings of love, the glances and the touchings, reached their great and logical conclusion in the egg of the bird, the calf of the elephant, or the child of the woman.

Mashupa and N'Tembi got to know each other well. They got to know each other at a distance, each knowing the form of the other, the other's walk and carriage. To each, the other was alone and clear, standing out, unique, even among a thousand. They got to know each other's faces; the smiles, the expression of the eyes, and the meaning of the smiles and expressions. Mashupa got to know the meaning of N'Tembi's downcast eyes, parted lips, and the quick breathing that made her white blouse rise and fall as he looked at her. They got to know their bodies. First with their eyes, and then with their hands, as the elephant gets to know the body of its mate with the trunk that is its hand. They got to know the sweet softness of their skins. The softness of N'Tembi and the hardness of Mashupa.

Over many days they did this. Little by little at first, with much drawing back on the part of N'Tembi, and then with less drawing back, and finally with none, but with a coming forward, as the ewe finally comes forward to the ram, the doe to the buck, the cow elephant to the bull. As there can be no immodesty in animals, there was none in N'Tembi when she placed herself within reach of her lover's hands and body. Governed by the necessity miscalled desire, they met and loved, hand to hand, lip to lip, breast to breast, loin to loin in the fulfilment of those natural laws which rule all living things. This is the law of life—its very cause. They courted in the bush-covered plots between the houses, or on the hill in the small room that N'Tembi had at the back of Senhora Ferreira's house, or in the small room that Mashupa had at the bottom of Senhor Abraham's garden. They courted wherever they could. They made love naturally like the birds and the animals because the time to make love was upon them. The earth, their mother which had nourished them for this, said, 'It is time you gave something back to me. Time you gave increase.' They obeyed her command because they could do nothing else.

The child was conceived on a hot night in the black shade of a cashew nut tree that was spread like a canopy, like a house, over the lovers. The air was fragrant with the perfume of the frangipani and stephanotis from a neighbouring garden; over a board fence hung the long white-scented bells of a datura. Below them, illuminated in the moonlight, great hawk moths hung, like humming birds, on invisible, whirring wings. The owls called, and the nightjars. The world was hot, aflutter with the summer loving of insects, beasts, and men. There were the whispers of other lovers who had left their houses to catch the light perfumed breeze. A spotted cat, sharing the night with lovers, assassins, thieves, and the guardians of the law, passed them, its white blotches alone visible.

N'Tembi's heart, and that of her lover, had been stirred, their blood had pulsed, throbbing in their veins. His hands had become urgent upon her. Her single garment, a white dress sprigged with pink flowers had clung to her body as, he sought it. The feral scent of their mingling sweat had joined the other aphrodisiacs of the night. Their breath had been hot on each other, and suddenly, the love play had merged into love; pleasure merged into pain, pain into pleasure, and one more life cycle was begun on the warm earth under the black, star-pierced tree. Another man and woman had served nature's great law of increase; their paths were now one, their past severed from them by an act that was irrevocable. As far as nature was concerned, their marriage was complete, for nothing is more complete than consummation, except death alone, its opposite. For there can be no coming back from death, no miscarriage, no abortion of the final drama which ends the life of man or beast.

Once their love making had begun, it went on, as was natural, but N'Tembi knew in her heart that the first time was when it had happened. She often said to herself as she worked, dusting, doing the laundry, and scrubbing the red granolithic stoep of her mistress' house, 'It was the first time.' She even made up a little song about it—'The first time was the time, but there will be many more for I am young and desirable and he is strong and loving.' There were many more words and much detailed description of her love making. It was a song she could not have sung in the convent, because the good sisters knew her language too well. And she laughed to herself, thinking, 'If the Mistress only knew what is in my heart and my belly or the words that come from my tongue unbidden. They come like water from a spring in the rocks. As clear and strong and as beautiful, but only to me. Only to lovers.' In her heart there was no question, in her mind no dilemma, because she was now a woman. No longer a girl, a flower; but a woman, a fruit containing seed.

To each the other was beautiful, and their beauty had

67

merged to produce the one that was coming which made them two no longer, but three. The 'I' in their minds became 'we,' and the 'we' was more than the two of them together.

Here was the thing of which all women are well aware and watch for, whether they know it or not. It did not need the comings and goings of Mashupa, which he thought so secret, to inform N'Tembi's mistress of what was in progress. The quick, nervous abstraction of N'Tembi had changed to a slower rhythm. Her eyes no longer sparkled like agates in the sunshine—they were soft. Her laughter, once so gay, was muted. She moved with more assurance, spoke more seldom, her mind occupied with dreams. Pregnancy clothed her in a mist.

It was at this time that Senhora Ferreira said to her husband Eduardo, 'Soon we shall lose a good maid.'

He said, 'Why?'

'Because she is maid no longer. Soon she will go the way of the other good maids we have had. You have only to look. It is apparent to all eyes.'

He laughed because he was a good-tempered and full-blooded man and said, 'Theresa, I am not the kind of man who looks at the bellies of my maids.'

But when N'Tembi came in, he looked and said, 'You are right as usual.'

Though neither of them said anything, both Senhora Ferreira and N'Tembi knew that the other knew. So the Ferreiras were prepared in their minds, for her going and thought of a new maid. It was always like this. A young girl came and for three or four years she was good. Then her womanhood flowered and she called to men with her eyes, her perfume, and the way she walked. She did all this without knowing she did it and the men came to her silent call, to the whistle of her swinging hips. They came because they were men, and her goodness, day by day, became less strong as the call of the woman she had become grew stronger. For only young girls and boys are good, as we call it, their virtue balanced on the precarious pinpoint of their years. Desire comes upon them, and then more and more desire, till it consumes them. Religion is the counter force that must hold the ball of morality balanced upon the point of lust, but sometimes it fails as the pin trembles in the hurricane of passion.

N'Tembi grew, swelling like a fruit. First she had been a bud, then a flower—now she was a fruit with seed in her womb. Man-seed that was held in her body, as the pips of an apple are held by the core of its flesh. And, at last, when she could be silent no longer, she spoke to the Senhora, bringing Mashupa with her.

'He is my man, my heart's desire,' she said with her soft, buck's eyes, the eyes of a fawn, brown, limpid as a forest pool, and gentle as are the eyes of all female things that are with young, with the tenderness of the motherhood that was upon her.

With her tongue she said, 'Senhora, this is Mashupa, the servant of Senhor Abrahams, and we wish to get married.' In her mind she sang of her love and its fruition.

'When will you be married?'

'Next Friday,' N'Tembi said, rubbing the bare calf of her left leg with her right instep. The words were spoken and she was ashamed.

'You have arranged it?' Senhora Ferreira asked.

'It is arranged with the priest,' Mashupa said, 'for next Friday, in the afternoon. It is my day off.'

'And mine too,' N'Tembi said.

For even a marriage there might be days when it would be impossible. It might be impossible if Senhora Ferreira had much washing to do, or Senhor Abrahams needed his car polished. Love, perhaps, could be snatched, but marriage had to be arranged and planned for. Some friends of each had been invited, only this had remained. To tell N'Tembi's Senhora. And now this too was done. It should have been done earlier, but N'Tembi had been afraid. If you planned too far ahead, if you counted on a thing too much, looked forward to it for too long, the gods, or Providence, or fate or luck might intervene. It was better to pretend that nothing was going to happen till the last moment. She said, 'The Senhora need not worry. I will work as usual. It is just for the afternoon.'

Senhora Ferreira said, 'I hope you will be happy,' and gave N'Tembi a hundred escudos—nearly five dollars— some dresses she had been meaning to discard for some time, and an old table for their house when they got one.

She said, 'Why did you leave it so late to tell me?'

'I was afraid,' N'Tembi said, 'and besides it was in my heart that Senhora knew.' She glanced down at her belly.

This was the truth, for it was hard to talk to white people of personal affairs. Often they refused to listen. But when a woman grew big there was no need for words.

All that remained now after marriage was to move into their house which they had, with great good fortune, obtained in the vicinity of the zoological gardens. It was a fine house, twelve feet square with a roof of galvanised iron, which being third-hand, and pierced by the nail holes of the previous uses to which it had been put, had a slight tendency to leak in the rains of summer. But it had a chimney made of iron pipes and a great cashew tree to shade its door. The child would be born within the city limits, but among the first sounds that reached its tiny ears, would be the roar of the caged lions and the bark of the baboons in the zoo.

She thought of the house, the baby, the possibility of one day having a sewing machine that she would carry home upon her head with her child slung in a coloured capalana on her back. She thought of Mashupa catching the bus to work each day like a business man. All this was in her mind as she spoke to her mistress with Mashupa at her side.

N'Tembi was married in a white dress which she had bought second-hand, with a veil made from a lace curtain. She had two bridesmaids dressed in pink cotton, and her friends came in European clothes, some of them wearing silk stockings and high-heeled shoes. Several had lipstick on their mouths and looked down with disdain at their simpler compatriots who watched the ceremony dressed in native costume—wound in the check and striped table-cloths, which were the intermediate costume that separated them from the near-nakedness of their mothers and the Western dress of their more sophisticated contemporaries.

Mashupa wore a white linen suit given him by his master and a grey felt hat. He had brown shoes and blue socks, a pink shirt and tie of a rich purple.

The service resembled in every respect that which was employed to unite white people in holy matrimony, and the blessing of Father Thadeus was given with the same words, and in the same voice that he employed in this office, whether he united the greatest in the land or the simplest handservants of the near-great, for in Africa no white man is of small account, this being especially true in the Colony, where a few thousand white-skinned people control the destinies of six million black.

The marriage went well, the priest blessed them and was happy to see them united in the church as they had been in the flesh. He was an old priest and wise in the ways of mankind. It was, perhaps, better to be spiritually united first, but if that did not happen, this too was good, and a sacrament no less a sacrament because what had gone before should, in strict morality, only have come afterwards. 'The indigenous peoples,' he always said, 'are like children. They do not understand these things.' But priests who were less wise in the ways of men, judged their brown people as they would have judged the white, and forgot all that the white had taken from them in custom and in culture, leaving a void which they were as yet unable to fill in its entirety.

The indigenous people, los indigenas, had had ways of controlling the ardour of their young men and maidens which, though not seemly to their white masters, worked well among them, and led to more happiness than misery. A girl in the kraals of the forest seldom had a child before marriage. To do so was to disgrace her parents, her clan, and totem. By doing so, she became an object of scorn and fingers were pointed at her when she passed. She would have no child, but would choose a lover and a playfellow. It was the custom that they should be free with each other, and lie together, but never to such an extent that a child should come of it. Their white masters could not believe that a man could lie with a maid and not deflower her. And since they could not understand such customs, they thought them evil. But the girl and her lover had love and release, and at the same time learnt a measure of restraint, which is no evil thing. During this period they were faithful to each other, touching none other.

The best white people thought of the natives as children for whom they held a trust. The good white people thought of them as domestic animals to whom they should, even if only out of self-interest, be kind. The simple white man said: 'Oh, they are just Kaffirs. They are like dogs and have no imagination or feelings.' And this must amuse the natives in a sad, secret sort of way, for most of them are poets, naturalists and botanists, and have very many skills of handicraft, till they are destroyed by being civilised. The other white men, the bad and the stupid, thought of them as baboons. As half men and brutes, and treated them as such, thus showing their fear of them.

But there are two troubles about the Kaffirs. First, there are too many of them, and they are getting uppity. And next, there are not enough of them to do the work of our new industries—so much profit is being lost from the lack of hands. So this is the white man's quandary, too many or too few of these half baboons, who, if they were full baboons, would be useless to him, and who, if they were full men, would threaten his position. So half baboon it is, the will of God and man, and so it must remain.

To none, not even the priest who acknowledged them as people and the possessors of souls (though perhaps of souls of the second or inferior class) did it occur that the natives were men and women with the loves, hates, desires, and aspirations common to all mankind. True, their culture was primitive like that of Europe in the time of the Cæsars. They lived in basket huts like those of our own ancestors. They slept, as our ancestors did, on mats and skins with pillows of polished wood under their necks. Their food was that of our ancestors, of hunters and simple cultivators, so that all that stood between their culture and our own was two thousand years of time. But time, in culture, is a variable factor and there were those among them capable of leaping those years in a single lifetime, just as there are still among us some who can abandon our way of life and go back, going, as we say, native and becoming white Kaffirs. Only a few white men do this, and when they do, the cause is less the call of untrammelled sensuality than a mechanism of escape from an intolerable civilised present into what seems to them a backward but bearable past.

Natives, however, in great numbers, are becoming white, in the sense that the culture they seek is a white culture, their aims white aims, and their hopes white hopes. They are black only in their skins. Under their skins, their blood is red like that of the white man and the yellow. Under their skins they are men.

So, without sanctions, without indunas, chiefs and elders, the young brown people who come to the towns are at the mercy of their natures and nature is very strong in them.

Because the white man did not believe in them, they have lost belief in themselves. The white man said, 'You must not do this'—but gave them nothing in its place, so they did not do it, but did more. And many girls had children who were fatherless, for not all men were like Mashupa. Many had become infected with the white man's custom of going from woman to woman, having learnt it in the mines, where they went with harlots because there were no good women of their own kind. Women who went with one man only, because they loved him, and who, as often happens among natives and seldom among white people, killed themselves in shame if they were deserted and dishonoured.

Of lobola, the giving of cattle to N'Tembi's father, nothing was said, though Mashupa knew that his father had cattle and was ready to give them to him for the purpose. Mashupa said nothing because N'Tembi was a new kind of woman, a modern woman, who could read and write and calculate, and he thought to suggest such a course would shame her and make her think that she appeared, in his eyes, a naked girl of the kraals—one who wore nothing but a kilt of breyed skin. It was her great knowledge and education that had fascinated him as much as her beauty. Her slim suppleness, that was like a peeled wand that has gone golden brown in the sun, or her eyes that were like a buck's eyes, or her breasts that were like small, sweet brown melons, or her waist which, pressed together between his hands, was no bigger than a young tree, or her nose which was small and wide-nostrilled, or her lips that were wide and deeply sculptured—not put on flat like those of the white people—or the lining of her mouth which was like a purple flower, or her teeth that were set in her pink gums like rows of pips in a mealie cob. All this had drawn his body to hers, and made it one with hers. But it was her mind that had fascinated him—it was the new mind of the Kaffir people, of the unbelievers, who, refusing Mahomet, had taken to the Lord Jesus, not realising that this was a religion that the white man had used up and abandoned, and given to them worn out and second-hand, as he gave them his worn-out clothes.

N'Tembi had said nothing of lobola to Mashupa though her father was poor and needed it, because she was afraid it would be an obstacle between them and she wanted marriage before the birth of her child so that it would be legitimate and could be baptised and go to Heaven. In addition to realising the error of the custom she knew that in her case it would have done little good, for her father's land was poor and sour, the grass long and harsh, when there was grass, and more cows would only have added to the thinness of the cows that were already there. Because, though the cows might increase in number, the land upon which they grazed grew no bigger. And she had learnt the white man's ways of seeing cattle as money, instead of thinking of them in relation to their numbers alone, irrespective of their condition. She had learnt this by going to the butcher with Senhora Ferreira to buy meat and seeing the fat meat cost more than thin, and learning that fat oxen were worth often twice as much as thin oxen. Of this, indeed, she had written to her father, and her letter to him about it was stored in the basket that hung in the roof of his hut with his other strange and magic things. But the knowledge that was in it remained unread, lying dead in the carefully written words.

The priest, Father Thadeus, would have said lobola was bad, because to him it represented the buying of a woman for money. A thing that cannot happen among the white people where it is only by a happy accident that the old rich men, and the bad men, obtain all the most beautiful and desirable young women. He did not understand, and few white men do, that in the cattle resides the life spirit of the tribe. In the cattle, cows and heifers, and in the women and the girls, lies the power of increase. They are the twin wombs of the nation. When they give up a girl, they give up a womb. They give up increase. They give up the two willing hands that worked in her father's garden and will now till the soil of a stranger.

In giving up a girl, the tribe and family loses strength. So ten cows are given in exchange. Ten cow wombs, which are less than woman wombs, and these ten, or their increase, or both, can be used to get a woman for another young man, replacing the one they have lost. But most important of all—she must be of a different totem, so that the blood of relations is not bred to the blood of relations.

In this way, since the beginning of time, had the Kaffirs obtained women in exchange for horned cattle. In war also they took them. Killing their husbands, and often their sons, lest they grow up into enemies. They took them, and from them bred children of their own. Each tribe, as it rose to mastery, absorbing another, so that south of the Zambesi, there are no true tribes to-day, no true blood, but many nations which are nations only because this blood or that, is the strongest.

Among the Thongas, who are also known as the Shangaans, the nation of Mashupa and N'Tembi, there is much Arab blood that comes down through the centuries, from the time when the Arabs held dominion along the coast, but holding it, still paid tribute to the great black kings of the interior with whom they traded for ivory, wild animals' skins, gold, wax, and fragrant woods and herbs.

In the blood of the child that N'Tembi nourished in her belly were many strains. The black strain of the Negroes of Central Africa predominated, and added to that were the admixtures of blood that had come through conquering and being conquered, for in both, the women of the defeated were taken. Of many of those tribes and races, there was no record, not even in song and saga which is the history of the barbarian, but the blood was there. There was also the blood of Arab slavers, of Indians, perhaps even traces of white blood from some old Portuguese adventurer or shipwrecked sailor. For in the blood of any man, white or black, is the blood of thousands. Each man is the product of two people, each is the result of the union of a man's seed and a woman's, so that by a process of multiplication, hundreds, thousands, millions of men, and before that, pre-men, had gone into the construction of this curled foetus. Back in its past, there might be Roman soldiers, Greeks, Persians, Indians and Malays, Phoenicians, Turks, Mongols—the unbelievable mixture of the Mediterranean littoral, of the near and far East, sieved out and filtered by the colander of trade and travel, of war and shipwreck, of conquest and slavery, of passion and lust, so that no man could say, with exactitude, what strains there were in this child. The only certainty was that it would be born a pale yellow and darken in tone as it aged. A Kaffir baby that would suck white milk from its mother's copper-coloured breasts and to all, except that mother, resemble every other Kaffir baby of its own age and sex. But to N'Tembi the child within her was her joy, her reality. Without the ability to formulate the thought, she felt, by instinct, that she was the vessel that held the very fluid of life within her—the everlasting fluid that has flowed since life began, that flows in the egg of the fish, and the womb of the elephant passing from one generation to the other, floating life—blood, sperm, and ova in the salt embryonic fluid, as a child sails a boat in a brook, upon its surface.

Chapter Ten

THE HOUSE AND THE LOVERS

The house was beautiful to Mashupa and N'Tembi. It was theirs and theirs alone. It belonged to a Goanese Indian to whom they paid rent each month, but having paid it, the place was theirs—a kingdom of their own. More, the Jew, Mashupa's master, though much despised by many, had with great goodness of heart lent him a bicycle with which to ride to work each day. This saved the bus fare, and the money was saved for a great purpose yet to be decided upon.

N'Tembi was happy preparing Mashupa's meals at night when he came back. She cooked rice, tomatoes, fish, ground nuts, peas, beans, cassavas, yams, mealie meal, and kaffir corn. Meat when she could get it, stirring it in her iron pot and seasoning it with biri-biri—the red, hot peppers of which he was very fond. While she worked, she sang, like a bird near its nest, with happiness.

The child, a girl more beautiful than any child that had previously been seen upon the face of the earth, was born with the aid of white sisters of charity from the Convent of the Sacred Heart. There were no complications of any kind, both parents being young and healthy, so that nothing marred their happiness.

In their hearts were the dreams of possessions. They wanted a bicycle of their own, a gramophone, and a sewing machine. They also wanted a bed such as white people slept upon, although the mats they used were more hygienic, having no cracks or joints to form a refuge for vermin. Some cooking pots they had, a kaffir pot of black iron with three legs, an old saucepan, and a kettle. Also four cups without handles and two glasses. They had six cans which had once contained Heinz's tomato soup, to which Mashupa had affixed convenient handles of twisted wire.

They had the love that burnt up in them at the sight of each other, and the warm nights to consummate it. They had the dense shade of the great cashew tree to protect them from the sun and nothing was wanting in their lives.

When he was away from her, working at Senhor Abrahams' house, peeling potatoes or washing his big Nash car, Mashupa dreamed of the softness of N'Tembi's body in his hands, and her warm breath in his face. He dreamed of her supple golden limbs and was in haste to return to her, pedalling his way home like a lunatic when his work was done. And she, who had been tending her child, singing to her, and cleaning the house with a brush made of a bundle of long, stiff grass tied with string, was waiting for him, as desirous of him as he was of her, so that their life was a long honeymoon which would, among white people, have been considered indecent, but which seemed natural and pleasant to them. God, indeed, appeared to have blest them, as Father Thadeus said when N'Tembi told him of their happiness. 'God,' the old priest said, 'means man to be happy and it is only man's sinful ways which prevent all men from being as happy as you are.'

Mashupa's happiness amused Senhor Abrahams, who said to his wife: 'Only natives can be happy like that. They are the children of nature and have no wants that cannot be easily satisfied. Food, a woman, and shelter are enough.'

'They are polygamists or would like to be,' his wife said. She was a very virtuous woman.

To which he replied, 'Most men would like to be and the Kaffirs are fortunate, for they can be if they can afford it.'

To which his wife made no answer but it was on her tongue to say that few white men, with sufficient means to satisfy their desires, confined their attentions to one woman. So that the question became less one of taste and morals than of economics. And although in principle the authorities were against polygamy among the natives, they did not really discourage it, for the desire for wives made the men go out to work to earn the money necessary to obtain them.

The child was baptised by Father Thadeus. The name they chose was Louanda Maria. The sprinkling of holy water from the font was the only mystery suffered by the child. Later there would be the confirmation ceremony. Here, then, was the first real break with the past, the first Christian child born to this unending line of heathens. Her parents spoke of it with awe. By it, tradition had been smashed, broken and crushed underfoot like an empty egg shell.

For a year things went well like this—a golden day following each golden night. The moon growing and waning, the seasons following one another. The leaves and fruits growing and falling again, and time having no meaning, once Mashupa had left his master's house. For only the white man is the slave of a ticking clock, only a white man bears his master everywhere with him, a devil sitting on his wrist. Mashupa and N'Tembi did not talk much except of themselves, their friends, and the people they had worked for. Their past, which was native, they both ignored. For them both, life had begun when they left their kraals behind them, when they had put clothes on to their bodies and carried their shoes in their hands to wear in public.

But if Mashupa and N'Tembi did not speak of their kraals, the people in the kraals spoke of them, and the news of their marriage filtered through to Mashupa's father in the north, and to her father in the south. Each asked his informant about his child's name, each asked something that neither N'Tembi nor Mashupa had asked each other. Mashupa's father asked, 'What is her totem?' N'Tembi's father asked, 'What is his totem?' And no one knew. Then one day a man related to N'Tembi's father came to Mashupa's father's kraal. When M'Queni asked if he knew Shibiti's totem, he said, 'Yes, I know. It is the same as mine.'

'What is it then?' Mashupa's father asked.

And the man said, 'It is the elephant.'

And Mashupa's father got up from the stool by the fire where he was entertaining the stranger with meat and kaffir beer, and left him without a word. For his totem was also the elephant, and thus a sin had been committed against the spirit of his ancestors and against the clan. Every law and convention forbade marriage into the same totem.

Nothing, not even murder, could be more serious than this. Murder and adultery and theft were crimes against people. This was a crime against the spirits, against the gods, and the gods were careless in their vengeance. They spread their net wide and not only the guilty parties would suffer punishment. All the clan would suffer, all his people, and all hers, unless something was done.

Already he saw the finger of the gods in their lives. His fourth wife's baby had died before it had been shown the moon—not a serious thing, but a great waste of time and effort. But two calves had also died, and the mealie crop looked as if it would fail.

Truly, the spirits of their ancestors were angry and the doctors must be called.

This was what came of the new-fangled ways of progress. Had Mashupa stuck to old ways, and paid lobola, this could never have happened, for in the formalities preceding a marriage, such an accident would have been impossible.

He called his great men, his indunas and captains, his wizards and wise men. He called them from afar, sending swift runners through the forests and mountains to the farthest kraals. And they came, with their sticks and their spears in their hands, and the wizards brought the appurtenances of their trade, all their tricks in little rawhide bags, their bones and their drugs, their charms and their herbs. Their poisons in bucks' horns stoppered with wild bees' wax.

They collected in M'Queni's kraal. When a black ox had been slaughtered and beer had been brought in great red kaffir pots by the women, he told them of the disaster that had occurred. He told the tale first in simile and hyperbole, saying that, as all men knew, in the world of spirits the crocodile must not mate with the crocodile, and that if this did happen everything went wrong in their lives. The rivers dried up, the fish died, the buck no longer came to drink. Then he became more open and said elephant must not mate with elephant. And, finally, he told them what his son had done and asked the advice of all, but chiefly that of the wizards, since the spirits were their concern.

For two days the matter was considered and discussed, and finally a decision was reached, which was no decision at all. They said that Tembula, the greatest wizard in the land, must be consulted for this was a great matter affecting not merely their own tribe and clan but all the people who were turning from the old ways to the new. A man must be sent to Mashupa to inform him of his duty. But what man? The distance was great. The time was short and the spirits angry. All who had come to the meeting told tales of disaster, of illness, of poor hunting and failing crops, of cows giving no milk, of goats killed by leopards, of empty traps and young women suddenly barren. Till they had heard the news, they had been unaware of their manifold misfortunes.

While they asked one another which man should go, one appeared among them. The wizards, claiming credit for his appearance, asserted that the spirits had unquestionably sent him. He came dressed in the clothes of the white man —a suit of grey, striped with red, with a grey hat upon his head and yellow shoes upon his feet. He had put them on when he saw the great gathering under the council tree.

'I will go,' he said. 'I am Querane who is known among the white men as Henrique. I am visiting friends in the vicinity and I heard of your troubles. I am of the old kind though I wear the clothes of my servitude. I work to gain money to buy wives, and wish to return to live among my people. I am wise in the ways of travel and can go fast, as fast as an eagle can fly. I have worked on the mines in Jo'burg. I know Lourenço Marques like the palm of my hand. I have been to Pretoria, to Kimberley, to Pilgrim's Rest, and to Cape Town. I will take your message for money.'

Querane had only been back from Lourenço Marques for a month and was tired of the bush kraal. He had told his tales, shown his possessions, been admired by the girls, and had had his will of many of them, but they were not to his taste. They were ignorant Kaffirs and the town called to him. The town where the girls wore high heeled shoes and lipstick and oiled their hair till it lay flat. The town where the various pleasures of vice were so easily found and so cheaply paid for. Here was a way to return and make money by so doing. He said, 'Because of my love for my people and the serious nature of the event, I will curtail my well-earned rest by the fragrant fire of my kraal, and return to the white man's town, seek out this man Mashupa and his wife and give them your message. It is certainly a great piece of good fortune that the spirits should have sent me visiting in this vicinity.'

'Tell him,' the old chief said, 'that he must go to Tembula for counsel. Tell him that if he fails disaster will overtake his family and tribe.'

'And the money?' Querane said. 'I must have money and the witch doctor, Tembula, must be paid.'

'How much?'

'Ten pounds for me and twenty for him. That should be enough.'

'You shall have it.'

'You will trust me?'

'I must. The gods sent you and the gods will strike you down if you fail. Besides there are the police. I know your chief and your kraal, Querane. You will not steal.'

The old man was right. He would not steal, but it was a pity—a wonderful chance. But the gods, whom he still feared, and the police, were too much for him. Either alone perhaps, but not both together. All the same it was a bit of luck that he had heard that there was to be a big indaba and had come attracted by the thought of an abundance of meat and beer. This gave him a wonderful excuse for leaving his kraal. The gods had called him to save these people.

Thus Querane came to the little house where Mashupa dwelt with his wife and child, with the money folded in a little leather bag.

He said, 'You are Mashupa, the son of M'Queni who is sometimes called the Lion of the North?'

'I am Mashupa.'

Querane held out his hand. 'I am Henrique,' he said, 'who is known in his kraal as Querane. I have ill news for you. It seems that your wife N'Tembi'—he bowed to N'Tembi who had come to the door of the house with her child in her arms when she heard her name—'and you both belong to the elephant totem.'

'Elephant,' Mashupa said. 'N'Tembi, is that your totem?'

She stared at him defiantly, her great eyes flashing, 'What if it is? What are totems to us? We are not Kaffirs!'

'Elephant,' Mashupa said.

'It is a heavy thing,' Querane said, 'and the king, your father, sent me to tell you that you must visit Tembula the wizard and obtain his counsel. Here is money.' He produced the little bag. 'Eighteen pounds,' he said, 'which I, at the risk of my life, have brought you from your father's hand. I have come a great way to tell you this.'

'Yes,' Mashupa said. 'It is something I never thought of. An accident. An arrow shot into the forest that has pierced the heart of man.' His face was pale grey with fear.

'You will not go?' N'Tembi asked.

'I must go.'

'We will see the good Father,' N'Tembi said.

'We will see him, N'Tembi, my heart, but what can he do?'

'Your child is a Christian. You are a Christian baptised in the faith.'

'Aai,' he said, 'but I am also a man. And a man has many roots. By this act my roots are severed. There is no place for me to lay my head. I have no kraal.'

'But all that is over, Mashupa.'

'It is over, but it is not over. How can yesterday be over?' he asked. 'It is past. It is past as a river is passed when it is crossed, but the river remains—the water is still there.'

'You are mine.'

'I am yours. My soul belongs to the Lord Jesus, but my spirit is not my spirit—it is that of my fathers.'

'It is over,' N'Tembi said again.

They gave Querane food and he looked at N'Tembi with admiration. This was the kind of woman he desired. Clean, beautiful, well dressed with high-heeled shoes upon her feet, oil upon her hair, and able to read and write. If this poor fool went to find the wizard, she would be alone.

He said, 'You have my sympathy. I will do what I can to help you. To help is my religion. Is it not said that all men are brothers?' It was wonderful to him how, in helping others, he so often helped himself.

'Not to-morrow,' Mashupa said, 'but the following day I must go if Senhor Abrahams will permit me. To-morrow I must tell him.'

What Querane did not tell them, was that he had not come by a quite direct route. He had gone a couple of hundred miles out of his way to inform Tembula, the wizard, of the situation and to tell him of the amount of money Mashupa had available. The wizard had given him two pounds as a commission, a splendid feast of beef and beer, and the choice of three young girls for bedfellows. Tembula was delighted with him. It was a good thing to have a great witch doctor as a friend. Tembula was added to M'Queni, the chief, as another important man who was indebted to him. It was wonderful the good a man could do if his heart was pure and his mind clear. Tembula, of course, being a wizard, had been too clever to give him any money. He had simply told him that he would reduce the charge he made, by two pounds, which enabled him to keep the difference.

Chapter Eleven

· THE DOCTOR

Mashupa considered it a great marvel that Tembula was prepared for him when he came.

When he came to his kraal, the wizard was seated on a carved stool. It was made of tambouti, a hard wood which is yellow in colour with a black heart. It was round and had three legs, like a white man's stool. But the seat had a long handle by which it could be carried, carved to resemble a snake's head, and covered with the skin of a great puff adder. It projected between Tembula's legs and looked as if the snake was issuing from his loins.

Except for a little kilt of monkey's tails and a necklace of green beads and men's teeth, strung alternately on a piece of gut, the wizard was naked. Beside him stood his newest and youngest wife. A mere girl with breasts no bigger than eggs, who offered him beer from a calabash. In front of him was a dark wooden bowl. Its rim was carved with symbols which resembled the signs of the zodiac. It was filled with water and in the water floated a bean at which the wizard stared intently, not even looking up when Mashupa stood beside him digging his great toes into the dust.

'Greetings, Wizard, great one, master of the storms and maker of rain,' Mashupa said.

'You are Mashupa the Thonga,' the wizard said.

'I am Mashupa, the son of M'Queni who is a king in the north.'

'And trouble is upon you—heavy trouble.'

'Truly, the trouble is heavy.'

'And you have come to consult me.'

'I have come.'

'All this I know,' the wizard said. 'I saw it in my bowl of water. And the bean, which is the seed of life floating in the magic water, that is the carrier of life, holds the answer. For days I knew you were coming, for days I have worked with the bean, the water, and the bowl. I have also consulted the bones and other magic things which cannot be spoken of, for it is many years since so heavy a thing has taken place.'

'I did not know,' Mashupa said.

'Only a child so young that it has not yet learnt to go out of the house, can say "I do not know." A small boy able to herd goats knows. You did not know because you were seduced by the new things and forgot the old. It is not that you did not know, but that you forgot to think.'

'I forgot to think,' Mashupa said.

'And now you must pay the price. Have you the price?' he asked. 'The price of my magic?'

'How much is your price?'

'Ten pounds,' said the wizard, 'for my advice.'

'I have ten pounds,' Mashupa said.

'And then there is the medicine.'

'How much is the medicine, Wizard?'

'Eight pounds,' the wizard said.

'I have it too,' Mashupa said, 'but that is all that I have.'

'It is enough,' the wizard said.

He held out his hand and Mashupa put the money into it. Eighteen hundred escudos, eighteen notes of a hundred each, for though the currency is Portuguese, they speak of it in sterling, the money of the mines of the Rand. Five escudos to the shilling and a hundred to the pound. Eighteen pounds was a great sum to Mashupa. He thought of his father giving it to Querane to bring to him. He watched Tembula count it. Now the money was gone. He watched the wizard stuff the roll of notes into a little bag that hung from a thong among the tails of his kilt.

Tembula drank the beer the girl gave him, and said, 'Sit.'

Mashupa sat on the bare, smeared ground in front of the hut. When he sat, the head of the stuffed puff adder was only a foot below his face. Though he knew it was dead, his heart beat more quickly, for its mouth was open. Its curved needle fangs lowered as if ready to strike. Its eyes, made from polished black pebbles, seemed to stare into his own.

'I have prepared medicine,' the wizard said. 'Strong medicine, and I have consulted with the spirits of the dead.'

Mashupa was silent. What, indeed, was there to say? He had come to listen and not to speak.

'They say,' Tembula went on, 'that there must be expiation. A life of suffering and danger—for twelve moons must this go on. And then, if you still live—you will be free of your burden of sin. It is against this time of danger and privation that I have prepared the medicine. Knowing that you were coming, I have it ready in a pot. Bring the pot, girl,' he said.

The girl went into a hut and came back with a pot of baked, black clay of a strange gourd-like shape. It was fastened in a basket of reeds, with a long rawhide loop so that it could be slung over the shoulders, and stoppered with a plug of wood surmounted by an ivory knob. Tembula set the pot beside him on the ground and continued.

'When you were a child, Mashupa, you herded goats with the other boys of your father's kraal, and you learnt much of the ways of the wild creatures of the forest. Then, when you were older, you herded calves and learnt more. Then you herded cattle. The bulls, the oxen, and the cows, and hunted bigger game. It was no longer mice and locusts and meerkats; it was buck, lynxes, and jackals, and by hunting them with spear and kerrie, with bow and arrow, you learnt much. You also learnt of the medicinal herbs of the forest and the edible herbs, the roots, and the berries. I recall all this to you because you must recall it to yourself. You remember how hard it was, how hungry you were? You remember how cold it was sometimes, without blankets, without a kaross, naked as the day you came from your mother's womb, that is the gateway to the world? You remember the fireless nights? But at least you had company. Now you will be alone. You will have no fire, no blanket, no weapons. All you will have is your hands, the pot of medicine that I shall give you, and the knowledge of how to make more such medicine.

'Take it,' he said.

Mashupa took the pot.

'Open it.'

Mashupa opened the pot.

'Smell it.'

Mashupa smelt the pot. 'It stinks,' he said.

'Of what does it stink?'

'Of elephants,' Mashupa said. 'It smells as the place smells where elephants have stood.'

'That is what it smells like,' the wizard said. 'And when you smear yourself with it, from head to toe and beyond the toes, to the very soles of your feet, so that your foot, which exudes a stink of its own, shall no longer smell of man, but of elephant, can you go safely among them. They cannot smell you if you are near them. And if you do not move, they will not see you.'

'Elephants,' Mashupa said.

'Yes, elephants. Are you not of the elephant totem—you, and the woman you have taken? Whom you married according to the white man's custom which does not count since she was a forbidden one?'

'I did not know it,' Mashupa said.

'Yet, it is so, and the spirits demand payment. This is what they demand. That for twelve moons you dwell naked among the elephants.'

'My wife and child?' Mashupa asked.

'You must leave them.'

'I will not,' Mashupa said.

'Then why come to me for help? Stay with your wife and child, stay there and be driven mad by the torment of the spirits!'

'They have tormented me,' Mashupa said.

'What they have done is nothing to what they will do yet. What they did was enough to send you to me. Stay then, Mashupa. Wait till you are driven mad, wait till you turn your hand even against those you love most and slay them.'

'Slay them?' Mashupa asked.

'It is possible,' said the wizard. 'Them or others. If you stay, there will be blood. There will also be death and disaster in your father's kraals and your woman's father's house. That is what the great ones have foretold. Go, and you may be saved because of my medicine and my secrets.'

'They will kill me,' Mashupa said.

'They may kill you,' the wizard said. 'They have killed others. But once they are used to you, you may be safe among them, being naked and weaponless, and smelling as they smell. There is your choice, Mashupa, son of M'Queni—a possible death from the kings of the forest, or the certainty of madness if you remain. Madness, which will drive you to the killing of women and children, and of men.'

'It is a heavy thing,' Mashupa said.

'There is one heavier thing,' the wizard said. 'There is death.'

'Here there is the chance of death.'

'There is always the chance of death. But wait,' Tembula said, 'wait young man.' He stood up and said, 'If you think I speak of the things I do not know, you do not think correctly. All great and true wizards have lived naked in the wilderness as you will live. For thirty-six moons I lived as a wild man. As an animal with animals, for that is part of the training of a wizard. There are many doctors in the land to-day, little men who were not called by the great ones, but who took to doctoring as a way of extorting riches from the simple. They buy their medicines, and knowing nothing, invent things which would sound plausible only to a child.

'No,' he went on, 'I, like the other great doctors of the past, have suffered to learn my art. We suffered and starved, shivered in the cold nights, and were scorched in the hot days. Were bitten by insects till we became immune to them, so that to-day I can take a scorpion in my hand. It does nothing, because it can do nothing and it knows that I am its friend. Honey I ate, and locusts and worms, and mice and what was left on the lion's kill that I disputed with the carrion eaters, the jackals, the hyenas, the vultures and the eagles of the air. Roots and berries—even leaves have I eaten. And only then, when all this was done and I was purified, was I prepared for the great ordeal by the doctors, which was to go alone into a swamp and there kill, with my bare hands, the great python whose skin adorns my person on occasions of importance. I found it,' he said, 'and seized it by the neck. It cast its coils about my thigh, about my belly. Its eyes, that were like stones, looked into my eyes. It opened its mouth and I beheld its fangs that were like assegais of ivory. I saw its flickering tongue, the red valley of its throat, but my hands were iron bands, and I held it till it died with its eyes still open. Then I skinned it and dried the skin and softened it with grease and ash. When all this was done, my fame was known and from that day it has never waned, but grown day by day, till men come from all parts of the land to see Tembula, the wizard. They come from the mountains of Lebombo, from Maputo, from the Zambesi, for in all this land there is none to compare with me for wizardry or wisdom. The other wizards are as sparrows compared to me that is an eagle. So they come from the North and the South, from the East, where the Sun is born, and the West, where it dies.

'Now,' he said, 'is your heart strong? Will you go or shall I return your money to you? For money that is not earned I will not keep, lest it bring me ill fortune.'

'Keep the money,' Mashupa said. 'What can I buy with it in the forest?'

'Then you are going?'

'I am going, but I go in fear. In fear of the forest. In fear of the heaviest thing, which is to bid farewell to my beloved and my child. Oh! Tembula, how does a man tear his heart out of his body? How does a man break with his hands all that he has built up? How does he crush the bread that he has baked into crumbs to be consumed by the ants?'

'He goes with the strength of the warrior,' the wizard said.

'I must go unarmed with nothing in my hands?'

'You have my medicine. And now that you have decided, I will tell you all the ingredients thereof. All, that is, but the most secret. First, is the fresh dung of the elephant and with this, to bind the wood ash that is the second ingredient, is the fat of the sea cow. Mixed in with it is the pus that is found at the root of the elephant's tusk, round the ivory as it enters the softness of the flesh of its lips. There are also the eyelashes of both elephant and buffalo, and the spleen of an inyala bull killed by the light of the waning moon, and diverse herbs, fruits, and roots. Smear this upon yourself, over your hair, over your hands and feet, over your loins and belly, smear it particularly on all those parts which have a strong and particular smell. Smear it under the armpits, and on the flanks and on those parts that are not seen. This will cause you to smell as an elephant smells. The ash will cause you to be grey, like an elephant. The rest, the other things are magic and beyond your understanding.'

'And when the pot is done?' Mashupa asked. 'It is not

a very large pot.' For eight pounds it seemed to him the pot should have been larger. But it was certainly a wonderful piece of magic that the wizard should have been able to see into his purse and know exactly how much money he had.

'When it is done,' Tembula said, 'if you still live, it will be simpler, for your initiation to the clephant people will be accomplished. Also being among them, you will have no difficulty in smearing your person with the mud from their wallows and the fresh dung you will pick up in their sleeping places. Use both freely, for they cost nothing, and you will be safe. Eat as you learnt to eat as a boy, as a cattle herd. Eat honey and bee grubs, eggs and small birds, insects and mice, fruit and roots. Make snares for the little animals, but make no fire. Eat what you eat as it is, removing only the skins of the beasts, the feathers of the birds, and the scales of the fish. Eat lizards, eat the things that you find under the stones. This is my word and the word of the dead, of those who have gone from us but who yet remain among us. This is the word from those whose intermediary I am. So speaks Tembula, the wizard.'

Mashupa picked up his pot and slung it on his back.

'Farewell, Wizard,' he said, 'farewell, mouth of the dead. Stay in peace.'

'Farewell, Mashupa. I have done what I can to help you and can do no more. Farewell and go gently.'

So Mashupa left the kraal of the wizard.

When he had gone, the girl brought more beer in the calabash and meat on a flat, carved wooden platter.

Chapter Twelve

THE ROAD BACK

The journey back was not the same, though the road he followed was unchanged. Beauty had gone, with hope, from the world and it was black in the hot sunshine, as dark as the pools of shadow under the great trees. Going, there had been hope. Returning, there was only an emptiness.

Already a curtain had come down between him and his wife and child. He was a marked man, a hunted man. He must see them, tell them, and go. Hunted not by calculable forces, not by other men, not even by wild beasts, but by the spirits. He was a haunted man. He was no longer even the same man as he had been a few hours ago.

The wizard had caught his happiness as a child would catch a butterfly, and crushed it between his fingers. How N'Tembi loved butterflies, pointing them out to the child as they fluttered, yellow, long-tailed with blue eyes on their wings, over the veld. They were swallowtails, but the name was not known to him. To him they were creatures that flew, like himself, on the wings of joy in the sunlight.

Tell her. How was he going to tell her? Tell the incomparable one, tell his heart's desire that he must leave her for a year to dwell alone in the wilderness. He must leave his little house, the small garden he had made and fenced so carefully, where cassava, ground nuts, taro, chick-peas, and okra grew in opulent confusion among the flowers. The sewing machine would have to go back and in another year it would have been paid for. The music of the gramophone, that had been their next project, was dead before the first record had been played. He had often thought of that. Of sitting, when the day's work was done, with the machine on an upturned crate under the cashew tree and playing tunes to N'Tembi as she worked on her machine with the table set at the entrance door. The table the Senhora had given them, and the door that he had made. The old one had fallen apart soon after they had moved in.

As if the gods would prove his sin, as if they would rub salt into the wound of his spirit, he found, as he came to an Indian store on the road, a wedding party. A man, no longer young, with a new wife. A pretty girl, confident in her beauty and knowing the grip her slim, silken body had on the man who was with her. She sat on the ground on a mat of split bamboo. In her hand she had a long, newly peeled wand. With it she pointed to each bolt of material she desired. The storekeeper pulled it off the shelf and unrolled it holding it up against himself. When she nodded, he cut off a strip and passed it to a second Indian who hemmed the edges on a sewing machine. He hemmed the torn edges and threw it down to her. By this time she had pointed to another piece. Soon the ground round her was covered with brightly coloured cotton strips.

The ground was dusty with the earth brought in on the bare feet of the customers. But neither to the girl nor to Mashupa, who was watching, was the soil dirty. It was their mother, the earth from which they drew their sustenance. All he thought was—how lucky they are. They, who have held to the old customs, those whom nothing can tear apart. Then he thought of N'Tembi and the wonder of her numerous talents. It was because she was as she was that he loved her. A superior person. But what had it brought him? First love, and then this parting. The love was over except in memory now, and the parting imminent. He must come back. He must survive. It was not impossible. He was no longer afraid. Twelve moons, he thought, and then we shall be together again. But the parting that must come. Three more days and he would be home. Three days and she would meet him with the question in her great dark eyes.

N'Tembi met him at the door of the house with the child on her hip. Over her head was a spray of purple bougain-villaea. A year, a thousand years ago, Senhor Abrahams had given him a rooted cutting. They had tended it well and it was in flower for the first time. Behind her was the black-ness of the house, the door, the mouth as it were, of their home. She was dressed in pink. On her head was a mauve bandana. Round her neck, a string of pearly beads. Her feet were bare. Her pink-palmed hands were cupped up-wards round the child's golden thigh.

'Mashupa,' she said.

'Yes,' he said.

'You are back!'

'I am back.'

'You are tired.'

'I am tired.' It was impossible to express such tiredness. It was not just that his legs ached, that his body was stiff from sleeping on the ground. It was his heart that was tired. He sat down. She brought him tea with sugar and condensed milk in a white enamel cup with a dark blue edge and handle. They had two such cups.

'Well,' N'Tembi asked, 'what is the news?'

'The news is bad.'

The tea had revived him. 'He says I must go and dwell

for twelve moons among the great ones alone and un-armed. Only by this can my sin be expiated.'

'I have been to Father Thadeus,' she said. 'He says this is madness. You are a Christian man. You have done no wrong. He says . . .'

'N'Tembi,' Mashupa said, 'I am a Christian man, but I also belong to my people and I must go. For a week I will dwell here with you and our child. Then I must go. Senhora Ferreira will take you back perhaps. In twelve moons I shall be home and it will be over.'

'And the child?' she asked.

'The sisters will take the child till we are together again. The Father can arrange it or Senhora Ferreira may let you take her there.'

'The house?' she asked.

'The house we cannot keep. You cannot live here alone. There will be no money for rent.'

'So our life is ended—this is death!'

'While we live, it is not ended. Be of good heart, N'Tembi. You have friends. The Father will help us.'

'It is ended. Alone, I am cut in two. Alone, I am as one dead.'

Mashupa touched the stem of the bougainvillaea. How little it had been—how it had grown. Would the people who took the house tend it as he had done? The purple creeper had suddenly become the symbol of life. Life was like a tree and Tembula had set his axe to it. It might grow again shooting from the bottom. It might. Sinking his head into his hands, he wept. The tears ran hot, salt, like blood, down his cheeks and into his mouth.

N'Tembi put her hand on his shoulder. 'The Father says this is witchcraft.'

'I have broken the law and must pay.'

'And you paid him for this?'

'I paid him.'

'The sewing machine will be taken back—we shall lose what we have paid.'

'I will make more. I will work harder.'

N'Tembi picked up the pot that he had put down and pulled off the stopper by its ivory plug.

'What is this?' she asked.

'My medicine,' he said.

'It stinks. What foul thing is this?'

'It is necessary,' he said. 'I must smear myself with it.'

'With that filth? With excrement?'

'I must,' he said.

'And, because a witch doctor says so, you must leave me?'

'I must go lest worse befall. Lest the spirits, angry at our deed, overwhelm us both. This way I can bear the burden. I can carry the cross alone.' He began to see it now. The expiation took on a Christian pattern. He thought of the forty days in the wilderness, of the Calvary. He could sacrifice himself to save them, his loved ones, as the Lord Jesus had sacrificed himself to save mankind. The elephants were the devil, the wilderness was the same. He must expose himself to it before he could return. Life was now divided into separate pieces. This, the parting. The arrangements that must be made. The time in the wilderness —the temptation. And the return. To see light again, he must pass through the shadow.

How strange it was, having talked of so much together, the question of their totem had never come up. She would have laughed at it. She was emancipated. But he, he could not laugh. The cord that tied him to his people, had been weakened, but never severed. It went back into the mysterious past that was his heredity, into his upbringing as a child. Stay, yes he could stay, he could disregard Tembula's instructions. But if he stayed, worse would overtake him, overtake them all. To save them, he must go.

As if the gods were giving him a sign, there was a clap of thunder and the loud rip of lightning as it struck a tree nearby. The storm had come up unperceived by them. Many evenings in the summer there were storms and rain, but this one was a sign. If he decided not to go, it would strike the house next time. No, there must be no next time—he must go!

There was another crash. The lightning jagged a swift, yellow gash across the darkening sky. Then came the thunder-claps and the wind, ice-cold from the south, reached out its hands for the big cashew tree, turning up its leaves as a man might raise a woman's skirt. The rain came in great cold drops. He stood in front of the door between the storm and his wife and child. The heavens opened and the rain fell in sheets. Squall after squall, driving in on to the earthen floor. He pushed N'Tembi back and closed the door.

She put the child down and came to his arms. Warm, fluid, soft, perfumed in the hot darkness of the hut. They became one flesh, moulded into each other, one as nearly as two people can be, as much one as mating animals, but with a desperate fury that only man can know. For only man understands the passage of time. Only man knows that this thing must end, that there can be no full possession, only a temporary fusion where, for an instant, the pulse of one is the pulse of two, where the heartbeat of one is drowned in the heartbeat of another, where, for an instant, the blood roars in the ears more loudly than the surf upon a strand. Where, in the midst of the savage storm, in the turmoil of emotion, in the vortex of the typhoon, there is an instant's rest and peace. Only man knows this instant of security. The instant where he pauses like an arrow shot into the air before it falls—a moment of nothingness.

For a week it continued. A furious honeymoon. Their two bodies, destined to be parted, cried out to each other, clung to each other in desperation. The hut was the cave of wild beasts, it was the palace of kings, it was the final refuge. Without knowing it, they were making, not merely a new child, but a memory, searing it into each other's souls, burning it in with the wild passion of their embrace. It had grandeur, it had bestiality, at once savage and gentle, at once raging and tender, it was a challenge to time itself, to its passing, for by memory time could be defeated. By a child, more life could be thrown like a spear from the present into the future. They were not husband and wife, they were not man and woman. They were one.

Between these outbursts, they went about their business like people in a dream. The outside world, the people in it, reality, was unreal. Only they, their brown bodies clinging together, were real. The rest was a dream—the prelude of a nightmare. But even desire could be killed by exhaustion, and even pain ended in sleep. Only thus could they find the last remnants of peace, of escape from the horror that was to come—in exhaustion, in sleep, as they lay curled in each other's arms.

Chapter Thirteen

THE FOREST

Something must now be said of the forest and its greatest inhabitants—the elephants.

From a vegetal point of view, the world of the forest is many worlds, for the trees and the bushes, grasses, and the bulbs have preferences, just as men and animals have. There are men who are lake-dwellers, and there are men in China who live out their lives upon the sampans in the rivers; there are the Esquimaux of the snowy north and the black Negroes of the equator; and those who live upon the desert sands, the nomads of Mongolia and the Berbers of the Sahara. The gemsbuck is a desert-loving buck, and the springbuck a lover of the plains. The kudu cannot tolerate open country, but demands bush. So it is with the trees and the other green living things.

The green world is a world of its own, a geographical world, with islands of this kind of growing things, and lakes of that. With great lands covered with one kind of tree almost exclusively and joined to other lands of the same kind by an isthmus of similar trees, or separated from it by a sea of various bushes. There are botanical peninsulas, gulfs, bays, archipelagos. They are dependent on rainfall and drainage, on the soil beneath them, and on the altitude above the level of the seas for their character. At one level one kind of vegetation stops sharply as if it had been cut off with a knife, and another begins, or the two kinds may merge, bleeding slowly into each other. There are botanical friendships. Plants which like to dwell together in a happy, symbiotic association of mutual help. There are botanical parasites that suck the green blood of their hosts.

Thus, in the low veld where Mashupa was, there were great areas of grey hardekools—that the botanists call *Combretum imberbe*. Immense tortured trees whose pale trunks took on the form of elephants and rhinoceroses, and other strange beasts in the moonlight. In one, the face of a crocodile was unmistakable; another had the grinning mask of a wild pig, or a baboon. These trees have sparse, grey foliage, and get their name from the dense hardness of their wood and its quality of slow burning that is like coal. They grow in sour veld, in the tall, harsh grass that is only edible in early spring, and, for the other seasons, is deserted by the grass eaters. There were patches where the tree, that the natives call zopforra, the tambouti, grows, its foliage almost as dark as its wrinkled trunk, except in the fall when it turns crimson and scarlet. This is a hardwood too, good for the making of furniture and fence poles, its black heart timber being impervious to termites. Its smoke is fragrant, but likely to poison the meat that hangs above it. Its sap is dangerous and its dust and chips can make the workers in this wood sick from the venom concealed in its perfume.

There were areas where the chamfuta or mahogany, that look like giant chinaberry trees, grow in green umbrellas over short, massive trunks. In places along the rivers there grew a small tree whose seed is a great bean five feet long and five inches wide, that rattles in the wind when it is dry. There were patches where the two-sexed marula was to be found, that the natives call the kango, and of whose sweet fruits they make an intoxicating drink, and which, if left on the ground, and eaten by the elephants and wild pigs, ferments in their bellies, and makes them reel with drunkenness. There were patches where the marsala or kaffir orange grew, its round, hard-shelled fruit a favourite dish of the baboon and kudu. There were the hornless isotso trees that bleed the gum of commerce. There was the xingoya bush, a shrub from which string is made, and the zand hlopfu that is used for axe handles, and whose name means elephant-resisting, and the nhlaro nhlato, a big tree found near water. There were grassy stretches between thickets of managa and nthwa nthawa, where the yellow fever trees grew in livid beauty. There were vast areas of dry sakari, dense bush hung with lichen that the Kaffirs used to tamp the charge of their muzzle-loaders. There were simbiri belts, waterless, birdless, bedded with dry leaves that crackled under foot. There were patches known as qwazine, dry forests of little trees that grow close together smothering all other life. And here and there, dominating the forest, were its kings, the simao—the giant baobabs or cream of tartar trees.

In the forest there was also the up and down world of the woodpeckers and the parrots that moved in the vertical plane of the tree trunks, and the monkeys that swung, one-handed, from the lianas. And above them were the great circular worlds of the upper air, where the vultures, the eagles, and the marabous hung poised, awaiting death below them. For not only the bare-necked vultures are carrion eaters; so are many of the noble eagles. The falcons alone being clean feeders, quick killers with beak and talon.

Up there, above Mashupa, who was as small as an insect to them, the great birds hung on outstretched pinions, staring down with eyes that could face the sun unblinking, into the sea of bush below them, awaiting accident, illness; awaiting the lion's kill, the hunter's bullet, the female thing weak in the throes of birth, from which they would first tear the living eyes, and when it was blinded, turn to the soft parts of the belly, rending the thin skin of her udder and other parts, while she bellowed in agony. As one falls like a stone from the air, others, circling near that one, fall too, and others who had seen nothing but the falling of their kind from the upper skies, but know that some-where below them a life has ended, or is about to end, follow them down. And with them come the kites and the carrion hawks and crows. Bloodstains on the veld will bring them down to investigate. They will find dead things even when they have crept under the bushes to die, for there is a trail of insects to such animals—of ants and beetles and of small carrion eaters, rats, mongooses, and the like, which bring the butcher birds, drongos, bee eaters, and little hawks. Their activity brings the larger birds—each thing attracting some greater thing that hopes to eat or rob it.

Up there the birds waited for death. An animal's death or a man's, for both are meat. Mashupa, lying wounded would have been meat to them and they would have sat on the trees surrounding him, their heads lowered into the grey shoulders of their wings, staring at him and waiting. Coming down sometimes to peck at him and then flying back with slow, heavy wing-beats to perch, like horrible fruits, again.

The world of the forest is many worlds. All are interdependent but none know it. The tree is dependent on the rain to descend from the heavens into the earth and dissolve the minerals that are its substance in the depths, but the baboon and the monkey do not know this and blame the tree for its lack of fruits.

The fruits are dependent on the bees for the setting of their seed, but the bees do not know this, and while fetching their nectar on swift wings, perform an unknowing act of fertility.

The dung beetle is dependent on the dung of the elephant and the buffalo for the dung ball that is the cherished home of its young, but it does not know that dung is dung. To the dung beetle, its ball of dung is beautiful.

Under the trees the buffalo grass that grows in wide-leaved shoots is dependent on the tree for its shade, but reaches always for the sun which would, if it were not protected, kill it.

The great carnivores, the lions and the leopards, the maned and spotted lords of the night, are parasites upon their prey. As much parasites as the ticks that cling to their ears, and cluster under their tails, but the lion and the leopard do not know this, they think they are nobles. And the bucks themselves, and the elephants, and other grass- and tree-eating things, are parasites on the green things they consume, like giant aphids.

The green things of earth alone are not parasites for they draw on nothing alive for their sustenance, but nurture all living things. The greatest of all parasites is man, who lives upon all living things. The things that grow, the things that run, the things that fly, and the things that swim. He consumes them all. He consumes his own kind in war, but he does not know it. For it is not only the cannibals that eat the bodies of men. Others drink of their sweat, and the blood that is the life of a man. And eat their time, so that they have no time to think, which is the function of man, but must run and scurry all day long, and into the night— but never upon their own business, always engaged in the service and to the profit of another. And these are the men we call civilised, these consumers of men, and the men who allow themselves to be consumed.

In the forest there are many worlds. The world of the tree-tops and the world under the tree-tops in the canopy of shade. The world of the bushes, and the world under the bushes, in the holes in the ground and under the stones; and each of these worlds is subdivided into numberless little worlds so that each is a solar system in miniature, revolving slowly with the force of the seasons—the spring, the summer, the fall, and the winter. And each thing, great or small, in these manifold worlds in which they move, sees a different world. For the world of the elephant is different from that of the ant, and it is doubtful if an ant can comprehend the bulk of the elephant, or the elephant the minute smallness of the ant, though elephants will run before them when they come in their thousands, and hundreds of thousands and myriads, through the forest destroying, like the Zulus, all living things in their path. Ants are the terror of the forest. Before them elephants and lions run, even lionesses carrying but one cub in their terrible jaws and leaving the others to be consumed by the jaws of the ants. All things will run before the marching armies of the ants. Elephants, lions, and buffaloes, like rabbits running from a dog, but they cannot comprehend the world of the ants. Even men run before the ants and wild, naked women, carrying their naked children in their arms, for the spears of their men will avail them nothing. An ant cannot be killed with a spear. There are ants that eat the houses and clothes of men, and ants that eat the men themselves when they are buried to the neck in the ground with their eyelids and lips cut off with knives, which is the way some tribes torture their enemies.

And there are bees which give honey, but can also sting great animals, even men with weapons in their hands, to death; and mosquitoes that can draw all the blood out of them, and flies that can do the same; and scorpions and spiders that can kill men, and serpents whose bite is death. All these live in the forest, and to each it is a different world, one constructed for his sole benefit. To an ant, the spoor of a small red duiker is a deep pit. To an elephant, a tree of medium size is a blade of grass to be swept aside. To a man, all living things are things that should be made to cease to live, because of the meat that clothes their bones, or skins that clothe their meat, or just for the sport of it. The sport of killing, so that his spears shall drink blood, or his bullets smack with a pleasant sound against the bone and flesh of a beast.

It was into this world of the forest, of elephants, bucks, buffaloes, and insects that Mashupa was precipitated by the superstitions and customs of his race. By them he was dropped as a twig might be dropped by a bird into the current of a river to drift, to sink, or by some miracle, to survive. A man alone, even a savage, as natural man has come to be called, is not equipped to combat the wilds alone. He requires the company of his family or tribe to assist and support him by the diversity of their crafts and skills. He needs other hunters to help him kill, boys to drive game, to make traps, and herd cattle. He needs women to weave and to tan, to cut thatch grass, and cultivate his little gardens, and to cook. But Mashupa was alone.

Chapter Fourteen

THE SMALL BEGINNING

Now the life of an elephant is a drama, for few other things in the world are so great, or live so long except, perhaps, a whale in the ocean, some reptiles, certain birds of the air, or a tree in the forest. So that when we think of a tree, and the things it has seen, standing there, rooted to the ground by its tap and subsidiary roots, and the smaller roots and the searching hairs that spring from them, we can also think of an elephant. Think of him as a moving tree, who also sprang from a seed, one so small as to be invisible to the naked eye. From a sperm as small, almost as the sperm of a man. We can think of this sperm actively meeting the ovum of the cow, in a warm womb the size of a mastiff's kennel, where it grows, over a space of months, twenty months for a cow calf, and twenty-two for a bull, into a baby elephant that is clothed with long, sparse hair, like that of its extinct relation the mammoth.

In the museum of Lourenço Marques, in a small un-guarded bottle on a shelf against a concrete column, is the minuscule foetus of an elephant. A mouse-size elephant, that looks like a shrew, which is not a mouse, but the world's smallest and most courageous carnivore. How this small thing was found, in the mountain of guts that was drawn out on the ground beside its dam, is a mystery. But there it is, the smallest elephant in the world. An elephant reduced to mouse size, in a bottle, such as we buy medicine in at the corner drugstore. And at one time every elephant in the world, and every man, was even smaller than this— mouse size. And before that, even less. But in each, in man, and mouse, and elephant, is this latent growth, the power to become what God had meant it to become. The power to live and increase its kind upon the face of the earth.

A man looking at this little elephant in a bottle, becomes very small in his mind, mouse-size, as he sees himself as he once was, inside his mother, and realises his relationship to all the living things in the world, since one and all were like this once, and unrecognisable in their species, the one from the other. For at one time the foetus of man is scarcely different from that of his cousin the bear, or, for that matter, to one who is not a scientist, from his other cousin in the tree of life, the elephant himself. And all are held in a bottle throughout their lives, by the circumstances of life, that holds them enclosed, as though they were behind glass, for a man cannot truly get out of himself or beyond himself, any more than a goldfish can remove itself from its bowl.

Here, in this unformed form, all life is one, and all men unrecognisable to their own mothers, who carry them from place to place as they move. The black baby is not yet black, nor the white one white, and the archbishop unrecognisable from the harlot, and the hunter and the clerk of one flesh. But all have in common the quality of life, the pinkness of their colour, and the cord that feeds them the transmuted food of their mother, and joins them to the past that is hers, as they join her to the future that is not hers, but belongs in the days to come.

So, the protagonists of the story, the elephants, and the boy Mashupa, the girl N'Tembi, their child, the Chef de Poste, and the hunters, and the other living things that cohabited the world with them were all of one small beginning. There was a time when all were alive, but none were living, and with each the drama of life began when they issued into it. And the first act done to them was to bathe and cleanse them so that they could begin it. This the cow

101

elephant did to her calf, and the other mothers to their children, none knowing what was in store for them, but each overwhelmed by her love for what she had brought forth.

The baby elephant, that was to become the lame one, was born on a small island set in a swamp, where his mother had gone to wait, when her time was near.

He was woolly, and the wool had a red tinge, such as the beards of most men have in the sunlight, and he was not as big as the biggest kind of dog, but bigger than the small kinds. He had no sex, or at least it could not be seen, because he was what the men of science, who name such mysteries and thus explain them away, call cryptorchid, which means that he had no visible sex organs. But he was male. All maleness was latent in him.

On each side of his mouth were the tiny white spears that would one day be tusks. He stood swaying on legs like short logs; and waving a little trunk that was like a little piece of hose pipe, as if he was surprised at it all. And his mother, with her great trunk, pushed him forward towards her front legs where her milk was waiting for him in two teats beneath her chest. There, because of his hunger, and instinct, which is another mystery, not explained by a name, he folded back his little hose pipe over his woolly back and drank with soft, pink lips. While he drank, his mother stroked him and blew gently upon him.

This first milk, like the first milk of all mammals, was colostrum, with a high sugar content, and would flow as such for a week or more until his infant bowels were cleansed and he could digest the more ordinary product. At this time his little trunk was not of much use and would not be for three or more months. It now was put on slightly to one side to make his drinking easier.

One day he would eat his last meal as we all must, man or elephant. Each, as much as the man condemned to death in his solitary cell, only seldom do any but murderers choose their final meal, as death is likely to come upon them unawares, like a thief in the night, or to approach them by degrees, stalking them like a Dyak head-hunter, or lingeringly, with illness that prohibits rich foods. So here the assassin goes one better than the rest of us.

Then, when death comes, as surely to the cleric as to

the noosed assassin, as surely to the hunter as the hunted, as surely to me as to you, do we all return to the dust of which we are made. taking back the life stuff with us into the ground from which it sprang, in form of the food consumed by us, and the parents who bore us before we came. As surely does this happen to the man who lives his three score and ten years, as to the elephant that may live two centuries, or the giant baobab that has lived five thousand years.

But between these two points of departure, for there is a departure into death, into change, as much as there is a departure into life, comes life itself—the life of a butterfly that may only last a few hours, or those lives that may last for centuries. But each life is fully lived unless it is cut off by accident. For the seconds of a butterfly's life in the sunshine are as hours in the life of a man, or as years in the life of a tree.

Every living thing is made of what it eats and what it drinks. The lion is made of many bucks, the leopard of many baboons, and the man of many oxen and sheep, whole herds and flocks of them, and truck loads of vegetables that are made of water and minerals, and barrels and hogsheads of whisky and gin, if he is rich, and barrels and hogsheads of beer, if he is poor.

The elephant is made of many tons of branches and leaves and roots and bulbs, and long before he was weaned, before he was even six months old, the little elephant began his long life of vegetal destruction, the swift tearing, and breaking down, of what had been so long growing up. At first pulling off, with his little garden hose of a trunk, small twigs and putting them into his mouth and spitting them out again because what he really liked was milk, and he could not imagine what prompted him to pluck branches in imitation of his elders.

After a month in the isolation of the swamp, his mother led him back to the herd, where, for the first time, he saw other elephants. Great ones, small ones, some even of his own size with whom he was soon playing. And some considerably bigger like his own tuskless brother who was to be his companion, but who then had been his senior and superior, vastly older than he was, since he was only a month old. This gap had been slowly lessened by time until now, at a hundred and fifty, his brother seemed no older than he was himself.

It is questionable how much a young thing, man or elephant, can remember of its youth. Mashupa could remember his mother's breasts, and standing to drink from them, and the capacities of the elephant approach those of a man. So it is probable that the young elephant retained memories of his mother's udder with its two fountains of milk; of her great belly, that was the roof of his house; and her legs that were its support, and something pleasant to play under, rather as a child plays under the dining-room table, or the wild bushmen seeks a cave in which to dwell. Each, the playing child, the animal, and the hunter, seeking food, security, shade from the sun, shelter from the rain, and privacy.

The life of the baby elephant was happy. He was now too big for his mother to pick up and carry in her trunk as she had done when he was younger and fell into an ant-bear hole that had collapsed in the rains. His mother was the centre of his life and often, when she walked, he followed her holding on to her beautiful long tail with his trunk. His tail began to grow longer hairs and they were white, like those of his older, tuskless brother, which was a rare thing among elephants, and made them stand out from the others, though they got no honour from it the way a mul-tiple-tusked elephant gets honour—becoming a kind of mascot to the herd.

So his tail grew and his little tusks grew and when he tried them on the pillars of his mother's legs, she slapped him till he squealed, and then soothed him, rubbing him over the face and his little round ears, with her trunk. Thus his life went on for years. A peaceful marching and counter-marching through the forests and swamps and over the hills of Africa. Sometimes they came across fields of kaffir corn, and mealies, the corn of America, that had come to Africa with the slave-ships from that land, and had prospered there. The natives ran about yelling, but were helpless, when they devastated the gardens that were all that stood between them and famine. A life that was an idyll, in which he fought mock battles and made mock love, mounting on the backs of small female elephants in imita-tion of the great bulls, which effected nothing, save the strengthening of their backs and prepared them for the days that would come later in their lives.

And then when he was nearly twenty years old, and half-grown, the male power came on him with some suddenness, as puberty comes with a boy, and he felt different. And the other elephants felt different towards him, so that, when he was playing with a young cow, a big-tusked bull struck him so hard that he fell to the ground.

And it was in this year that war came to the herd. Men with guns came upon them. A half-caste Portuguese brigand and his native hunters surprised them and slew many, including his uncle. And the herd fled crashing through the forest, trumpeting and screaming with pain, fright, and fury. He saw his uncle fall. He saw two big bulls come to him, one from each side, and raise him up and carry him along with their tusks under his belly, marching him off with their heads turned inwards. They got him away, but for nine days of agony he stood holding on to a great tree with his trunk, to help his weakened legs support his body. Then he fell and never rose again. But many others were killed, and many were wounded, some of whom died, and some recovered, but were, after their experience, not to be relied upon. For their tempers were deranged and they were liable to sudden unreasoning fits of anger.

It was here that the young elephant first learnt three new smells. The smell of powder, the smell of man who was nearly white, which was different from that of the natives, and the smell of elephants' blood, that was also quite new to him. The only other blood he had smelt was that of a lion's kill occasionally. Not often, because lions tend to leave the country when the elephants come in. And the blood of bush pigs that the elephants killed whenever they came upon them, because there is a hatred of them in their hearts, for which there is no apparent cause.

In this war which had come upon him in his twentieth year, there was a strange human parallel, for among men, too, war now seems to come every twenty years, when a new crop of young men become ripe for death as their manhood flowers.

But of this he could know nothing, nor was it even true then, for men were less civilised and the urge for suicidal destruction not so great among them, for they were not so bored that they were ready to do any mischief at another's bidding, merely for a change and to break the terrible monotony of their cushioned lives.

In France, Napoleon had just broken up the great camp at Boulogne, which was to have been his base for an attack upon England. And, in North Africa, the United States had just victoriously concluded her war with the pirates of Tripoli. But these wars did not compare with those of our days, for though many were killed and injured, the lives of most citizens continued their uninterrupted courses.

In those days, when the great-tusked one was twenty, the world was still a balanced place, with many cultures and modes of life, and plagues and fevers that kept the people from increasing too fast. So that, though many died, few starved. Whereas to-day we have wars instead of plagues, and, despite them, people still multiply and many are hungry to the point of desperation. Only in America is there not hunger that approaches famine. For to-day, in our wonderful world that is filled with belts and wheels and pulleys that go round and round, with plastics and other magical things, most men go hungry. And what is the good of an electric toaster if there is no bread?

It is hard to imagine man, with all his techniques and appliances for killing, turning back the pages of history to examine the peaceful lives of certain savage tribes and using this knowledge to his present profit. He could look with advantage even on the despised Kaffirs. For until the coming of the Zulus, who learnt their trade of killing from the white man, Kaffir wars were not much more than games, raids for cattle and girls in which few men were killed. A pastime in which all, even the cattle and the girls, benefited from the change of society and the outcrossing of blood that would strengthen their progeny.

And all this happened, this wonderful progress of a century and a half, in the lifetime of this elephant and his brother. So that, had he been a man, he could have seen it all. The wars, the revolutions, the discoveries from Benjamin Franklin to Edison, from Pasteur to Freud, and, having seen them all, would have had a perspective we can never attain.

Still, war remains war among men or elephants, and though it had gone on since the beginning of time, it was new to the young bull and made a great impression on him, since its coming coincided with life becoming impossible for him in the herd, the big bulls setting upon him whenever he approached the young cows who had formerly been his friends and playfellows. So, with some others of the same age, and in the same predicament, he left the herd and they formed a small association of bachelors waiting for the strength that would release them from their bonds of celibacy, when growth, height, weight, strength, and length of tusk would insure them the possession of the cows they now desired.

To this end they waited, playing and wrestling among themselves, as athletes do, strengthening themselves for conflict and victory. They butted their heads against each other, wrapped their trunks about one another's forelegs, in a kind of elephantine half nelson, and made controlled lunges with their tusks into each other's vital parts. One day they would do in earnest what they now did in play, just as children playing in the streets with toy guns, in our man's way of life, turns to real guns and bombs and bloody battles, because this is the predestined way of man, until his heart is changed, and love replaces greed.

One day, the young elephant left the bachelor herd and joined up with an ancient, solitary bull that he met feeding in the forest at some distance from the others. This bull taught him all he knew by demonstration, and probably by actual conversation, for there is little doubt that animals can communicate with each other. This ancient bull had only one tusk, having lost the other in battle or smashed it against some giant tree, when, already loose in its socket, it had become still further weakened and had fallen out. How old this elephant was, it is impossible to say, but perhaps he was two hundred years old. Certainly he was a hundred or more, and might even have been born about the time the first white men landed in South Africa. At any rate, he was wise in the ways of the forest and found an apt pupil in the young elephant who joined him. Such an association is not uncommon among elephants; the pupil learns from the more experienced elephant, the old elephant has the benefit of the young one's company. It was from this old bull that he learnt the trick of moving in a circle and coming back to stand hidden, sideways on, beside his own spoor, so that a hunter who followed him, would be bound to pass within reach of his trunk. For the old bull always did this no matter how tired he was, and he tired easily now; or how safe it was, for it had become second nature to him, and the young bull acquired the habit.

When they moved along the elephant roads, the old one went first, testing every foot of the ground with his trunk, and every few yards raising it many feet into the air to search for food or danger. They moved through the forest with a silence that was unbelievable. Not a twig cracked beneath their feet, not a leaf rustled as these immense beasts proceeded along roads beaten hard by their kind over centuries of history, and the centuries that preceded history as we know it. These paths are narrow at the bottom, for an elephant sets one foot directly into the spoor of the other, each leg walking, as it were, in single file, so that there is no central ridge in the road such as one finds in a hippo path. But above the road, looking towards the sky, the bulk of the passing elephants makes a wide path, pruning the trees by the friction of their vast bodies against their branches, and by plucking a mouthful of food here and there as they go by.

These roads once traversed all Africa. They were followed by the Voortrekkers, the pioneers, and since the elephants marched along the contours of the hills, never climbing more steeply than was necessary, most elephant roads are seldom so steep that a car could not follow them in second gear. One could almost say that the roads of Africa have been engineered by elephants, since engineers with their levels and theodolites have been able to do little to improve upon them. Long before the white man came, every poort and pass in the mountains, and every ford and drift in the rivers, were known to the elephants, and used by them in their passage across the land.

The old elephant also taught him other ruses, such as that of passing through the herd. This stratagem consisted of coming upon a big breeding herd from the rear and passing through it, upwind, so that the herd follows in their path and obliterates the marks of their passing with their own multitudinous spoors. When they did this, the herd which had been feeding noisily, screaming and trumpeting, the mothers washing, beating, feeding and caressing their children, pulling down titbits for their soft mouths from the topmost branches, and putting them into the small grasping trunks, fell silent as they looked upon them. For even the biggest herd bulls were small compared to the great, one-tusked elephant and made way for him, as, silently as a butterfly, he marched slowly through them, his trunk swinging before him. Or, if he raised it to test the air, every trunk went up, trunks in hundreds reached into the air, turning and twisting this way and that, writhing above the bush like a great company of black, rearing snakes, for this silent monster was a king, a survivor whom they recognised from their earliest years. And behind him, the young elephant walked sedately, enjoying the feeling that the eyes of all were upon him and his great companion.

This was a period when, like a clerk in an office, he desired marriage, but could not afford it. He had to build up a store of capital, which, in his case, was physical strength, that would enable him to obtain and keep a wife. It was an apprenticeship to the full seriousness of life, and during it, he learnt again that the bulls were the quarry of men, of men with guns; some of his old companions, with ivory that was already sizeable, fell before them. He learnt too, that men made war on men. And he saw the devastation of villages by Arab slavers and half-castes, and gangs of slaves, both men and women, marching along the elephant roads, linked together by forked poles that were set about their necks and pegged there, so that even by night they wore them. He heard the crying of young women slaves whose babies had been thrown away so as to conserve their mothers' strength, and the curses and groans of the men, and the sound of whips, and the cries of the flogged in the night. He saw the tusks of elephants carried upon bleeding black backs towards the sea, and learned to correlate these things with the hunters, and to fear them. He saw dead men, women, and children, and dead elephants stripped of their meat, and in his mind a picture was formed, which was consistent, though meaningless to an elephant, who could know nothing of the uses to which either slaves or ivory were put. When he was thirty, soon after the Battle of Waterloo had been fought, he returned to the herd.

There now followed some thirty years of activity, of fighting, love making, and breeding. And in this, too, his life was comparable to that of a man who spends twenty years growing up, twenty years in furious sexual activity, a further twenty, when love is more of a habit than a necessity, and the rest of his life, its evening as it were, in a state of relatively solitary reflection. The fires may be burnt out, even the embers are no longer warm, but life, though life upon a different level, continues.

It was this last period that he spent with his elder brother wandering in the wildest parts of the land—two gigantic living monuments to their kind. Mystical, sacred beasts, to the indigenous natives. Great animals whose lives were governed by an ever weakening will to live, and the series of reflexes acquired over a life of more than a century that caused them to continue. Their organisms had the custom of life.

Many cows he had served. Young, frolicsome cows, old wise ones; many calves he had begotten; many fights he had fought, avoiding serious injury, but often killing his opponents with a thrust of his tusk into the roof of their mouths, or driving it into the belly, below the basket of their ribs, or from behind in pursuit, between the legs into the intestines where the testicles were carried inside the body. How often had the madness of musth come upon him, and caused the fury of his fights and loves. The dark brown, odorous secretions had run from the hollows near his eyes, and been rubbed off upon the trees he passed, a love sign to the herd cows. That had brought them to him. But running into his mouth, for the glands near the eye were above the corner of his mouth, the dribbling, evil tasting secretion enraged him further. Cows he served when in musth or not, but only in musth did he seek battle, only in musth had he a mad desire to kill.

He had been hunted by men and wounded by them. He had killed men. The white man, Pretorius, others in different parts, and many Kaffirs over the face of the land. This hatred of men, this desire to live uninterrupted by them, was possibly his only motive now. This, and his love for his brother and companion, was all that was left of a long life in which everything else was spent. There is no doubt that he had memories, as an old man has, of places and things; that he was driven, by habit, to certain places at certain times. That even living was a habit.

Chapter Fifteen

THE ELEPHANTS

In the thick grey-green bush, the great elephant stood resting his aching ivory upon a tambouti tree. His immense tusks had become a burden to him, weighing him down, straining the bone into which they were socketed. They were dark in colour, almost black, blunt from digging, and sometimes even dragged upon the ground, ploughing thin furrows on each side of his head as he walked. Once his pride and ornament, they had now outgrown their use, and were a burden and a danger to him. It was for them that he was pursued, for them that more than sixty years ago he had been wounded. Because of them he had become a killer of men, a destroyer, and, therefore, doubly a fugitive, a criminal with a price upon his head.

Beside him stood another big elephant, his brother who had been born tuskless. These elephants, except when moved by some obscure passion to vengeance, avoided men, and lived either in almost waterless deserts, or in swamps which the hunters feared to penetrate.

Over the years they had acquired the ability to go without water for much longer periods than ordinary elephants. Necessity having become an `acquired characteristic, to which, upon many occasions, they owed their lives.

For years they had been hunted, galvanising men into dangers and perils, because of the ivory, which could be transmuted into gold, that the great one carried in his mouth. The ivory which, ceasing to be an ornament in the mouth of an elephant, an instrument of power, a digging tool, could become, by the processes of applied science and handicraft, the embellishments of the fashionable woman's boudoir, the dead witnesses of her toilet. Little trinket boxes, hand-mirror or brush backs, or the silent stretchers of glove fingers, that were themselves also the product of living animals—the soft tanned skins of bleating kids. It could be cut into piano keys and knife handles or turned into billiard balls.

These elephants had lived through the great days of the ivory hunters when the prices were high because the demand was great. The time when, in Dieppe alone, there were eleven factories that manufactured piano keys, billiard balls, chess-men, and other objects of art and virtue in ivory.

African ivory also went into the decorated sword hilts and scabbards of the samurai of Japan, was carved into gods, into devils, into the little indecent figurines that came to Europe in the wake of war and rapine, part of the loot of the East. In the eddies of trade, ivory was borne from Africa on the great ships of the Dutch East India Company and the John Company to the West to Europe, and to the East to India, and from there found its way by sea and caravan to China and Japan.

Ivory from Africa for centuries had gone into churches and temples, into private collections and museums, into bars and taprooms, even into the mouths of ageing men who used ivory plumpers to extend their sagging cheeks.

The maiden crying over her music lesson, was only the last echo of the scream of an elephant, dying in Africa, that had reached across the world, losing power and significance as it went, weakening as it went. The raided slaves, both men and women, who, shackled together had carried the tusks across the forests and deserts, had wept and cried too, and had died under the whips of their Arab masters. For ivory is born of pain, horror and crime. Like gold, like jewels, ivory is a weapon in the devil's hands, tempting men and women from the path of virtue. The agony of the hanging ivory Jesus on the miniature wooden cross, and that of the elephant who died that it should be made, are related, for the maximum of pain, reaching its crescendo in man or beast, can go no further; the ultimate is reached, and having been reached, is stilled, as strength passes with the flowing blood into death, which is merciful. For death has no superior.

As in every facet of every jewel that we see in the windows of a jeweller's shop are reflected the faces of the women who desire it, as in the past of every old and great stone there is at least one crime, so, in each snooker ball, in every ivory carving, is a story of danger, greed, pain, and death. Each, as you hold it in your hand, could tell you a tale of Africa, for most of the ivory of the world comes from Africa. Even that carved in the East has travelled across the Indian Ocean, or through the China seas into the hands of brown and yellow craftsmen. Some eastern ivory comes from long-dead mammoths frozen into the Siberian tundra, a little comes from India and Siam, but most is African, and to obtain this ivory, elephants by the hundred thousand have perished.

Between 1840 and 1850, three thousand tons of ivory reached the Ivory Floor in London each year. Between 1860 and 1890, twenty-one thousand tons came in. The tusks averaged only twelve to thirteen pounds in weight, so that during those years, between fifty and seventy thousand elephants were killed annually. Through this holocaust, these two great elephants had lived, surviving all others. Monsters who, having reached maturity, had outgrown it, and moved into a sphere of existence which bears no relation to time as we comprehend it. They were living monuments of history. Pachyderms, whose immense, wrinkled hides were yet too small to record all the events of the eras through which they had lived; the discoveries, the battles, the kings and queens who had reigned and died, the empires that had been destroyed. Full brothers, born of one dam and one sire in the same great marsh in the Zambesi basin. They stood with trunks entwined. Behind each was a pile of dung, each piece of brown oval, the size of a small football, that would scarcely have fitted into an ordinary bucket. The top pieces were darker than the lower, wet and shiny with mucus from their bowels. Hovering about the balls of dung were mosquitoes—little brothers of the anopheles, the malaria bearers.

At the bottom of one heap, at the base of the cone of dung, was a dung beetle, risking death by trampling, in order to fulfil her destiny, which was to breed, to lay her eggs in the ball that she was constructing—the dung of the greater grass-eating animals, the elephants, buffalo, and white rhino, being necessary to the continued existence of her kind. With the little pellets of the bucks they could do nothing. The black rhinoceros, who scattered his dung with his hind legs, was useless to her. The dung beetles are the poor relations of the iridescent, sacred scarabs of ancient Egypt.

White cattle egrets were perched on the high, sculptured backs of the elephants. Tickbirds, the farmers call them. They picked the parasites from the cracks of their skin with long, yellow, dagger beaks, while they waited for them to move and flush locusts and other insects from the ground, as a spaniel flushes game for its master. The elephants were the great spaniels of the tickbirds, and in reciprocity, the tickbirds were the white-winged guardian angels of the elephants, warning them of danger by adding their flight to the cries of the grey lowries that the hunters call 'go away birds.'

The elephants' ears were turned back at the tips as the ears of some dogs are, and only came up when they moved their heads sharply. When they charged, their ears rose high above the level of their backs, like the black sails of a pirate ship, fourteen feet or more, from edge to edge.

About the elephants was a sweet scent, a perfume that is unmistakable to the hunter, of elephants at peace, which differs greatly from the strong, acrid smell given off by a herd that has stood in fear. Sometimes their stomachs rumbled. Sometimes, their great ears, their edges torn by their passage through the trees, bored with holes bitten into them by ticks, flapped with a clapping sound. Their eyelids rose and fell with a somnolence induced by the burning heat, and in the middle of each eyelid was a long hair, that was a kind of feeler, an antenna, protecting the eye from harm in the darkness of the night. Their small eyes were golden brown, the colour of light sherry, with black pupils.

At intervals, unclasping each other, they tested the air with their trunks, raising them into the fickle, shifting winds of midday. This was out of habit, for they were safe enough and knew it, since hunters wait for the steady air of the morning and evening, and rest, as the elephants do, in the heat of noon. Having raised their trunks they plucked a few leaves and thrust them into their gaping mouths. They did not eat as cows and young bulls do, noisily with many tearing and cracking sounds, but plucked the leaves gently, one by one, or stripped them of their foliage, as a boy might strip the leaves from a willow wand by running his hands along it. In silence lay their security.

Then they stood still again, immense, sculptured, angular with age, with entwined trunks. They stood as children might, holding hands, as they had themselves stood a century or more ago as calves in the shadow of their mother. For the very old, both among animals and men, have much in common with the very young. Their ardour is consumed;

while the ardour and heats of the young are not yet come to fruition, so that one part of each, that part which yearns to the female or male of its species, is not extant or is dead, and any love that they have is without that element of fury which distinguishes the mating kind of love from any other.

These two elephants who had, in their youth, fought bitterly for primacy, now loved each other as they had when calves. Loved as men might, who love each other with a love surpassing the love of women. For in that part of them, they were already dead. The glands that had caused it atrophied. The part of their minds that had claimed it satiated. The herds that had been theirs, and yet proclaimed it in the family likeness they had stamped upon them, knew them no longer, save at a distance and then only upon occasion.

That had happened many years ago, when the cows no longer responded to them, finding their weight upon their backs too heavy to be borne; when the sharp young tusks of the less mature bulls had been too quick for them, when they were tired of fighting for mastery and of killing their rivals. For each had killed more than one of his own kind in combat. When the noise of the calves about their pillar legs had become intolerable to them, when, in fact, their families had bored them, when the effort of the act of love had become greater than the pleasure of it, and nothing forced them to it but habit. And then habit had weakened, till at last it disappeared.

Leading up to the place where the elephants stood was their spoor, but it was only a single spoor, that of the lame one with the tusks, for he walked behind his brother, and always set his feet exactly in his brother's footprints, leaving them only when they halted to rest side by side or sometimes when pursued. So that, generally, where the going was good, there would appear to be only one elephant. This spoor, apart from the eccentricity of lameness, was like that of all old elephants, very smooth. The wrinkles and lumps that are found in the sole of a young beast wear down and disappear with age. This spoor had been brought in, measured with a stick set across its circle, by many scouts, the spies of the forest, who seek elephants for the white hunters, and set the trackers on the spoors they have found. And often the hunters had not believed the sticks they had brought in and had beaten the scouts. There were no elephants whose feet were two footprints and one hand-breadth in diameter. But some had followed them, and been lured to their deaths in the deserts, or had been killed. So much so, that the natives believed this elephant to be tagati, bewitched, with the power of turning himself into two elephants, for some had beheld them together. It was also believed that sometimes he had tusks, and sometimes he had none, and that one part of him was inhabited by the great king T'Chaka, and the other by the king of the Matabele, Moselekatse, who had been his captain, and they now said, if a white man came upon this great and incredible spoor—'It is not worth following. We know of this beast from our fathers, and if we do come up to him, he will have no tusks and will kill us.'

For this was the plan of the elephants when followed. They would go fast, running, so that their feet 'dug in,' as it is termed, the dust from the oval hind foot where it presses into the ground causing a little arc of sand to rise in the spoor of the front foot into which it has been placed. And even when they ran, did the second elephant, the one with tusks, try to put his feet with great exactitude into the footprints of his brother. Then, when they had run enough, and the hunters were tired beyond their strength, at the end of several days, and they were at a great distance from water, the elephants would find a place for their stratagem. The tusked one would go on, for his was the lame spoor that the hunters had been following, and the other, the tusk-less one, would hide himself near the spoor and wait. When the men came, tired and hot, first the tracker bending over the spoor, then the hunter with his gun and gun bearer, and finally, some way behind, the boys—such boys as could be persuaded to join in the enterprise—the tuskless one would strike. He would let the tracker pass and the hunter, but the hunter only a yard or two. Then, raising his great trunk, that was like a tree, he would smash it down on the hunter's head, and then seize the tracker and dash him to the ground. In the beginning, he had sometimes trodden on his victims and knelt on them, squashing them as if they were grapes, so that the blood and juice of their bodies spurted up over him. But later he abandoned this practice, as he did not like the mess of man-juice upon him, or the stink of it when it turned putrid, or the flies that it brought on to his feet, knees and chest, and which, being far distant from water, he had to bear for many days till he could find a pool deep enough to bathe in. When the deed was done, he rejoined his friend and brother, and only for that short distance where there was none alive to follow him (for the surviving boys had long since fled with their story of the disaster), did his spoor overlap that of the lame one.

Other elephants killed in other ways in this great and never-ending war between the elephants and men. Some picked men up, and setting them upon their tusks, tossed them into the air as a child tosses a ball, and then knelt or stamped upon them. Others impaled them with their ivory, still others held them down with one foot and then pulled them limb from limb, or even played with them, tossing them backwards and forwards between their fore and hind legs. Each had, as it were, a habit and technique of killing, which, if it varied in detail, remained constant in principle.

Behind the elephants were their heaps of dung. In front of them, below their pink-lined lips, were fragments of chewed leaves and branches, masticated by their great molars, that were like the plates of a grinder, into fibrous skeins which resembled the chewed residue of cane spat out by the field hands of a sugar plantation, magnified a hundred times. So that one might have thought that it was done by a giant worker in the woods, a man as tall as a house, with jaws of brass and teeth of iron. For these skeins were more than a foot long and as thick as a strong man's wrist. They originated in the leaves and branches of the trees under which the elephants stood and reached for with their trunks, that were at once hands and noses, and to which, because of their near-sight, was added the function of a kind of eye. An elephant's sense of smell being so exaggerated as to go beyond smell, almost into sight. Even things near to them are not clearly seen and something directly in front of them is almost invisible, unless it moves, because of the way their eyes are set on the sides of their heads. Charging, they tend to move in the chord of an arc rather than directly forward, with their weapon raised curled above their heads. A curled trumpet sounding the charge and the mort. This inimitable, one-fingered, omni-purpose object is a weapon, trumpet, hand, and nose, all in one. It is a vacuum cleaner that can suck in water or dust and blow it out again, that can pick up the smallest nut or bend down trees as thick as a boy's body. It can snap small trees as if they were matchsticks, sharply, and the sound of breaking trees near a herd of elephants feeding in the night is like the sound of rifle shots. But the trunk is more than a nose. It is an extension of the mouth as well, the corrugations of its under side being developed from the palate ridges. And these tender ringed parts are the favourite feeding places of the ticks.

With this nose, the elephant can smell further than any other beast. Can smell a field of millet two miles away; by its touch, feel its way in silence, step by step, through the thickest bush on the darkest night. This weapon, to which the natives give the name of hand, is like the hand of man, both the instrument of love and death. With it, the bull caresses the cow, and the cow the bull, running their trunks like loving serpents over each other. With it, they kiss each other, even putting their trunks into each other's mouths. With it, the mother beats, strokes, and washes her calf. With it, she calls and threatens.

In it, live white maggots, harmless parasites upon their great host, emerging only when death comes, as fleas leave a dead dog, for when no warmth or comfort is left to them they must go. Their world is destroyed. For, to a maggot, a pocket of pus is a home. And this maggot world is simply another sphere of life, a part of its whole, as much a part as the soaring of the eagle or the rise of sap in a tree.

The trunk of an elephant can be considered the Achilles' heel of all their species, living or extinct, for should the trunk be damaged seriously, the elephant is rendered helpless, and must die.

Almost immune to all sickness, mankind almost his only enemy, there seems no reason why elephants should not live forever. Reaching an age of puberty at twenty, an elephant attains its full strength at fifty, so that to estimate the chances of its living—if unhunted—a century is probably an underestimate. And, assuming a century, certain favoured specimens may, according to some authorities, reach double this age since there is no known cause for the death of an elephant, no known disease. Nor does it die as most herbivores die, of weakness when their teeth wear down to their gums and they fall prey to a lion, or of starvation stuck in the glutinous mud of a half-dry water hole in the winter. They die by water—even in it, because when their time is come they seek it, and majestically, without struggle, they fade from life into death, imperceptibly into mountainous putrescence.

It is thought, however, that sometimes an elephant may die of snake bite. That, when feeding in the trees, a mamba or a tree snake may strike it in the soft membrane of its trunk. Or it may get bitten in its thin-skinned parts, between the legs or the toes. An elephant, unless very weak, cannot get stuck in the mud because its hind legs are jointed so that they move forwards, bending at the joint we call the hock in a horse, towards the forelegs instead of away from them, which enables them to pull out their hind legs by the traction of the front. In addition their feet contract in size as they take their weight off them, so that when an elephant raises its foot from the mud it is smaller than when it pressed it down and comes out easily.

Nor are elephants affected by climate or altitude. They can live in the hot lowland swamps or in the cold, mist-shrouded mountains with equal facility, and their diet is the most varied of all vegetable eaters, for with their trunks they can feed on the branch tips of great trees and with their tusks dig out roots and bulbs. Their only rival in the possibilities of geographical distribution is man himself, who lives both at the pole and the equator, and like man, when forced by circumstances, the elephant can change the habits of his life, and indeed has done so, for even as recently as in Selous' time elephants were diurnal and lived in the open glades of the savannah country, in parklike lands, where they were hunted on horseback. Whereas now, they are nocturnal, forest creatures, fearing both the daylight and the open.

These two elephants had made the transition, but the memories of their childhood and youth were of the open veld and went back to the time when all Africa that supported vegetation, from Egypt to the Cape of Good Hope, was the range of their kind. To-day, except for the protected few who inhabit the forest of Knysna at the Cape, the remnant of a herd in the Addo Bush on the Sundays River, where Pretorious was employed to thin them out at the request of the orange planters, some in the Kruger National Park, and others in the protected area of Maputa in Portuguese East, their homeland is limited and becoming daily more restricted as civilisation surrounds them, and the rifles of the hunters confine them to those spots where the danger of hunting them becomes out of all proportion to the possible rewards of success.

There are wild elephants in Rhodesia, the Caprivi Strip, in West Africa on the borders of Angola, and in it. There are elephants in the Congo, the Sudan, Kenya and Uganda, Abyssinia and Egypt. But there are less than there used to be.

There are wild elephants at this moment being exterminated in Portuguese East Africa, within forty miles of Lourenço Marques, to make room for white settlers. But, to the north, there are still places where they roam in their hundreds, and will continue to do so because this land, so favourable to them, is deadly to man, being the haunt of the malarial mosquito and the dread tsetse fly. In addition, there is country that is, in many parts, unhuntable owing to its character, its vast impenetrable marshes, its woods of small trees growing so thickly together that a man can hardly pass, but which, to an elephant, presents no greater obstacle than a field of wheat.

A further factor in their preservation is the light ivory of the cows which makes the game of shooting them not worth the candle or the risk. And with these cows run young bulls, also not worth the danger or trouble of shooting, but big enough to serve their bull purpose and breed calves. So that it is only the big bulls that are doomed, and they are already so rare that the tusked one, whose story this is, would, by many, be counted a figment of a hunter's imagination; the product of fever, and of that exaggeration which is common to hunters when they meet, and sit talking by their campfires in the night.

These two monsters lived in the great wild area that lies between the Limpopo and the Zambesi, mainly in that section of it which is known as the district of Querida, but going far beyond this area at times, into Rhodesia and Nyasaland, as their spirit, born of instinct, memory, and thought, moved them.

Chapter Sixteen

THE TREE

Among the baobabs, the great trees of this part of the forest, was one greater than all the others. This tree was a monument among monuments, a leviathan among leviathans, an elephant in the tree world, towering above all others, rooted not only in the soil, but in antiquity. It was an immense tree already when Carthage fell, when Cleopatra courted Cæsar. Its pear-shaped fruits, covered with soft, green, plush-like down, had hung from its branches, as they do to-day, when the Lord Jesus hung upon the wooden cross. It was among the greatest living things in the world. Among the giant redwoods, the whales of the arctic seas, and the elephants, and the giant tortoises. So old that time no longer applied to it. So ancient that it could be referred to in geological, rather than in historic or geographical, terms.

It was not without reason that the ancients worshipped in groves of trees, and not without reason that the early Christians felled them, for the influence of a forest monster is beyond description. Each has an atmosphere. Near each, by the accident of its age alone, much of moment has occurred. For a great tree in a forest, like a lone tree on a plain, is a rendezvous with destiny. A land and death mark, a love mark. At once a nuptial and a funeral monument, and as such, sacred. Each solitary giant, a sylvan god, an impartial witness of acts both good and evil, for a tree knows neither right nor wrong—its only law is growth. It has no preference for blood or sperm. It fears nothing but flood or fire, and the great baobab was beyond the reach of either. The shadow of its branches and the strength of its roots had destroyed anything inflammable near to it, and it was beyond the reach of flood, as it was beyond the reach of time.

It was what it had been a thousand years ago, four thousand years ago, a landmark and the home of a myriad of humming bees. A perch and nesting place for the birds of the air, and a larder for the honey-loving ratel. The ground about it was blood-soaked with massacre, but it showed no sign, the air above it had vibrated with screams, but it was blue and clear by day, and a star-pierced bowl of indigo by night. It stood where it had always stood since it had been dropped as a seed, fortuitously, at one of the cross-roads of Africa. All it had ever done was to stay alive, to grow, to survive.

This tree was history itself, a living testament of events. The evidence of some was cut with knives into its soft bark, etched, tooled as a manuscript might be tooled so that the record would stand for those that followed to read and wonder. It stood at a great, secret cross-roads in the forest world. A cross-roads known only to the animals and a few solitary hunters, to the tribes that, at various times, had inhabited these desolate parts, to the Bushmen, who had lived a stone-age life here, till exterminated by the Bantu, and who alone, with the wild animals from father to son, through an endless chain of mothers, had cohabited with it since its small, unknown beginning. For even a baobab, an elephant, and a whale must begin.

These cross-roads by which it stood ran north and south parallel to the mangrove-clothed coastline two hundred miles away; and east and west, again roughly, from the coast into the interior, to Mashonaland and Matabeleland, into what are now called the Rhodesias, and beyond them towards Angola.

For the trackless forest is not trackless, it only seems to be so. It is a network of paths, great and small, that would appear, could we see it as it really is, to resemble the criss-cross lines that vein the palm of a man's hand. Some greater than others, as they are in a palm, but totalling a multitude, and ranging from the great roads of the elephants to the tiny mouse runs that tunnel the thick grass.

For thousands of years the bees had nested in the baobab, so that part of it was an immense, humming hive, a store-house of sweetness, rich with wax and honey gathered from the flowers of the forest and borne to it on swift, transparent wings. And never, since the last Bushman died, by a Bantu spear, had the dripping combs been robbed, for the Bantu, though they are great lovers of honey, deemed it a sacred tree, so the bees had gained by the Bushmen's death. To the Bushmen, nothing was sacred, that being an idea beyond their hunting culture. Only the moon in its round fullness affected them, and that only to dancing on their flat, stamped dancing grounds. But they had slept, making their little nests like those of birds, in its shadow, and had loved each other there, lying, little yellow men and women, in each other's arms. As men and women, or as animals that resembled men and women in form, or as something between the two, neither men and women, nor yet quite animals.

But the tree drew men to it by its size, by the magnetism of its grandeur, by its age, by its situation. It had been for centuries a meeting place, a rendezvous. Arab slave caravans, on their journey to the waiting dhows, had rested here and the same caravans, outward bound, filled with cruel hopes of human captures, had separated here going their different ways. It had been the silent witness of lustful and cruel scenes, of wild, black women forcibly taken, of men killed in their sleep by murderers who crept upon them unawares. Other men had been brought to bay there, and had died, with their backs to the smooth, purple buttressed trunk, that had stood behind them like the wall of a castle.

And now the baobab had become Mashupa's refuge, drawing him as it had drawn the others, and armed with his amulets, and the enforced purity of his life, he had no superstitious fear of it. Or perhaps, having so many others, this fear was dwarfed into insignificance. So that his bare feet had beaten many little paths to it, from all directions of the compass. It was the centre of his new life, the place where he built the little shelter that was his home.

The elephants avoided the tree, partly because they did not eat its leaves or fruit, and partly because they feared the savage stings of the bees who were its keepers. But the bees, dangerous to those who interfered with them, were quiet with Mashupa, the lost one, and their hum was a comfort to him in his loneliness. And the names and words engraved upon the tree were a solace to him, for he had learned to respect written words, attributing magic to them. They were a bond between him and N'Tembi who could read and write like a white person, so that, looking at the names and the dates cut into the bark, he found comfort and security in them.

The names had been carved by those who passed simply because the first name, that of Pretorius the hunter, had been found there, and the idea had seemed good to them, suitable, and carving their names had satisfied something in them that they did not fully understand. Moreover, carving had passed the time for them, and had impressed their native companions of the chase. All over the world men carve their names on objects too big to carry away, thinking, perhaps, in this way to establish some kind of ownership. Branding trees as they would brand the hide of a steer with the hot iron of their hope for immortality. In all carving and graphic art, there is magic. There is even magic in scrawled obscenities, and in hearts pierced by sculptured arrows.

But Pretorius had not carved his own name. Someone else had done it to commemorate the fact that he had been killed some five hundred paces away. His remains lay there, among the yellow fever trees of the pan from which Mashupa drew his water when a shower filled it.

It was to these fever trees that the great tusked elephant, with his brother, repaired every twenty years or so, to feed and reap the branches of his revenge. It took twenty years, almost a generation, for the trees to recover from the blows they dealt them, smashing them with their feet, butting them with their massive heads till they broke like twigs, tearing them with the great hawsers of their trunks, and feeding upon the flesh and blood and the minerals that had once been the hunter. They savoured the small branches, the salad-like young shoots, with the dressing of ancient anger. So that some of what had been the hunter had completed the circle of nature, had become food to the searching roots of the yellow fever trees, and entering the sap, which is the life-blood of the tree, had become green leaves, which in turn became the food of the elephants, and digested by their tremendous organs, were scattered again over the land where once this matter, clothing the form of the hunter, Pretorius, had trodden in search of game.

And it was into this world of the forest that Mashupa thrust himself. A man thrust back naked into the womb of time. A man alone there, an Adam in an angry Eden. For in this world of the forest that was once a garden, all things hated man, the arch destroyer of their peace. Without weapons, without fire, with only a red pot of elephant dung mixed with fat and wood ash to protect him, Mashupa entered the forest.

But of all this, he was ignorant. He had not seen the great tusked elephant, or his tuskless brother, or the spoor of the one that was the spoor of two. Many elephants he had seen but not these. That was yet to come. That day lay waiting to be born in the inexorable womb of time.

Chapter Seventeen

THE WORLD OF GHOSTS

Mashupa had become a wild man. He was no longer a sleek boy whose powerful muscles rippled under a coffee-coloured skin, shiny with health. He was emaciated, his eyes enormous in their sunken sockets. His flesh, denuded of fat, hung suspended to his corded muscles. His ribs stood out like branches from his flanks. His body was plastered with Tembula's medicine. His nails were worn down to the quick from digging for roots, his hide scratched from the thorns that he had to contend with as enemies, naked, in the forest. To him a blue-headed tree lizard had become a meal, a leguaan or iguana, a feast. Beetles, caterpillars, large moths, the curious things found under fallen logs and flat stones, wild fruits, berries, and roots were his food. Sometimes he got honey. Sometimes, driving off jackals and vultures from a kill with a rough club, he ate offal.

He lived a life that had less comfort than his most primitive ancestors, less than the baboons, the only manlike creature who shared the wilderness with him, for they, at least, moved in companies of their own kind.

Only the immense courage and will that is man's heritage enabled him to live. His thoughts, other than those of food and safety, were of his wife and child, of his life before this time of expiation, and the necessity of surviving it. Elephants he encountered almost daily and, while he avoided them, he lost some of his fear of them, because as long as he wore his covering of mud and excrement and remained still while they passed, they took no notice of him. If they saw him at all, it was as a curiously shaped and leafless stump such as abounded in the forest. They relied on scent, and to them his scent was that of an elephant.

The secrets of the forest were opened to him. He saw elephants making love, the bull mounting the cows like immense, grey cattle. He saw snakes curled, twisting together in the slow rhythm of their passion. He saw the mating dance of the shy nyala, the bull fringed, dove-grey, striped with white and the cow a rich chestnut-brown. He saw bush pigs. He saw buffalo, solitary old bulls, almost hairless with great horn bosses. He saw tortoises. He found their eggs and ate both. Mice he ate and rodents of all kinds. He made traps for mongooses. He ate birds' eggs and young birds. He ate ground hornbills and guinea fowl when he was lucky enough to kill them with his throwing stick—a rough-knob kerrie he had fashioned. He had, except in his heart, ceased to be a man. He had only one aim, to obtain food and shelter from the storms and wild beasts, to remain alive.

What he consumed was returned directly to the soil, except for the small portion his body retained to serve its function of living, and even that, when the time came, would return to it, as did the leaves and branches of the trees, the bodies of the insects, reptiles, and mammals that were his colleagues upon whom he preyed and who, should the occasion ever offer itself, were ready to consume him.

In the forest, weaponless and alone, a man was no master; his varied talents were unspecialised. Mashupa was strong but not so strong as an elephant. He could climb, but not as well as a monkey. He could swim, but not so well as an otter. He could run, but not so swiftly as a buck. He could dig, but not so deep as a mole. He had teeth, but could not bite like a lion. He had nails, but they were not weapons like those of a leopard.

He was, as all men are, though many forget it, a creature living on the natural products of the ground, but because he was so alone, his position was emphasised. He moved on the surface of the forest beneath its canopy of trees. About him the green things were alive, as he was, the difference being one of degree, sensibility and movement. He moved swiftly on the surface of the forest, they moved slowly in the vertical plane. But both had this in common— should the plants cease to move downwards towards soil and rocks where they found their substance, or upwards towards the light, or should he cease to move in the horizontal plane, both would return to the ground from whence they had sprung.

Growth, death and birth in the forest, was a neatly adjusted balance, which, if changed by man, or circumstance, such as flood or fire, at once sought a new equilibrium. It again became balanced, though the proportions and the ingredients of the second balance might differ completely from the first.

The strong are not necessarily victorious, and even in the forest, there are more mice than lions. In the forest Mashupa was a mouse. A thing so small, so unimportant, that his comings and goings made no impression, either good or bad, upon it.

Mashupa's loneliness was intolerable. He was no hermit sustained by faith and mystic dreams, but a man tortured by his manhood, by his dreams of woman, by his thoughts of N'Tembi's aching loneliness that must, he knew, equal his own. He longed for her warm, silk-soft body, for the naked body of his child. He longed to hear their voices and the sound of their bare feet scuffling the dust. He longed for his home, his bougainvillaea, the six little cans for which he had made handles of twisted wire.

Sometimes, when he could bear it no longer, he went towards the nearest kraal nearly forty kilometres away, not approaching it closely, but going close enough to hear the occasional crowing of a cock and to watch, in the distance, the blue spirals of smoke that rose from the cooking fires.

Once, in the evening, he heard a girl's voice. She was singing loudly as she swung down a path; perhaps to combat the loneliness of the place; perhaps, because she was happy, returning from her lover. It is coming back that a girl sings. When she goes, she goes on silent feet, coyly—as coquettishly as a mating buck on its little dancing hoofs. But afterwards, her full heart rises into her throat, and like a bird, she sings. Yes, she had been to her lover. Of that he was sure, and so tormented was he by the thought that for days he could think of nothing else.

Always, when he could rest, he stirred his mind that seethed like an ant's nest with the stick of his memory. Pictures came to him of N'Tembi's beauty. His hands groped in the empty air for her body. He thought of what Father Thadeus had said. He had said—'You are a Christian and free of the trammels, the thraldom of these traditions.' And he had answered him saying—'It is true, but my people do not understand. At my door will be laid the death of every child, the sickness of every beast and woman. Me they will blame when a spring dries up, when the crops fail and the game is scarce, and that I cannot bear.' Believe. He did not know what he believed. He only knew now what he wanted—his wife and child and to live to consummate this reunion.

Four times the orange moon had risen over the fringe of the forest, setting the edge ablaze with glory, rising like a fire out of the pale indigo of the evening, growing and fading to silver as it rose into the sky. Four times had it waned, growing smaller and smaller. Now it was rising for the fifth time, a thin, white sickle 'in the star-pierced heavens. Four times, and he was still alive!

He mixed more medicine in his pot, adding a great ball of elephant dung to the mixture of water and black clay. It had stopped stinking to him now. He was used to it and his man smell was utterly lost in the sickly smell of the excrement with which he smeared his body.

A man who no longer smelt like a man was not a man. He, Mashupa, was a man no longer. He was part elephant, part of his totem, a thing as much separated from his fellows as a cadaver, a thing that smelt of putrescence while still alive. A dead thing, with a living, suffering heart. He lay down in his nest of leaves and slept till the cold of the dawn woke him.

In one of the early dawns through which Mashupa shivered, another scene was taking place. It was taking place in his father's kraal.

There, at the gateway of the cattle enclosure, the kraal within the kraal, its hub and centre, they had placed Talifa, the old induna, his grandfather in the maternal line. They had put him there because he was too old. He could no longer eat properly, and his words were nonsenes. His last act had been to stand up for Mashupa, the boy he loved. His last words had been to say that this expiation was useless, that the boy was not to blame, only time was to blame, and that the times had changed. So that this old man, who should have been conservative, clinging to the customs of his fathers, was more free in his thoughts than the younger men, and so was thought to be mad. He was so old that he knew that many things which men think matter a great deal matter not at all, and that many things which they deem of no importance are of the first importance. This being the definition of madness among men, they carried him as the darkness faded to the gateway of the cattle kraal—into the pathway of the bulls, the cows, the heifers, and the oxen. In the pathway of all the horned animals, except the calves which were kept apart from their mothers, so that they should not drink all their milk in the night.

In the kraal the young men stirred up the beasts, talking to them, telling them what they must do. It must be remembered that these cattle were the descendants of other cattle that were used in war, running with men into battle and goring their enemies with long, sharp horns. It must be remembered that these cattle were more than cattle, and not only represented the wealth and honour of the clan, but also were intimately confused with the spirits of the departed, so that as they were more than cattle, they were also more than men, being part spirit.

When the beasts were sufficiently disturbed and were milling about, the bulls pawing the ground, throwing up the soft, dusty, trampled dung on to their dewlaps and snorting through wide nostrils, the cross poles that formed the doorway of the kraal were drawn aside and the cattle—a great parti-coloured stream, led by the bulls, galloped out. The old man in the gateway was no obstacle to them. He became as nothing under the weight of their cloven hoofs. He was nothing, his long life was ended in a manner that was traditional, and his spirit, crushed out of his flattened body, entered that of the crushers and he became one with the herd. As they galloped away, the old man was with them. Strong again in the multi-coloured herd. Strong as the strongest bull, and the bulls stronger because of his spirit.

The kraal was now empty of life, and silent, except for the calves lowing for their dams in the smaller subsidiary kraal that was attached to it. The tall, irregular barkless poles of the trees sunk into the ground that walled the kraal were white, like bones, in the early morning light; and the dust that had risen from the milling herd had sunk again into the brown velvet bed of its floor, which was raised as high as a boy of ten above the surrounding ground with the piled, tramped dung of many years. Under that dung, and protected by it, and the horns of the cattle, were the grain pits where kaffir corn and mealies were stored in sealed containers, as a reserve against famine. The boys had gone off after the cattle, to herd them and collect the cows that were now drifting back of their own accord, drawn by the cries of the hungry calves and the pain in their distended udders; for the milk cows had run out with the others. Their hoofs, too, were red with the old man's blood.

But before the first cows came back, the men had collected the remains of the induna in a mat, and scattered wood ashes on the place where he had fallen under the hoofs of the cattle, so that the returning cows hardly noticed the smell, and only one of them put her head down and roared, as cattle do when they smell new and bloody death.

The women and girls took no part in this event, for women belong in the fields and have no rights in the kraals which are taboo to them as long as they are nubile. Little girls and old women may have dealings with cattle but a young woman during her periods may not even look at them, and, should a herd be in her path, she must not pass through it, but go round the beasts. Should a drop of woman's blood fall in the kraal, the whole herd might become sick, and for an infringement of this taboo women have been put to death. If, however, the oxen are sick, they are sometimes put in charge of young maidens, who must herd them naked, and without returning to their homes, sometimes for as much as two months together.

So the women were out of it, but knew of it, as they built their cooking fires. They did not speak of it because it was not to be spoken of, but it was in all their minds. When they heard the rush of the cattle, they covered their eyes with their hands and sighed, for something they had known all their married lives had gone from the kraal. A tree under whose shadow they had lived as young women had been cut down. True, the tree had given little shade for many years, but it had the reputation of shade. There were stories told of the once dense shadow its leaves had given, and each story emphasised the vanished glories and the wisdom that had passed. The leaves in the spring came singly now, where once they came in green battalions. But anyone looking at the tree could see what it had been. The older women remembered, the younger only remembered what they had been told, but they had been told so much and so often, that they believed they had seen for themselves.

A sigh, like a gust of wind in the trees, went over them as they turned their heads towards the galloping herd, and then their eyes went back to the pots where the morning meal was cooking.

The name of the great bull, who had led the herd out of the cattle kraal, was Mabata-bata, which means the one with many spots. He was an old bull and tame only with the herd boys who sharpened his horns and took him to fight the bulls in other neighbouring herds where he was always the victor. This was one of their sports.

Mashupa knew Mabata-bata well. He had known him when he was a calf and he had been a boy. He had herded him. He had even been there when the important question of his castration had been discussed, and had been reproved for his vehemence in protesting against the suggestion. Yet, perhaps, he had been instrumental in saving the bull's virility. Perhaps the weight of his small, treble voice added the hair's weight to the discussion which had decided the question. For the Thongas castrate their cattle and choose the bulls they will keep, with the greatest care. This spotted bull was the calf of a black cow with white blotches that had been one of the lobola cattle paid for Mashupa's sister, Amatotata, by a white bull of the royal Zulu kind belonging to the old man who had just died. His ancestors had been stolen when the Zulus, fighting among themselves, had neglected to leave sufficient guards for the beasts. These cattle were the descendants of the white cattle of T'Chaka—notable for their beauty, endurance, and intelligence in battle. They were white, with black ears and muzzles. Their skin, under the white hair, was black, and on their flanks and bellies were small, black patches and flea marks.

Thus, the past had reached out to crush Mashupa's grandfather under the hoofs of his friend. But the bull, Mabata-bata, who would let Mashupa pull ticks from his eyelids without moving, knew nothing of this.

The old man had joined his ancestors. The weakened juices of his body, the blood of his viscera, were on the great, cloven hoofs of the cattle as they walked with lowered, uneasy heads over the pale, winter grass.

He had joined the herd spiritually and physically, enriching them with his presence and his wisdom. Crushed flat, trampled, at the gate of the kraal, he now dwelt in the kraal, and wandered over the forest as the cattle grazed. Made long ago, as a child in the womb, out of the African soil, he had now returned to it. Earth to Earth.

One by one the cows were milked into receptacles hollowed out of soft wood, by boys who milked with one hand, and kept the calves away with a little stick in the other. They tapped the black, dewy noses of the hungry calves, letting them suck a little to draw the milk down, and then forcing them away while they milked. For these cows would not let down their milk unless their calves were there. If a calf died, it was skinned and the skin stuffed with grass, and put beside the mother while she was milked. Some of the cows had a string which was passed through a hole in the membrane that separates the nostrils. It was used as a twitch is used on the lip or ear of an obstreperous horse, to keep them still if they were too wild to handle. When the boys had gone, they allowed the calves access to their mothers, and once freed of restraint, they butted, tugged, and sucked till the last drop was drawn. The boys poured the milk into gourds set on stands, made of small trees pruned to have three prongs, which would hold it out of the way of the dogs and poultry till it turned sour. These calabashes had an opening at the bottom which was closed by a wooden plug, the residue of whey left in them being sufficient to cause the fresh milk to curdle at once.

At this stage it was eaten with carved, wooden spoons by both men and women. When the whey, which they called mulaza, separated, the cork was withdrawn and it was drunk by the men and herd boys. The solid portion called ntjhwamba, could be eaten by all with the exception of women who were having their periods. For them it was taboo, as were all milk products. This taboo applied also to women who had been confined, until their child had been presented to the moon. The milk that came from a cow for the first week after calving was taboo to all people, except children, who might drink it boiled, because children were not yet people.

The boys milked the cows. The calves drank their mothers' milk. The women cooked at their fires. The men stood or squatted in the sunshine, waiting for food. The blue smoke rose, fragrant, into the still air. Everything was as it had been. Life went on in the kraal. The death of the old induna had only interrupted it. It had changed nothing. Besides he was still there. To-night they would feel him among them as they stood to watch the herd re-enter the kraal.

Chapter Eighteen

A BLACK GIRL'S HEART

A black girl's heart is red, like the heart of any other human being. Preserved in formaldehyde, bottled in spirit in the College of Surgeons, this organ, that beats so violently under a brown, velvet skin, would be indistinguishable if set among other, Nordic, hearts ranged upon the shelf.

N'Tembi's heart was sore, her belly ached with emptiness, with the void of Mashupa's going. Her house was a mockery, her child at once her only comfort, and a continuous reminder, because of her likeness to Mashupa, of his absence.

When she had done with crying, her eyes dry because there were no more tears to come—when her little stores of food, saved for the celebration of the anniversary of their marriage, were consumed, she returned to the service of her mistress who, though not glad about the circumstances which had brought about her return, could nevertheless not bring herself to regret them. One man's meat was, indeed, another man's poison. It was sad about the boy Mashupa, but one could always do with an extra maid. The child was a nuisance. But if you had girls, and you had to have girls, you had, after a short interval of time, babies

133

on your hands as well. They were like animals, these people female animals, cows, mares, bitches, and if you had them, you had their calves, foals, and pups. There was, indeed, no alternative, which was perhaps just as well, for besides its being the will of God, the black children of to-day were the servants of to-morrow. So, while one might deplore, one accepted such things as a part of life. The idea of love, of affection, between the indigenous people, never entered her head. They paired off, coupled, like animals in season, and that was all. It was not something one talked about or even discussed. As the sun set each night, so a baby came every year. This was almost certain among the natives who had accepted as much of white man's culture as was permitted to them. Under primitive conditions where polygamy prevailed, she believed, they only had a child every three years, giving suck for that length of time and avoiding conception till the first child was weaned. The natives had many curious and revolting customs. Imagine a three-year-old child standing at its mother's side to drink like a calf from her dugs. There were many other things she had heard about their courting and marriage customs. They were talked about in bated breath by the ladies of her acquaintance. 'Did you hear? Did you know? My husband told me . . . They say it is not unusual for——'

But her laundry was beautifully done again, her lingerie was ironed to perfection, and, while it lasted, she was content.

With Mashupa's going, N'Tembi's life fell apart. Her world was empty. Senhora Ferreira had given her work again, and a room where she could live with her child. And she lived there in a tormented dream. On the outside, on the periphery, as it were, of her dream life in which she worked, ate, slept, and tended Louanda, was Henrique, the stranger who had brought the news from Mashupa's kraal. She hated and feared him because of his importunities. She knew, as he knew, that time was against her, and the force of life with him who pursued her. She clung to him because in some way he was a link with Mashupa, and sometimes, with him, she almost forgot Mashupa. That part of her life was drawn like a circle about its centre, which was her longing for her husband. But it was not only her husband, it was her husband as a man, and the stranger, as she called him in her mind, was a man. Outside this second circle was a third. That of her religion, her training, her belief in virtue. And outside this, again, was a fourth in which dwelt all the necessities and longings of all women of all time. The female blood that called to male. The instinct to seek a new mate when the first was gone, the female capacity to fragment life, to cut it into segments, as a sausage is cut, so that each piece is separate, and what happens in one segment of no concern with the others that precede or follow it.

As Mashupa moved like a ghost in the forest, so did she move as a ghost in the city; moved in a dream in which what she did was without reality to her. What she did was not her. The real N'Tembi was Mashupa's. This thing with its desires was something apart. If it happened, it would not happen to her, not to the real her.

Her mistress discussed her situation with her friends, and they were much amused. 'They are all the same,' they said. 'They never become real Christians, and if one man goes, they take another. They are like baboons, like animals.' They smiled and shrugged their shoulders with pleasant disgust.

And then, one warm night, after it had nearly happened, even the stranger never knew how nearly or he would have forced her more, N'Tembi gave notice. She had had news of Mashupa. This news which had excited her led her to allow more liberties than usual from her lover. This news, because it brought Mashupa, her husband, vividly into her mind, made her resist the liberties that she had encouraged.

Legally, her mistress could have held her to her contract, but since she did not really need her, she let her go without even asking where she was going. It seemed unnecessary. Since there was a man, she would go to him. But among the Kaffirs, perhaps because their ideas are not entirely controlled by thoughts of profit and loss, by money and wish for gain, the heart often dominates the mind. It dominates what we call the soul, the spirit, and slowly N'Tembi's bruised heart took control of her numbed brain. She knew where Mashupa was. Four hundred kilometres to the north, in the district of Querida. If I get there, she thought, people will tell me. Not white people, who would know nothing of such things, but people of her own race who would know the story.

Like water piling up behind the wall of a dam, her hopes, fears, wishes, her desires climbed centimetre by centimetre. The scale of going or staying was now evenly balanced—a hair's weight would send her north.

The hair had come in the form of a man she met in the native market when she accompanied her mistress there to purchase fresh garden produce. She spoke to a man from the north who had seen a man, who had seen Mashupa! It was enough.

The man had said Mashupa was living in a great hollow tree like a baboon. He said he had been seen by a young man setting wire snares for buck.

Mashupa, her husband, living in a tree like a baboon! Without a word she had answered her mistress's call and had held out the basket she carried to be filled with fruits —papayas, avocado pears, and mangoes. That evening Senhora Ferreira was giving a small party. She would have a fruit salad in the American style, served like the picture she had seen in the *Ladies' Home Journal* that had been given to her husband by the first officer of a freighter with whom he did business. It was after the party that N'Tembi had given notice.

N'Tembi had a plan. Her wages would suffice to get her to Querida. After that, everything was in the hands of the Holy Virgin who, also a mother, would no doubt assist her. Her faith was boundless. Her remaining effects, the few she had kept, she sold, telling no one of her real intention. Then, carrying her child on her hip and a roll of blankets and her cooking pot on her head, she took the bus to Villa Theresa, its northern terminal. There, in answer to her prayers, she found a truck belonging to an Indian trader that was taking goods to his store at Querida.

N'Tembi now knew where Mashupa was. Not exactly, but within a hundred kilometres or so. She knew he was in the wildest and most north-westerly part of the district of Querida, and, once there, others would be able to give her the information she wanted.

What was she doing? Running away from temptation? Going to seek her husband? She did not know. She only knew that she must go. She passed through the Administrative Post without any notice being taken of her. She

136

went north again on a truck with a gang of men who were working on a timber concession. When she reached their camp, she left them and went to a nearby village where the people were kind to her, giving her, as is the Bantu habit, food and shelter. All knew about Mashupa. They passed her on down little forest paths that grew wilder and ever narrower. She saw elephant spoor and dung, she saw the devastation they caused among the trees, and at last she came to the final village. Beyond this no man lived except Mashupa.

The story she had heard was a lie, no one had seen him, but hunters had picked up his spoor on two occasions. So he was still alive. The bird that had fluttered in her heart since she had begun her journey was now stilled. He was alive.

'You cannot see him,' they said, 'for that would destroy his purpose.'

'No, I cannot see him,' she said, 'but I can live near him.'

'How?' they asked.

'I will build a little hut in the wilderness and wait.'

'How will you build alone?' the Chief asked.

'I do not know,' she said, 'but God will help me. He knows why I am here.'

'We will help you,' the Chief said, 'for this is a sad and heavy thing. Your man alone in the wilderness is contending with the spirits of our fathers. It is impossible for us to help him, but you we can help.'

So, at a small spring, one too small to supply the wants of even a modest kraal, they built her a little beehive hut of saplings thatched with grass. They felled trees to make a fence about it, setting them with their trunks inwards and the spikes of their thorny branches outwards, as a defence against the animals of the wild. They would help her with food—mealies, sour milk, ground nuts, kaffir corn, and pumpkins. The men cut the poles for her hut and cleared a small land for her minuscule garden, fencing it with trees they felled. Women helped her cut the thatch grass to cover her house. The Chief gave her seeds of kaffir corn and pumpkin; ground nuts and cassava roots to plant.

N'Tembi, because she was a woman, worked in her new nest, the thatched beehive hut that held her and her child. She cleaned it and tended it. It was her home. The past was forgotten. She slept on a mat of split bamboo with the child warm against her belly. A cotton blanket covered them. Her neck rested on a wooden pillow.

Sometimes a villager would come to see her. Sometimes, though rarely, those who came brought news or rumours about Mashupa, of how he was faring, of how thin he had become, of how, if by chance he saw a hunter, he fled from him like a wild thing. And all the while her mind and her heart and her body cried out for Mashupa. Cried out and ached as though the cries and the aches, and the tears in the night, could bring him to her side.

While she waited for the hut to be built, N'Tembi lived in the village which consisted of six kraals that stood about a hundred metres from each other in a circle whose centre was a large mhohlo or elephant wood tree. The water was carried from a well dug in a marsh almost a kilometre away. Natives seldom build near water because they know, from long experience, that such a site is unhealthy, though they do not know why.

The kraals of the village varied in size according to the richness of its owner. Each wife had to have a separate hut, all had store huts, and roofed structures where they kept their grain, and woven baskets containing nuts and beans hanging from branches, and everywhere there were small, half-wild chickens. There were no cats. In their language there was not even a word which meant cat. There were many dogs, yellow, mouse-grey, and black, prick-eared, greyhound-like animals descended from the Egyptian greyhounds which had penetrated into the interior hundreds, or perhaps thousands, of years ago. They had smooth, harsh coats. They did not lift their legs as other dogs do, and could not bark. They were hunting dogs that slunk continually at their masters' heels. They were half-starved and lived on the offal of the game they hunted and on the human excrement that was voided round the kraals. For this purpose, the women went to one side and the men to another.

In every kraal there was the cattle enclosure, or kraal, where the beasts that were herded by day slept at night on their powdered dung which rose continually higher above the surrounding ground. The soil round the huts was smooth from the tramping of many feet, and kept swept with brooms made of branches and grass.

Almost everything these people had was made by them.

138

The huts of saplings tied with bark, and thatched with grass. The bows with which they hunted were hewn out of special trees. The bow-strings and strings of their traps were woven from the fibres of the baobab. The arrows were made of a kind of bamboo reed and fletched with vulture's feathers. The arrow and assegai heads they forged from iron ore with a bellows made of an inflated goatskin. The clothes they wore were made of dressed skins, cattle skins and buckskins—little aprons worn before and behind, and a sort of leather skirt worn by the women. Their sleeping mats were made of split reeds, their pillows of hard, polished wood, their bedding of nyala and kudu skins, their pots of baked, red clay. Most men had knives and axes of European or American manufacture, some had iron cook pots, enamel cups and bowls, some had woollen or cotton blankets, and one man manufactured arrow-heads by beating out six-inch nails on an anvil made from a piece of rail. But they could have managed without these luxuries,

Her life in the kraal brought back memories of her childhood to N'Tembi. The crowing of the cocks, the scream of a burnt dog in the night—a dog that, sleeping for warmth near the ashes of a fire, had got too near it. The sound of mealies being rhythmically pounded in a stampblock—all threw her back into the primitive culture from which the good sisters had taken her as an infant. As she helped the women in their work, she even came to understand Mashupa's dilemma, for the spirit of the forest descended on her, and her Christianity was insufficient to save her from her superstition, though she prayed both night and morning.

Her hut was fifteen kilometres from the village—a good two hours' walk along seldom frequented paths—and it was with many fears that she went to live there. Some days a group of larger children brought her food and hung it in a basket in the tree midway between her hut and the village. They feared to go further because this was what they called 'the land of the elephants,' though few had been seen nearby for some time. It was an area in which whole herds sometimes lived for weeks at a time. 'If they come, I shall return,' N'Tembi said.

'You will be welcome,' the Chief told her.

The days passed into weeks, the weeks into months in a blur of time. She worked in her garden. She collected fallen branches and game dung for fuel. She fetched water from the tiny spring. She fed and cared for her child and waited, with a woman's animal patience, for time to pass, in a strange, mystic amnesia. She waited as women wait for a man to return from the wars, or to come out of prison. She waited, and sometimes, as she waited, she sang in the high, throaty voice of the native people. A sweet, wailing voice that carried far into the silence of the forest. She sang because she was sad, she sang to ward off evil spirits, she sang, as children whistle in the dark, to keep up her own courage. She sang because she was a woman, young and nubile, singing as a bird might sing, with her heart in her throat. And the birds in the trees heard it, and rose from the twigs on which they were perched.

Sometimes N'Tembi heard the police whistles blown by the villagers. Whistles that they carried on little cords around their necks. They blew them as they walked the forest trails to tell the elephants they were coming and the elephants, disliking men, moved away.

So N'Tembi lived, and the child lived, and her hut was ringed about with little paths. The heap of the ashes from her hearth and the refuse she threw away grew in size. The growing midden, the change of seasons, and the increase in the size of her child, and the child in her belly, were her calendar.

Sometimes when loneliness overcame her, she visited the village carrying Louanda on her thigh and the new child within her. But usually she stayed at home, lost in her dream, and overcoming her fears with prayers. And often, as she worked in her small garden behind its barrier of thorns, she sang. For as happiness induces song, so does sorrow, and all the sorrow of a woman alone was in her throat.

It did not seem to her that she was doing a remarkable thing. She was doing what she had to do. Fleeing temptation and moving towards her husband, as if, by her prayers, her proximity, and the greatness of her love, she could protect him from the dangers of the forest. Twice she heard elephants in the distance. Once the wild trumpeting of cows nervous of some suspected danger; and once they were nearer, she heard them feeding in the night. The sharp cracks of breaking branches sounded like rifle shots in the inky darkness.

But the dream state of pregnancy was on her so that time ceased to be time. It was a sort of purgatory that lay between the happy, heavenly past with Mashupa, the hell that he was now enduring, and the future where everything would be wonderful once more.

Baboons she feared, and carried the spear the Chief had given her when she went abroad, for baboons are fearless of women, and it was believed that they would attack and rape them upon occasion. Baboons there were in quantity, many coming to drink at her spring.

Of all this, Mashupa knew nothing, but his loneliness was now a little mitigated by a young baboon he had taken from its mother. He had found her plucking at an arrow that had pierced her flank, passing right through her. He had killed her with his club for meat, and then discovered the baby clinging to the long hairs of her belly. He was going to kill it too, but thought to save it and eat it later. He fed it on wild fruit and grubs, and found himself unable to destroy it. It was a female and he spoke to her continually, though at first the sound of his voice had sounded strange to him. But it was a relief to speak and to have company, something that loved him, that slept, curled like a child, in his arms. She soon followed him about, and the strange pair, the wild man smeared with clay and dung, and the little baboon, wandered together in search of food along the game paths of the forest. When she grew tired, she would jump on to his back. Rested, she would slide down his leg and follow him again running on all fours, but standing erect at a tree occasionally and often indicating edible berries and bulbs by her excitement.

Once, when drawn by some instinct in the direction of the village, it was the baboon that led him nearer. Perhaps she knew that this was the area in which she had been born. And it was here that for a second time he heard a woman singing. But this time it was no girl returning from an assignation. This time it was the full-throated voice of a woman. His heart stood still. His belly rose into his mouth, his knees became weak. He thought the spirits had driven him mad at last, for the voice was the voice of N'Tembi. She sang a song of grief and loneliness. She sang his name —crying out, 'Mashupa, oh Mashupa!' into the air of the forest where not a leaf moved in the burning stillness of the afternoon.

He went forward, slowly creeping through the undergrowth like a hunter, and then, through a screen of trees, he saw a hut in a little clearing. At the door of the hut was N'Tembi with the child upon her hip. What had brought her to him? How had his silent cries for her penetrated so far? What agency of providence had brought her here to comfort and to tempt him? A great cry rose in his throat. He throttled it back, raising his hands to his own neck as if it was an enemy. He must not go to her. But he could watch her from afar. His life had a centre again. Once more the wheel could spin. The linchpin was back upon the axle. Picking up the little baboon, he turned away. He was a man again. No longer a half man, moving in a world of beasts and spirits.

Chapter Nineteen

THE MILLS OF GOD

Driven by some obscure motive of memory or instinct, driven as a bird is driven to migrate, the two great elephants began to move south. Like battleships, but silent as butterflies, they drifted slowly, eating their way, resting trunks hand in hand, waving branches over their backs to keep off the flies, bathing when they came to water and drinking, and going without water when there was none, but always silent and unhurried, always with the spoor of the tusked elephant in that of his tuskless brother, they came on, drifting giants, as silent as thistledown. Each step brought them nearer to death, as each step all their lives had done, as each step a man takes, or a child, is one step towards the change from life to death, from the known into the unknown, from the bacteriological and metabolic changes we know as life, into similar changes which we call death, when the spirit passes from the body, and the body goes back into the earth.

It was twenty years since they had last been in the vicinity of the great baobab and the grove of fever trees where the tusked elephant had been wounded and lamed. It was time to go again. But the trees were rooted in their swamp so there was no hurry. The march of the elephants was dignified, majestic. Its silence, impressive. It joined the other silences of the forest, that were so silent that silence was more obvious than noise. It was a place where noise, in the hot summer stillness, would be a relief to human ears. But there were no human ears. There was no life, or so little, and that so muted, that it appeared non-existent. Only the two pachyderms appeared to live, and they only when they moved. When they stood screened by bush and trees, they looked like anthills. But still they moved, with precision, without haste, but with certainty. Once again the great baobab was exerting its magnetic power. As it had drawn many men—Pretorius, the hunter, the Arab slavers, the half-caste brigands of the frontier in the past, and the long-dead Bushmen; as it had drawn Mashupa to its giant shadow, and Carew and his love; as it had drawn N'Tembi, not to it, because she did not know of its existence, but to the area where, though it remained invisible, its spirit dominated the surrounding bush, it now called to the elephants.

Mashupa was puzzled. Had the gods, the spirits in whom he no longer fully believed, weakened in their desire for revenge? Had God, in whom he almost believed, answered his prayers and those of N'Tembi? Had Father Thadeus's prayers for intercession found an answer? Had his grandfather, whom he loved, and did not know to be dead, been able, because he was so near death, to persuade the spirits to mitigate his lot? Had the Virgin Mary, the Holy Mother, thrown her mantle over him and his little family?

But God or gods, Virgin or spirits, providence or luck, had suddenly changed. The baboon had been the first thing. Fresh meat, though it was raw, in quantity. The baby baboon for company, and above all, the iron head of the arrow which he had fashioned into a knife by splitting a short branch to hold the haft and lashing it with the baboon's green guts. And now there was the final thing. The greatest of all, that N'Tembi should have come to dwell near him in the wilderness, and that, though he was alone, he was no longer quite alone. That, though he could not speak to her, he could watch her and the child from afar.

To this end, he went back to the vicinity of her hut and circled it, finding how far she travelled beyond it. She did not go far. Three hundred metres was as far as she had ever gone to collect her burning wood. There was no reason for her to go further, for the forest floor was littered with broken timber, smashed and left to rot by the elephants when they had stripped it years ago.

Here, well beyond her range, he made a little hide, out of branches, and came to watch her, holding his baboon between his knees. Soon there was a narrow path leading from the baobab to the hide. Beyond it was the no man's land between his paths and N'Tembi's. From here he could see her go to the spring with her pot upon her head, watch her fill it, bailing up the water with an empty tortoise shell, and carry it home, her hips swinging, her back erect against the weight of water on her head. He watched her collect wood and inhaled the smoke of her fire. Sometimes, when the wind was right, he thought he could smell her body, for living as he did, his sense of smell had improved immeasurably. His nostrils had widened, and now twitched like those of a dog when he scented game. He watched her bathing at the spring, pouring the water over her naked, golden body. He watched her bend, her breasts falling forward, as she bathed the child Louanda. He heard the soft voices, and sometimes she laughed. He saw that she was with child again and his heart almost broke with anxiety, with pride. Above all things in the world, she was his heart's desire.

He wondered how long he could resist the temptation of going to her, and here he detected the subtle hand of the gods. The gods had been kind with the knife, and the baby baboon, and the sight of N'Tembi, but more than this, he hesitated to take. To take more would be to challenge providence. The finger had been offered him, but that did not mean he could seize the hand. He knew her comings and goings. He knew when she went to fetch her food for he watched her come back with it. And here, he did succumb to temptation. Once, when she had gone, carrying her child, he crept into the hut to savour the perfume of her body, of her living. To see her meagre comforts so that he could carry a picture of it away in his heart.

That had been his intention, but he did more. From her fire he stole a living ember. A thick stick with a glowing end of ash and coal. Three times on his way back, he stopped to make fire, to revive and strengthen it, and to gain more coals. When he got home to the rough shelter he had built, he made a hearth, scraping out the ground in a hollow and flanking it with two large, flat stones that he found near the baobab. Now there was something alive beyond the baboon baby. Something of hers, part of her hearth was his, part of her warmth was his. Into the flames, as he blew them up with his lips, he could cast, not only meat to sear it, but his dreams. In the coals he saw visions of his wife, and dreamed of the past. Something of the warmth of her body came to him from the fire as he held his hands towards it. And in his dreams by that fire, he was nearer to her. True, Tembula had forbidden fire. But God had sent it by N'Tembi, to temper the bitterness of his lot. God was greater than Tembula.

So they sat night after night—the clay-plastered man and the young baboon, with hands extended to the flames. Its light was reflected in the leaves and branches of the shelter, illuminating it with a rosy glow. By his side were his knife, his club, and the throwing sticks that he had been able to fashion. Life was better now, his ancient boyhood skill with the sticks had returned. He could hunt the guinea fowl, francolin, bustard, ground hornbill, and dove, as they came to the pan to drink. He could cook them, and his shelter, because of the fire, had become a home. He saw many elephants, but evaded them by his stillness in their presence, and the magic of his plastered mud. At night, on several occasions, he heard them feeding, but such sounds no longer made him afraid. He had fire.

It is fire that makes man, separating him from the animals. First came a weapon—a club, which even the great apes have been known to use. Then fire which all beasts fear. There is something of God in fire. Then receptacles, so that water could be carried. And dogs, tamed for hunting. Last came seed, planted instead of gathered wild, and the flocks and herds of tamed beasts. But the king of all these is fire. The saviour and the destroyer.

When N'Tembi returned, she knew someone had been in her hut. Her fire was not as it had been. The thick branch she had left had been replaced, and there was a strange smell in the hut. A smell of elephants. She thought of Mashupa's medicine that Tembula had given him, of her disgust when he had shown it to her. But that disgust was now changed. Nothing now could have smelt more sweet to her. He had been there. She was no longer alone. For a long time he had been watching over her and their child. This she knew now, and knew why lately there had been a feeling of comfort in her heart. That was why she had sung as she did when she bathed. He was watching her, she thought. Watching the body that was both hers and his, that she had given to him so freely. He had seen her beauty again. In his mind, his hands had been on her, caressing her skin. Her heart beat faster. She gathered Louanda into her arms and held her tightly. The child that had come of the man, that was part of him, the only part of him that was now left to her. She searched the forest for trace of him. She found his spoor. She found his hide. She found the little track his bare feet had beaten to it, the hollow where he had squatted for hours at a time.

Now she knew. Now she was happy. All she had to do was to wait. She was reunited to him in spirit, bound to him by his eyes which could see her even if she could not see him. The rest was only a matter of time, a matter of the waxing and waning moons, the growing and the falling of the leaves and the fruits of the forest, the mating and the moulting of the birds of the air. Waiting was a thing that a woman was fully equipped to do, since her life was always one of waiting, one of periods and pregnancies, of cycles. Six moons had already passed. Half the time was gone. There would be so many such cycles and then it would end. Her child would be born in the village. It would be born as its ancestors had been born—as she had. Savagely, cruelly, out of her belly as the women kneaded it, but she was not afraid. All this was as it had always been. Later would be time enough to think of baptism, of the holy rites of the Church, for now she was a wild woman again. Not as wild as Mashupa, but no longer tame, no longer the docile house servant of Senhora Ferreira, but a tribal woman, living at the fringe of society. At the frayed edge where man merged with beast and tree and insect, subject to the same dangers and vicissitudes.

Chapter Twenty

THE HEART'S DESIRE

Now the time that had passed during which Mashupa had courted N'Tembi, and had loved her, had had a child born of her, and had left her, with child again, the many months that all this had taken were as nothing to the great elephants. They were as a day to them, for as a day is half the life of a two-day-old child, and a year half the life of a two-year-old child, and ten years half the life of the girl N'Tembi, the two years of her courtship and pregnancy and the first five months of her new child's life were but an unappreciable fraction of the elephants' lives. A week-end as it were, in which the summer rains had come twice, and the winter drought had come twice, and the marulas and other trees that fruit had fruited twice. But all of it, in the multiple span of their years, was a mere nothing, something a little longer to them than the nuptial flight of a butterfly, though to a mouse it was almost the fullness of its life. In nature, there is no such thing as time, not to the elephant or the mouse, or the butterfly nor even to the inhabitant of the wilds, brown man, or white. The first having no watch but the crowing of his cocks in the dawn, and the flight of the doves to the water in the evening, and the second who, having broken two watches, says at last:

'To hell with time, there are no trains to catch in these parts,' and abandons the forelock of time, letting it run wild like a horse, and copies the simple Kaffir, the unbeliever, in his reliance on the cock crow and dove flight, and depends on his belly to tell him when he is hungry, and his heavy lids to tell him when it is time to sleep, which, as often as not, is in the full heat of the day.

Time then, for all these men and animals, was a different thing, as distance was. It was different for each, for N'Tembi who was pregnant, for Mashupa who was afraid, for the white men who, in Lourenço Marques, still rose at the summons of a clock. Different for the black peasant tillers of the ground. Different for the hunters who had to restrain their eagerness, holding themselves back, and the cultivators who, as they sowed, thrust themselves forward towards the harvest, and the hazards that stood between the seed they sowed and the crops they would reap. Different for old Carew, pondering on his last hunt, Maniero who thought of his friend Ferreira's wife. Different for the Indian merchant who wanted a great tusk to sell to the Spaniard, who wanted it for the Holy Father in Rome. All were trying to hurry time, or to contract it. Senhora Ferreira was eager for time to pass so that she could find a lover, and afraid of its passing because each day brought the beauty, which was her life, nearer to its end.

The great elephants, alone, were unconscious of its passage, for being beyond the age of love, beyond the seasonal drives of passion, such acts no longer punctuated their lives. Their heavy hides were equally resistant to heat and cold, so the seasons did not affect them as they moved majestically through both time and the forest.

But time was assuming a new importance to Mashupa. His love urged time forward with the whip of desire, but time was recalcitrant. Nothing could make the days pass more quickly. Indeed, as his desire, whetted by the sight of N'Tembi, increased, time seemed, in defiance, to stand still, the moon to hang unmoving in the sky at night, the sun to hesitate in its slow course from east to west. To pass the time, he carved a decorative spoon for N'Tembi. It had a twisted and perforated handle. One day he would take it to her. Later, when all this was over, they would look at it and remember. And, if at first it had been better to have N'Tembi near, now it was infinitely worse. The tips of his fingers ached for her. His loins were an agony. The call of the man in him to the woman, to N'Tembi, was greater than it had ever been.

Silently she called to him when he saw her, with every movement of her body, with every glance of her dark eyes when she turned them on the forest, as if she knew when he was there. Sometimes she threw out her open arms towards the trees as if she would call him into their embrace, into the warm security of her breasts and belly. Sometimes he thought he saw tears coursing down her cheeks. Sometimes when she sang, and the desire in her voice came floating through the bush, he thought he would go mad.

Surely he had suffered enough, surely the gods need not tempt him so hard. How was it that God, who gave man desire when He created man, should use it to destroy him? The gods themselves now seemed mad to him. The very gods who'd sent him the baboon, and the arrow that had become a knife, had also created the mother baboon whom it had wounded, and whom he had killed. The God of whom he had learnt, who cared for every sparrow in the air, for every hair of a man's head, was now confused with the malignant spirits of his totem of whom Tembula had spoken. The elephants loomed larger in his mind. There seemed more of them. There was more spoor nearer to him. Danger threatened him from all sides.

Then there was a great storm. As great as the one just before he left his home, where he had stood between the lightning and his wife, when he had covered her body with his own. It struck the forest, flooding it, killing the fire that he had, with the little shivering baboon clinging to his back, tried his uttermost to save. With the cold and the rain, fever had come so suddenly that he trembled, and shook, so that his teeth chattered in his head. And when the trembling had passed, he sweated water from every pore in his skin. He saw vultures, the birds of ill omen, on the great baobab. Driven from the upper air by the weather they had descended and were surely waiting for his end.

Only one thing was now possible. To his longing for N'Tembi as a man longs for a woman, was added his longing for her as a child longs for its mother in illness. For he was ill and again a child, and he was a man to whose body the woman called. He was all life, striving to reach a conclusion, before its own life is ended. As the flowers in the parched desert bloom and fruit in haste when there is an occasional rain, so that they may perpetuate themselves, before they are shrivelled by the savage sun, so did he strive to his woman, to the female of his species, to his wife, to his love, to his heart's desire, before it was too late.

It seemed to him that as he called, in the lashing rain, to her, so did she call to him. That her voice was raised in the voice of the storm, carried by the driving wind, the stinging rain, the small, sharp hailstones that beat upon him. Her voice was in the wild cry of the storm-driven bird, in the crash of falling trees, in the furious gusts of wind. Above all in the wind, for the wind in the forest trees cries out like a woman.

She was calling and he would go. He would defy the gods, the spirits. He would defy the Christian God, all gods, all men, all storms, all beasts and terrors. He would go.

In her beehive hut, N'Tembi trembled. The wind passed over the circular hut and round it, as water swirls past a rock in a swollen stream. The rain was silent against the thatch, but there was nothing to keep out the sound of the thunder, or the flashes of blue lightning that forked through the storm, splitting the purple blackness of the clouds. It came in through the cracks of her door illuminating her hut with a livid light that flashed, left a darkness deepened by its coming, and then lit it up again. She held Louanda on her knee. The child had her face buried in her breasts. She was crying softly. The piercing cries with which she had greeted the storm had weakened to this. Within her womb N'Tembi felt her new child move as if with fear. She had no idea how long the storm had lasted. A long time it seemed to her. But fear is a factor in time, lengthening it, just as happiness is also a factor, accelerating its passage. The storm stopped as suddenly as it had begun. The wind fell and there was a silence almost as menacing as the roar of the lashing gale. The only sound was the drip of the trees, as each rain-soaked leaf gave up its burden to gravity. Soon, when it grew hot again, and the water had soaked down into the ground and had been gathered up by the roots, the same leaves that now dripped water, would transpire it into the steaming atmosphere. This was the major life cycle that affected the life of the trees, as the circulation of the blood affects the health of man and beast. The sap that would rise was the blood of the trees. There was also the sound of running water, as the ground, unable to drink so much in one gulp, spilled it away filling every little hollow, and turned the game paths into streams.

This storm had been no worse than other summer storms, but N'Tembi was alone. And fear was slow to leave her heart. Then she smelt elephants. There was no doubt about that smell. There were elephants nearby. She held Louanda closer to her. She strained her ears, but all she could hear was the pounding of her own heart. But one did not hear elephants—they just came. In one moment there was nothing, and then there were elephants. Then there was nothing again, unless you heard the rumble of their bellies or the clapping flap of their ears. The smell grew stronger. There was a noise at the door as if something was trying to open it. She shrank back against the curved wall of the hut bending her body forward over the child in her arms. The door moved. It opened. A strange, harsh voice said: 'N'Tembi, N'Tembi!'

She could not speak for fear. The voice said, 'N'Tembi!' again. 'N'Tembi, it is I, Mashupa.'

'The voice is not the voice of Mashupa,' she heard herself saying.

'It is I.'

'The smell is of elephants.'

'It is I—it is I who stink of their dung.'

'Mashupa,' she said, 'Mashupa!' She saw him crouch over the little fire in the centre of the hut and blow the embers into a tiny, flickering flame. He threw a little dry grass on to the fire. It flared up and she saw him. But it was not Mashupa. This was a wild, mud-plastered man. So thin was he that every bone of his body showed. In the firelight his eyes enormous in their sockets, like eyes set in a human skull, stared wildly at her.

'N'Tembi,' he said, 'N'Tembi, my heart's desire!'

She came closer.

He took her hand and pulled her to him. His hand was like iron. As hard and harsh as the bark of a tree, his smashed finger-nails tore at her skin, his arms were as hard as stone with no cushion of flesh to disguise their power. The elephant smell overwhelmed her as he held her. The child slipped from her hip to the ground. The aching loneliness of months, the fears, fell from her as a cloak might fall, as a blanket. The smell of his sweat came to her nostrils dilating them. A mixture of man's sweat and elephant filled the silent hut. Filled it as the man and woman were united again in the blackness, by the heat of their desire.

Like the storm, he had come—as swiftly. And like it, he had gone back into the night. Like the storm, it seemed like a dream now it was over, but it had not been a dream. She raised herself on her elbow. Not a dream, but another sin. Because, according to custom, there should be no full union with a pregnant woman. But she was a modern woman, immune to custom. A Christian girl and free. But was she free? Since she had left town, she had gone back a long way along the road to her tribal, hereditary past. The hut stank of elephants. Elephants were their totem, hers and Mashupa's. He had broken his period of expiation. Tempted by her presence, he had fallen. But she, was she not equally to blame? Had she resisted him? Had she forbidden him? The thing which had been a dream faded and reality replaced it. It was real. Mashupa was real. What had taken place was real. The river that was Mashupa had burst its banks, flinging itself into the waiting pool that was N'Tembi. Unknowingly, she had meant this. Unknowing, she had placed herself where it could happen. And it had happened. Released from months of tension, she sobbed, at once excited and at peace, and at once glad and tearful. At once regretting what had happened and longing for it to happen again. Even the gods, the spirits, had not been strong enough to hold them apart. Nothing could part them now—not even death. Till death does us part, she thought. But was not this that they had suffered a form of death?

When Mashupa left his wife, he picked up the little baboon which he had left outside the hut. It clung to him chattering with fear and loneliness, its arms were about his neck, its face buried under his chin. Its furry body was warm against him as he walked. For the first time since he had left his home, he was at peace. The ache of his loneliness was alleviated. With her near, he could stand anything. Nothing was too much. And Tembula had said nothing against this. He had not mentioned women. He had said, 'Go alone,' and he had gone alone. He had not asked her to come and she had come. Perhaps the spirits had sent her. Perhaps God, because he was a Christian boy, had sent her. But now he feared nothing. To-morrow he would go, to watch her from his hiding place and then later, when his loneliness forced him to it, he would go into her hut once more.

Next day, when he went to his hiding place, he found that she had been there before him and had left a tortoise shell filled with mealie porridge in the fork of the tree under which he hid. She knows, he thought. She knows that I am here, and he lay down to watch her, and to listen to her singing.

The storm had meant nothing to the great elephants. It had not delayed their march. The rain rolled off their backs as it would off a roof. There was water everywhere now and they were content. The contentment of an animal is like that of a tree. If conditions are favourable to life and growth, it is content.

They moved neither fast nor slowly. They did about thirty kilometres a day, inexorably, moving towards their goal, the grove of fever trees. Last year the trees would have been nearly as well grown. Next year they would be very little bigger. But it was this year, it was now, that the strange spirit of memory moved them, urging them, as a yeast ferments when its time is come, when the conditions which cause its action are exactly right. In nature there is a great, though inexplicable, exactitude.

As they moved, the wet branches that they parted with their bulk shivered, and the raindrops that still clung to the leaves fell in short, sharp showers on the ground below. As they moved on silent feet, there was only a faint squashing sound of the mud as it was compressed by their weight. As soon as they had passed, each footprint was filled with water forming a tiny sunken lake. The kilometres fell behind them, joining the other hundreds of thousands that they had marched, the vast distances, over an immense period, consumed as if they had been eaten, digested by the great, grey pillar legs. Sometimes they stopped to drink at a pan filled with fresh rainwater. Sometimes they took water up into their trunks and bathed, squirting it over their great bodies, sometimes they bathed each other or stood resting with entwined trunks. In the darkness they were nothing, just patches of greater darkness, that moved with probing trunks through the forest. By day they were

153

scarcely more visible, grey ant-heap patches, in a vast sea of grey and olive foliage. Their eyes, like the eyes of most old animals and men, were empty of expression. Dark-pupilled, sherry-coloured, they showed nothing, seemed to see nothing. There was no fury in them, no determination, no anger. They had no thought of revenge—that had passed. There was only this urge, this reflex of memory, to perform an act whose cause was lost somewhere along the thousands of miles of trail they had traversed.

N'Tembi knew Mashupa was near. Knew also, because she was a woman and he a man, that he would soon come to her again. In two days, in three days, in a week, he would hold her in his arms once more She thought of the mud she had washed off her clothes and body after he had gone. The mud, which together with the smell of man and elephant, had proved to her that she had not dreamt. The smell of elephant was suddenly pleasant to her. Her heart beat faster when she smelt it. And now there were more elephants about. She saw fresh spoor, but none troubled her. She never even caught a glimpse of one, for this was only the edge of their territory.

The food she put down for Mashupa was taken each day. His spoor was fresh on the still, damp ground. She could see where he had sat, and knelt, had lain down in his little hide as he watched. Knowing he watched, she had tempted him with her beauty, combing the tight curls of her hair as she sat with naked breasts. Moving provocatively, swinging her hips when she walked with the red kaffir pot of water on her head. Without words, but with acts stronger than words, she called to him. Every movement of her body told him to come, each cried out to him that she was his, that she was waiting, that they were young and strong, and their love a power, like the flight of birds.

Since the rain, Mashupa had fetched his water from the pan near where the grove of yellow fever trees raised their livid trunks out of the mud. In the evening light their leaves were very green and feathery, their branches yellow, and their trunks a livid mauve. Sometimes a fish eagle sat perched on the tallest tree. One of the kings of the air, he stared about him, without fear of man.

The little path from the baobab to the hide, near N'Tembi's hut, was now smooth from Mashupa's running feet. And there was the new track to the pan of fever trees. He did not have to hunt so much for food, since N'Tembi managed to leave him some each day, which gave him more time to watch her. To watch his heart's desire, and to desire her.

It took the elephants six days to drift down to the fever trees. At last they saw them and, like two great, grey battleships, moved in on them. It was early morning when they came and the fever trees were stained with the dawn, red with the early light, as if they had been dipped in blood. The elephants moved into the pan and stood knee-deep in mud and water while they ate. They ate without haste the branch tips and smaller limbs, that were of less than one year's growth. As they ate, their mood changed, anger seeped into them as memory rose from the depths of their natures. Their eyes were no longer calm, but wicked. They now began to tear down the trees. They smashed them with their trunks, snapping them so that the forest echoed. They tore them down. They set their foreheads against them and smashed them. And then when they had done, they moved away. It was over. If they lived, they would come again when the trees had recovered, in twenty years.

What directed the accident of their moving? Why did they come to the east side instead of the west of the pan? What fortune brought them on to Mashupa's spoor?

Since he had been going to N'Tembi, he had used less medicine. He wanted to be attractive to her and he was also forgetful. Going for water into the middle of the pan where it was cleaner than on the edge, he had washed his feet, so that the smell on the path was the smell of a man, not of an elephant.

The elephants moved on the spoor, their scenting trunks swinging in front of them. Every breath increasing their rage. But still they moved slowly, cautiously, silently. The tuskless one in front, the bull with tusks behind, setting his feet in his brother's spoor. Why should they hurry? The man was tied to them by his spoor as surely as if he had been tied by a string.

Mashupa was watching N'Tembi when he saw them. First he did not see them. He saw something that might be an elephant except that it was too big. It was a giant ant-hill. But how was it he had not seen it before? Then the baby baboon in his arms screamed with fear and ran into a tree. They were elephants. They were the fathers of all elephants. They were the great beasts of whom he had heard. The ones that were inhabited by the spirits of Moselekatse and T'Chaka. The great ones. They were his totem come alive.

The elephants moved slowly forward. They stood like immense, grey stones at the edge of the bush, but towering over it. Their trunks had ceased to swing. They hung in front of them as they raised their heads. Their ears opened out wide on each side of their heads, like great, black sails. Their trunks went up, curled back. He saw the huge tusks of the tusked one, black against the clear blue of the sky.

N'Tembi, who till now had seen nothing, looked up from her little garden and cried out—'Mashupa, Mashupa!'

Mashupa ran towards her. Thrust her into the hut and stood at its door with her spear in his hand. The assegai that the villagers had given N'Tembi to take with her when she went abroad because of the danger of baboons. The elephants still stood with raised trunks, then they moved forward. He could see their eyes now. This was death. Death to them all. There was only one way to meet it, with a weapon in his hand. Mashupa was a warrior again. The present slipped back into the past. He was as his father had been, and his father's father, and the thousands before them. A wild man facing death, like a wild animal, with bared, iron fangs, his woman and his young behind him.

The elephants did not charge. They did not trumpet. They merely moved forward. Their feet made no sound. The only sound was the crackling of branches as they walked through N'Tembi's fence of felled trees. The tusked one advanced in front of his brother. Towering above Mashupa he straightened out his trunk. As it fell like a tree on Mashupa's head, Mashupa flung his spear straight into its mouth. The tuskless elephant came up, and the two of them walked over Mashupa's body and over the hut. It collapsed under their weight. The tusked elephant opened up the wreck with a sideways blow of his weapons. The tuskless one reached for the woman and tossed her out as a boy would toss a ball. N'Tembi had been holding the child, but she came apart from her in mid-air, and she fell screaming on her belly. The tusked elephant impaled her and threw her up so that she hung like a naked, brown fruit, dripping its red juice from the tree that had shaded the hut. With his trunk, the tusked elephant drew out the assegai from his mouth. The blade remained embedded in its roof. Mashupa had thrown hard and the assegai was an old one, a token spear, good enough to give a woman, but for serious use, the lashings should have been renewed.

The elephants now turned and went back to the fever trees. Everything had been done with precision and without haste, almost without anger, for the anger they had was an old, worn-out anger. They left as slowly as soundlessly as they had come. Neither coming nor going, had there been any sound but the futile challenge of Mashupa facing death. And the screams of the woman and the child. When they had gone, there was only silence in the forest and red blood turning brown as it dried in the sun upon the ground.

As the bush closed behind the elephants, the first vulture plummeted down and checked, to circle the clearing. Before it had landed, there were more vultures. More and more would come, some from as much as a hundred kilometres away. For hours new arrivals would continue to fall from the sky. Spread out widely at a height far beyond the vision of man, they were drawn together by the dark thread of death, thrown like stones into a whirlpool, into the central vortex of disaster. For a while they sat hunched on the trees. Like the elephants, they were in no hurry. Then, suddenly, they came down on to the bodies. First one, the boldest—then the others. In a moment the bodies were covered by them, fighting and screaming, as they tore at the entrails. Those on top of the bodies penetrated them and drew out their bald heads dark with blood and viscera. Two vultures were tearing the child that hung in the tree. It fell with a thud to the ground. They followed it down.

A single marabou stork joined the feast. It drove back the vultures from the woman's body and began to gorge, slashing off great chunks of flesh with its long chisel beak. Black and white, with a bare, scurfy neck, this long-legged bird was like some terrible priest, a priest gone mad. Its shoulders were bare of feathers and over its breast dangled a loose bladder of pink skin. Its underparts were clothed with swansdown feathers—fluff. The marabou of Fifth Avenue, of Bond Street, and the Rue da la Paix. Fluff from the belly of the carrion eater to decorate the bed jackets of penthouse luxury.

157

The sky was darkened above the feeding birds by the sweep of two gigantic shadows as a pair of king vultures came. Landing on the ground, they stood still for a moment, moving their red, bare heads in all directions. Then they came forward with their black wings outspread. As they came, the other vultures fell back. Even the marabou moved away when the carrion kings arrived.

Soon the ground round the bodies was covered with the feathers the vultures had plucked from each other, and their chalky excrement. By dark, little but bones were left. By morning there were few bones, for the hyenas, seeking the marrow, had come and cracked them in massive jaws, and the jackals had come. All that was left was food for the ants, and the flies. And they had come.

Chapter Twenty-one

THE WITNESS OF
THE ADMINISTRATION

In all events there is a sequence. Each event is at once an effect of previous causes, and the cause of new effects. When events A, B, and C have taken place, they must be followed by events D and E.

The seed that is planted, that is sown by the wind, by passing through a bird or a beast, is already doomed to destruction. It may fail to germinate and rot, it may germinate and die, or be eaten. It may grow and live the full span of its kind, but, in the end, the sequence remains the same in each case—the life cycle is completed. Birth, death, and more life again.

The lives of Mashupa and his woman, and his child were completed. But their bodies were still alive, transformed by the mutation of appetite into the forms of the vultures of the air, the carrion eaters of the forest, and the increased fertility of the ground where they had died.

Perhaps too, the spirit is everlasting and goes into some strange, spiritual reservoir which we, with our passion for nomenclature, describe as heaven, as life everlasting. Whatever it is, this quality of spirit, its disappearance is the only

158

thing that divides the quick from the dead. And into this world of ghosts and angels, Mashupa and his family had disappeared. Ghosts, black angels flying on sable wings, but as far as the material and official world was concerned, dead, and gone from it at the trunks and ivory scimitars of two rogue elephants.

This set up a new sequence, a new train of events, new ferments that caused typewriters to click, wires to buzz, and telephones to ring. Postal operators, clerks, ministries, the Governor-General—all received a faint vibration from their death. Barmen poured out drinks for those who discussed the news in the papers. For it was news, as all disaster is news. Hunters looked at their weapons. Gunsmiths hoped for a revival of business as hunting stories crept into the press. Girls shuddered at the thought of the mashed up bodies and bought new hats to comfort themselves. Nursemaids frightened children into obedience by telling them they would give them to the elephants who now, because they had followed an ancient instinct of revenge, were classified by the ignorant as devils.

Tembula rubbed his hands with pleasure. The priest, Father Thadeus, said masses for the souls of the departed. And the Chef de Poste sent for Maniero. That was the first thing he did after visiting the scene of the crime.

He had returned with a sad heart, for he loved his people, thinking of himself as their father, with a small, terrified, and starving baboon. The only thing left alive in that place of death.

In Lourenço Marques, Maniero was talking to Senhora Ferreira and her husband about the orders he had received from Da Silva. Senhor Ferreira was an importer and Maniero had for many years bought his ammunition directly from him. He got it at wholesale price and knew that it was fresh from the factory. The age of ammunition is a vital factor in the life of a hunter.

'It is strange,' Maniero said, 'to think that once she worked here. What was she like, Senhora?' he asked.

'A good girl, but an animal, like them all. Filled with lust like a cat.' As she spoke, she managed to come very near to the hunter so that his senses, alert from his life in the wilderness, felt the warmth of her soft body and the subtle odour of perfume, and-woman, that emanated from it. He knew what was in her mind. For a man who has lived much with animals is well aware of the animal in man, and woman. The part of him which was not the ascetic hunter desired her. His body was aware of its own, and her, demands. But his mind laughed at his body for the simplicity of its reaction. He was not a sensual man and besides, Ferreira was his friend. But he was amused at the tension and at his previous ignorance. One knew. Yes one knew but one did not apply such things to the wives of one's associates.

'Nature is a hard thing to deny,' he said. 'It is natural for a woman to desire a child, and a man is her means of obtaining her desire. Of course she does not know this. All she knows is her desire for a man. That is nature's great trick!' He laughed. 'I have often thought,' he said, 'that if the act were not so enjoyable, there would be few births.'

'That is a fine way for you to talk, Maniero!' Senhora Ferreira, like everyone else in the Colony, called him that. 'You, who have never married, or from what one hears, even been interested in a woman.' She tossed her head and filled his glass with Madeira.

'Ah,' Maniero said, 'that is true. I was born without the quality. Family life is a pleasure I have missed, but I have eyes in my head. I see what goes on not only among men and women, but the wild animals of the forest.'

'They are not the same,' she said.

'No, Senhora, they are not. The animals are more honest. But in the forest, one gets strange thoughts. And one sees great parallels. For instance, it's my belief that men, like elephants, come into musth. That they are overcome at certain times by a desire which is irresistible.' He laughed again. 'You know,' he said, 'sometimes when a man is jilted, he marries another woman at once. "On the rebound," they say. Well, it is not a rebound. It is not done out of pique or injured vanity. It is done because he is in a marrying mood, in the state that among elephants is called musth.'

'And women?' she asked.

'I am not a woman and do not understand them,' Maniero said. 'But there are also parallels which must occur to you.'

'You are very complimentary,' she said.

'I am very observant, Senhora,' he said.

160

'When are you going,' Senhora Ferreira asked.

'To-morrow.'

When he comes back, she thought. By then it will have worked. She knew she had sown the seed of desire. That he was aware of her as perhaps he had never been aware of a woman before. She moved so that her clothes rustled and her high heels tapped on the cool, red-tiled floor. She knew and he knew. Time for what she had begun to ripen, was all that she needed now. Time and opportunity. Time she had. The opportunity she would create as all women create it—the situation where effect must follow cause.

'And Carew?' Ferreira asked. 'What of him?' Maniero had often talked of him.

'Ah, Carew. He is coming with me.'

'That old man!' she said. 'He will be a danger to you.' Suddenly she was afraid for Maniero. Suppose there was no time.

'I can do with his advice,' Maniero said. 'Even if he cannot hunt. This elephant is no ordinary animal. But perhaps these deaths and the others should be laid at the feet of the man who first wounded him. Perhaps Pretorius, whom he killed so many years ago, is the real killer of these people.'

'Tell us about elephants,' Senhora Ferreira said. Abstractions did not interest her.

'Wait till I get back,' Senhor Ferreira said, 'I left my cigarettes in the car.'

She looked at her husband. Time pressed on a woman. She was thirty. Thirty for a woman corresponds to forty in a man. Both then are in their full power, but they have only ten years left in which to use it. She glanced at her husband's back as he went out of the door, then turning half round, pulled up her skirt and adjusted a garter. She held her skirt high, showing the whole of her silk-stockinged leg, and a small provocative piece of ivory flesh above it. As she dropped her skirt, she looked round at Maniero and found him staring at her. So he had seen. That would be something for him to think of as he sat by his fire alone in the forest. Nothing could have been simpler than this old trick of partial exposure. But the desires it was capable of arousing were older still. She lowered her eyes letting her long, black lashes fall on her cheeks.

'Oh!' she said, 'you looked.'

'On the contrary,' Maniero said, 'you showed.'

'You beast!' she said. 'Animal.'

'Perhaps we both are animals.'

She looked at him her eyes wide with meaning. That is something else he'll remember, she thought. She saw the flame kindle in him. She had started it now. The pressure of time had killed all modesty. There had been time for modesty before. There would be time later. Many years of time. But there was none now. She came closer to him so that he could touch her. She felt his arms round her. She felt his hand as she stood beside him. A minute, two minutes, three. It had all happened so quickly. Before that she had been standing at the window wondering. Now she was beside him and knew. She heard her husband returning and bent forward over the little table beside Maniero. His hand slipped from her. She said, 'Let me fill your glass again and then tell us.'

'Elephants?' Maniero said.

'The lame one,' she said.

'Yes the lame one. Well,' he said, 'you know the natives, the indigenas, claim that he is not one but two. They say one has tusks that are enormous, colossal, and the other is tuskless.' He tried to concentrate. 'They both have white tails. They are supposed to have come up from Zululand in the old days, and to be inhabited by the spirits of T'Chaka and Moselekatse. He, or they, have killed several men including the hunter, Pretorius, who just wounded him. But there may have been others that we have not heard of in Moçambique. His spoor is unmistakable. I have hunted him and lost him before. Carew hunted him in the old days. He drew a picture of his spoor for me.'

'Show us,' Senhora Ferreira said. She went to the bureau and got a pad and pencil. She brought them to him and stood so that she touched him, leaning over him as he drew. He could see the soft curve of her breasts above her dress, and the darkness between them. The shadows that vanished into an edge of lace. He could feel her flank and hip, her thigh, as she pressed closer with interest.

'And you will kill him,' she said.

'Those are my orders. I am to go on till I kill him, no matter how long it takes. But it will not be easy.'

'Are there really two elephants?' Senhor Ferreira asked.

'I do not know. In the forest anything is possible and

since this business is concerned with the spirits, no reliable information is to be obtained, even from the best trackers. And now,' he said, 'I must go.' He said good-bye.

As Senhora Ferreira said 'good-bye' she squeezed his hand.

They both wished him luck.

'I'll need it,' he said.

'You will have it,' she said. 'And you will come to tell us as soon as you get back. At once,' she added—her eyes on his.

'At once,' Maniero said.

Da Silva looked at the hunter. 'So you have come, Maniero,' he said. Barrel-chested, short and thickset, he stood balanced on the balls of his feet like a boxer.

'I have come. His Excellency the Governor-General said this time there must be no mistake. I am to remain till it is ended.'

'Yes,' the Chef de Poste said.

'I will kill the lame one,' Maniero said, 'whether he is one or two elephants, whether he is a ghost or not.'

'It is time,' Da Silva said, 'but Maniero . . .'

'Yes?'

'What you have said is dangerous talk.'

'What I said?'

'Yes. It is psychologically dangerous to be so certain, to direct your will with such vehemence. The human mind is a strange instrument. The will, when set, is like a bullet speeding on its course. It cannot enter the barrel again.'

'I am a bullet,' Maniero said. 'That has been my life.'

'Yet,' Da Silva said, 'you are not a killer. You do not love death. You do not play with your heavy ammunition, running it like gold through your hands, letting the shells trickle through your fingers, and rubbing their smooth, brass sides with affection like Von Artling.'

'Von Artling,' Maniero said. 'I have seen him too. That man loved his ammunition because each shell carried death in its brass belly. Certain death with him behind the rifle.'

'He was killed,' Da Silva said.

'Yes, by a buffalo. Despite his experience, he was careless.'

'That is what I am trying to say to you, Maniero. Von Artling was certain too.'

'Von Artling did what many elephant hunters do, Senhor,' Maniero said. 'He was careless with smaller game.'

'Well, all I say is, be careful. You will be hard to replace.'

'No man is irreplaceable. Least of all a hunter.' Then he said. 'To-morrow Carew will be here.'

'Carew, the hunter? Impossible! He must be over eighty.'

'Nevertheless he follows on my spoor. I am waiting for him. He wants to see the bush again before he dies. He wants to hunt once more. I think he hopes to die here. A fine man,' Maniero said. 'In his truck he has a barrel of spirits in which he wishes to be pickled like a cherry in brandy, if it should happen. A very considerate man, Senhor Carew, wishing to cause no one trouble.'

'The brandy will be stolen,' Da Silva said.

'He has flavoured it with gasoline and croton oil,' Maniero said.

'He cannot keep up with you,' Da Silva said.

'He will follow me. Hunt near me. He has arranged to be carried on the marches, and will only get down to hunt.'

'It is a strange world,' Da Silva said. 'Hunters who are all but centenarians, elephants inhabited by the spirits of kings, and the outer world boiling like a pot about to explode into war.'

'I do not like the outer world,' Maniero said. 'My world is the forest. Do you know what Senhor Carew said to me? He said—"Once more I must see the silence." Is that not a strange remark? But he is right. In the noonday heat of the forest, there is no sound. There is nothing to hear and you see the silence. The very leaves frozen on to twigs that are as still as stones.' Then he said, 'He has his old tracker, Siloko, with him and Siloko's son, now an old man too, and his grandson who is no longer young. More will join him, old men and their descendants. That man, Senhor, in the old days before the coming of authority, was like a king here. Once he fought with his people to rescue some women from the slavers, the Arabs and half-castes who dominated this coast.'

'I have heard of it,' Da Silva said, 'and so now we are to see a legend come to life.'

'I am eager to see him in the forest,' Maniero said. 'There is still much for me to learn.'

'You to learn?'

'Me, Senhor. In the forest I am still like a child. An

intelligent child, perhaps, but still a child. The forest is so old, so full of manifold mysteries, of secrets. The forest,' he said, 'is like a beautiful woman whom one can fondle, but whom, because one can never get to know her fully, one can never completely possess. Always there is some final reticence. Always still another veil.'

'They say you are married to the forest, Maniero,' Da Silva said laughing.

'Perhaps it is true, Senhor, for I see her as a woman. The tree trunks are her limbs, the waving reeds her hair, the stars at night her eyes.'

'A poet,' Da Silva said, 'a hunter and a poet.'

'Perhaps to be a hunter it is necessary to be a poet,' Maniero said. 'If, as I think, a poet is a man who seeks the truth and proclaims it.'

'When do you start?' Da Silva asked.

'In a few days. I must wait for Carew. I must send out my trackers—the spies of the forest. I must view the scene of the crime.'

'It is cleaned up now,' Da Silva said. 'I had to go myself. I could not get anyone to go with my assistant. I went myself,' he repeated. 'I took the doctor and the priest with me. We gave what was left a burial. The two together. All the bones mixed up. Even the doctor could not tell his from hers. It was a picture I assure you. The vultures still sat gorged in the trees. The bodies had been flattened like great bloodstained pancakes. The man must have died beside her. All their bones were cracked by hyenas. Of the child, nothing was left but the skull. The hut reduced to a small heap of broken sticks and grass. The little garden devastated, tramped flat, and everywhere the spoor and dung and feathers of the carrion eaters, the vultures, jackals, and hyenas, superimposed on the spoor of the elephants. Never, Maniero, have I seen such spoor—each the size of a small table.'

'The lame one,' Maniero said.

'Yes, the lame one, and to my mind another one as well, though the hunters I had with me denied it.'

'They are afraid,' Maniero said. 'If there are two, they say it is one. If there is one, they swear it is two.'

'Yes, they are afraid as their fathers and their grand-fathers were before them. It is time you came.'

'I shall kill him,' Maniero said. 'Then I shall retire.'

'What will you do?' Da Silva asked. 'You will never live in town.'

'I shall buy a little farm with plenty of water and grow pawpaws and bananas. I shall have some cattle, donkeys, poultry, and pigeons. Senhor, I love pigeons.'

'And hunt?'

'For meat—just for the pot. I think I have killed enough.'

'You know the rest of the story?' Da Silva asked.

'I know nothing beyond what you have said.'

'Well, according to los indigenas, the natives, the elephants will now be peaceful for some time since the revenge of their totem is complete. You see, these two, this boy and girl, married without knowing they both belonged to the elephant totem. This, as you know, is a crime against the gods, against taboo, against custom, and to expiate it, the boy, an excellent young man, was sent by the witch doctor, Tembula, to live among the great ones for a year. His wife, a beautiful young girl, my assistant tells me—he saw her once in the store—could stand the separation no longer, and went to dwell near him. Not to see him, but just to be nearer to him was her aim. She made a little garden. People helped her because her great love moved their livers to sorrow. And of all this, my friend, the Administrator of Querida, knew nothing. To speak of it was taboo. Even my police said nothing. The chiefs said nothing—only when it was too late did I hear. But imagine the tragedy, the suffering. Imagine the blow to our culture, for these were civilised, Christian natives. Imagine how they were torn this way and that, split in two by the conflict of the old and the new ideas. Imagine the joy of Tembula who actually condemned the boy to death by sending him alone in the forest. The gods and spirits— what did he care for them, Maniero? What he cared for was the blow he could deal to those who had accepted civilisation, had donned clothes and followed the teachings of our Lord. Think of the boy's sufferings alone and weaponless in the wilderness, living on rats and lizards, on honey, locusts, caterpillars, and tortoises. Think of him shivering and starving. Think of him, by accident, finding his wife and child in a little clearing and watching them. For this is what my trackers tell me he did, day after day, seeing her work in the garden, watching her give suck to

166

their child, seeing her kneel in her hut to pray to God for His protection and her own, and then, like demons, the elephants come, and all is gone. Love, and its fruit, hope and joy—all mashed into the hot, dusty ground. The very dust coagulated into mud by the blood of this little family that should have lived under my protection. This, my friend, is a love story, a desperate one of fear and hardship, of danger ending in terror and death.'

Da Silva sank his head into his arms on the desk. He looked up. 'This,' he said, 'is my great failure of responsibility to my people. For, somehow, I should have stopped it. If I had only known. But how many before me have said that! How many will again! For here were the forces of evil arrayed against the innocent. What could they do against a wicked sorcerer, the power of the mightiest beasts of the forest, the terrible forces of nature, the thunder and storms of summer, the cold of winter, the full panoply of all that is powerful and bad against this little family of Christians? What is the answer? Where is the cause, Maniero?'

'The cause,' Maniero said, 'is the transition of these people. These are the pains of parturition, the afterbirth as it were, of a new order that is being born. The man and woman were half civilised and half savage, half Christian, and half pagan. The elephants are only half wild now in the sense that they have learnt to hate and to fear man. The land itself is half tamed. Nothing is as it was ordained it should be, and nothing as we would will it to be. This is new to you, Senhor, but to me it is just another forest tragedy. The nest torn down is not that of a weaver bird destroyed by a hawk, but of a man and woman. Yet, in principle, it is the same. It is the story of the forest exaggerated into human terms. That is why I wish to farm,' Maniero said. 'To grow and cultivate instead of destroying. What am I,' he asked, 'but a Don Juan, a Casanova of the forest? Instead of making love, I kill, and nothing is easier than killing. So quick, so easy. Once, as a young man, I thought to conquer the forest. But as a man cannot possess all women, as in a sense, the more he possesses the less he has of them, so a man cannot kill everything, cannot master everything. As the sensualist is eventually overcome by his sensualism, so can the hunter be overcome by his habit of killing. Though I am not, as you said, a killer, the power of the hunt intoxicates me. Before I am completely overcome by that force, I must cease.'

'A cypher,' Da Silva said. 'An asterisk, a symbol, a signer of forms and papers—that is what I have become. And His Excellency orders me to end this business as if I had not for years pleaded that it should be ended. Am I not the laughing-stock of Lisbon with my little elephant revolts?'

Each man was now talking to himself. Used to silence, each craved a listener. Now, having spoken their innermost thoughts, they were silent. A murderer, carrying the ball of his chain under his arm, passed the window.

Da Silva saw Maniero looking at him and said, 'He is a good boy but he ran away. He wished to sleep with his wife, but I cannot have my murderers running away, so I had to put a ball and chain upon him. It is a ten-kilo ball. But I have informed him that his wife may come here once a month. After all,' he said, 'making love is as natural as murder.'

'There is much to be said for both,' Maniero said. 'But me, I long for my pigeons. I wish to breed pouters. At least their vanity is obvious.'

'There is much to be said for pouters,' Da Silva said recovering his good humour. Both men laughed. Maniero stood up.

'Senhor,' he said, 'I will kill the elephant or he will kill me!'

'Before you go,' Da Silva said, 'there is something I must show you. Come.' He led the way to a court behind the office, and pointed to a young baboon fastened, by a light chain attached to a belt about its waist, to a pole sunk in the ground.

'A young baboon,' Maniero said.

'Yes, it is all that was left alive there. She was hiding in a tree.'

'Mashupa's?'

'His pet, I think. A companion that he took to mitigate his loneliness. The only witness we have of the tragedy.'

'The witness of the Administration,' Maniero said.

Chapter Twenty-two

THE COMING OF CAREW

When Maniero got his orders and went to see Carew, he found him ready. He had been ready for some time. Mackenzie had bought him a truck. He had collected his canned provisions. He had rifles and ammunition. A double-barrelled Jeffries—a lovely handmade thing—and a Jeffries 404 magazine rifle. And he was waiting, like a bird preparing to migrate, for the signal, the sign, the sudden acceleration of the blood, the change of the winds, the cooling of the weather, for whatever it was that would suddenly, when the moment came, move him.

He did not know when that moment would be. He only felt that he must be ready, that one morning the feeling would come to him that he must be off.

So when Maniero came to say he was going, to say goodbye, or to see if the old man really wished to accompany him, the key of Carew's resolution fitted into the slot. The gear slid in from the neutral of his passive waiting, into action, into low gear, that would slowly build up, as the tension mounted, into high, into the maximum speed of which his ancient organism was capable, into the fury of the hunt, the last expedition, into the entrance of what he hoped would be his paradise, the triumphal bloody march into Esther's arms.

Lord, that was what his life had been—a thing of gold and scarlet, of brilliance, that must end in a final flare of glory, of action. That must end, as it had been lived, in the forest, amid the explosions of his guns, the trumpetings and screams of elephants, the wild cries of his men. Only this could warm his old blood enough to carry him through to the end. Only on the crest of the great wave of forest warfare, could he reach the heights he needed. Only thus, on the chariot of his art, could he attain the freedom that he desired. Only so, could he end the long tedium of his waiting. Suddenly he was sick of waiting for death. Suddenly he felt he must go and meet it with outstretched hands. Meet old death, where he had lived with life, meet him in the forest.

Without further word he said, 'When do we start, Maniero?'

'In two days,' Maniero said.

'Go first,' Carew had said, 'and wait for me at Querida. I will come one day after you.'

'Come with me,' Maniero said. 'I will wait a day.'

'I could go to-morrow,' Carew said. 'I am ready, but I wish to go alone. My heart is hungry for the forest, and such hunger I must slake alone. I am going,' he said, 'to meet my end, and my love. I am going to pray in the forest that is my church, and at first, I would prefer to be alone with my thoughts. You see, Maniero,' he said—he put his hand on his arm—'I am very old, I have much to think of and remember. Every foot of the way is ours, mine and Esther's. The trees I know, the loops and bends of the road, the rivers and pans, the very birds of the air are ours—hers and mine.'

'I understand,' Maniero said.

'You will wait for me?'

'I shall be there at Querida.'

'Send out your scouts, get everything ready. Get all the news, the stories. Collect my people if they are not already there.'

'All this I will do.'

'You are a good boy,' the old man said. 'If we'd had a son, we should have wished a man like you. But we shall have no children now.' Esther was alive in his mind again. Old, past bearing children, but alive. She was very near to him. Her voice was calling from the forest. Her hands beckoning from the trees.

Carew could not remember how long ago it was that he had last been at Querida. Thirty years anyway, maybe forty. He stopped worrying about it. A long time was good enough. At his age there was not much difference between thirty and forty years—looking backwards that is. Forwards, was another matter. The rope of his life was now about fully extended. It might stretch a little, but that was all. He'd lived more than a thousand and two months, more than eighty times since his birth the trees had bloomed and fruited, had withered in the winter drought, had dropped their leaves in a carpet at their feet to rot and nourish them again.

The first time he had seen Querida that he could remember was in the sixties sometime. There had been nothing there then, no streets then, no houses. They had come later—he remembered the first administration building had been a corrugated iron shack, an oven in which official after official, in that untamed land, had died. Why, he had buried one of them. The grave was over there by a great sausage tree. He looked towards it. It had not changed. It seemed no bigger. Its fruits hung from the boughs as they had then, some of them weighing five or ten kilos. Fruits which, if they fell on a man, could kill him. But now Querida was a town. It had lost its diffidence. It was no longer an outpost clinging precariously to the fringe of the forest. It had penetrated the forest, and for a few hundred hectares had tamed it. But always the jungle awaited its chance to return. Always the jungle bombarded the encroachments upon it with tree seeds, with termites, with snakes, mosquitoes, flies, tarantulas, and scorpions. Always here, as elsewhere, there was a ledger account between the credits of an advancing civilisation, and the debits of a graveyard, which, however floriferous and well-tended, continued to grow in size.

The main street was an avenue fifty metres wide, lined with neat, white-washed buildings. Lord, he knew them without even asking which were which. The big administration building, the police barracks, the jail, the church, the priest's house, the mission, the school, the hospital, the houses of the doctor, the District Veterinarian, the Agricultural Officer, the Accountant, the Assistant Administrator.

White, tin-roofed, with red granolithic stoeps filled with palms, ferns, and bignonias planted in green painted kerosene tins. In front of the houses, hiding them from the blazing white width of the avenue, were lines of trees. Flamboyants and jacarandas that would, in their season, splash the ground with their fallen flower petals of orange-scarlet, and sky-blue. Against the houses themselves, climbed bougainvillaeas—purple, mauve, and cherry-red, and the orange, honeysuckle-shaped flowers of the golden shower hung from the tall bamboos in the gardens in great cascades.

Here was the illusion of security. A doctor who, even if he could not save your life, could at least stand, watch in hand, by your bedside and watch you die. Here, too, was a priest to shrive you. The place had every amenity. It had about all, though in a small way, that civilisation, even that of a big city, had to offer. Palliatives, salves of soul and body for those who, fearing the wilderness, dwelt in the prisons that were called houses, and served men more wealthy than themselves.

The houses were linked to each other with telephone wires. Little copper veins that carried the blood of business, tragedy, and petty scandal from one member of the community to another. From the post office, wires led back nearly four hundred kilometres to the Capital. But these wires, too, were an illusion, for often the poles were down. Broken like matchsticks by elephants that used them as back-scratchers, as handkerchiefs for their mouths, as toothpicks on which to wipe their ivory. Who thrust them down in playful butting competitions, just for the hell of it, in perversity, or, perhaps, in some kind of anger at the encroachment of these straight, leafless, ill-smelling trees that man, their enemy, had erected in their territory. When they were down, natives stole the wire to make noose traps for game, or ornaments for their women, or for household purposes. The job of linesman at Querida could be no sinecure.

But there was beauty here, in the wide river that was the home of yellow crocodiles, in the neat, white houses in which men and women made love, quarrelled, bore sickly children, and from which they were finally transferred, by retirement or death. Beauty, a man-made flame of garden bloom, illuminated the village, spreading even to the native quarters that lay behind the white man's street.

It was here, in the native village, that the men, who had heard of Carew's coming, waited to greet him. Old men and women, young ones that knew of his exploits, curious ones, children, young girls with babies on their backs, ran forward in a brown stream when they saw his truck. Some uniformed native police, half police, half soldier, came to keep order.

Carew, getting down from the truck, waved them away. 'I lived here before there were police,' he said, 'and do not need you. My tongue and my sjambok are enough to keep order here!' The people laughed and cried out. An old man in a litter said, 'He has not changed!'

He told them he had come for the last time—for a last hunt. He said, 'I, who am a great hunter, and the mighty hunter Maniero, whom you call the bull because of his strength, are here to rid you of the spook elephant that has for generations caused you so much trouble.'

'Aai,' they lamented, 'even for such great hunters, the lame one will prove too strong.'

'That we shall see,' Carew said. 'We shall also see if the courage of the young men is equal to that of their fathers when we hunt him.'

'You will need strong medicine,' they chanted. 'Aai, the great hunters will need strong medicine.'

Carew spoke to one of his boys who brought him a leather gun-case with brass fittings. Taking a key from his pocket, he opened it and fitted the double-barrelled 600 together. 'Here,' he said, 'is the strong medicine.' He put two big brass shells into the breech, closed it, and fired at a great hardekool tree fifty yards away. The shots came almost as one. The explosion rocked the old man on his feet. The roar was like that of a cannon. Shaken with surprise, some of the crowd turned to run, some fell down, some cheered.

Slipping the gun over the crook of his arm, Carew said, 'Let the young men cut out the bullets with axes. Let them see how deeply they penetrated the wood of the hardest tree of the forest, and let them ponder on the speed of the shots, the accuracy of the aim, and the power of my medicine. Maniero is the bull, but I am the older bull and my horns are still sharp.' He patted the rifle breech. 'Now go, children,' he said. 'Go home and reflect, and when I call for men, let the cowards stay at home and brew beer with the women.'

The crowd dispersed. He watched them go. He told his driver to go on. He stood watching the truck, with the barrel lashed securely in the rear, go down the street throwing up the white dust with its double wheels. Then, carrying his rifle under his arm, he walked up the middle of the avenue—a small, shrivelled old man with a heavy rifle in the crook of his arm. He filled the street from tree border to tree border, so that, seeing him walk, you would have felt there was no room to pass. The first shots in the war of the elephants had been fired. The action whose end was in the hands of the high gods was begun.

Maniero was with the Chef de Poste when Carew came into the office. Maniero stood up.

'Senhor Carew,' he said, 'this is Sua Ecellensia Raimundo da Silva, the Chef de Poste of Querida.'

To Da Silva, he said, 'Senhor Carew, the English hunter.'

Da Silva said, 'I am not an excellency, not yet that is.'

Maniero said, 'Senhor, a little extra honour, a little politeness, does no one any harm. Where is the police corporal who does not like to be addressed as captain? And besides, one day you will be Governor.'

'One day perhaps, if I live, my friend, and these elephants that plague me are removed.' To Carew he said, 'I heard a shot.'

'Two shots,' Carew said.

'They sounded like one even to me,' Maniero said.

Carew laughed. 'You are a tactful man, Maniero. The Chef de Poste is His Excellency, and I fire only one shot when you, a hunter, know quite well it was two.'

'They came very fast.'

Da Silva said, 'Senhor, do you know it is forbidden to fire a rifle shot in the precincts of the town?'

'They are fired,' Carew said, 'they cannot be taken back. I was here, Senhor, before your father sucked his mother's milk. I have buried one of your predecessors, and I do not fire solid bullets costing perhaps ten escudos each to amuse myself. Those shots, your Excellency, are the first directed against the lame one, your enemy. They were token shots. In the forest it is necessary to use tokens and emblems.'

Da Silva laughed. 'Querida is yours, Senhor. Shoot as much as you like!'

Maniero said, 'I am of the opinion that there are two elephants. That they are brothers.'

'How do you know?' Carew asked.

'I do not know,' Maniero said. He put his hand over his heart and said, 'I feel.'

Carew said, 'Then there are two. I accept it. Senhor,' he said to Da Silva, 'a great hunter must have extra senses; seven senses perhaps, or he does not live to make a name. It is these senses which govern his life in the forest, make him know where game is, and what he will do. They direct his fingers, his eye, and the rifle in his hand so that all three are one thing. The trinity of death. There are two elephants and we will kill them.'

'I am worried about the brandy barrel,' the Chef de Poste said. 'If the people get at it?'

'To-night, Senhor, there will be an indaba and I will issue a tot, a thimbleful to any who dare drink it. The shaking of the truck will have disturbed the gasoline and croton oil very nicely. After that, Senhor, I think you can set your mind at rest.'

'You think of everything, Senhor Carew.'

'I have had many years in which to acquire wisdom,' Carew said, 'but the cup is about full now. There is room for no more. Almost I know too much of what is in the hearts and minds of both beasts and men.'

'A drink,' Da Silva said. 'Was there not a wise man, an American, I think, who said—"It is a long time between drinks?" '

This Carew was a strange old man. Small, like a jockey —a jockey of the forest. Like a withered leaf. Then looking closer, you saw that the texture of the leaf was of leather, its bony structure of wire and whipcord. They no longer manufactured men like these old ones. He, himself, would never be like that nor would even Maniero. With Carew you felt the presence of death, saw the dark wings of the reaper standing behind his chair as he sat, but there was that about him which stayed the scythe. It was as if even death, that he must have faced so many times, stood back and said—'Let the old boy choose his time. When he is ready he will come to me. I shall not have to mow him down.'

'Madeira,' he went on, going to a small cupboard and getting out a cut-glass decanter and three glasses. 'From one of the first possessions of our great Empire. How great it was once, Senhor Carew—Africa, India, China! How great Portugal once was!' He filled the glasses—'To success, cavalheiros, gentlemen.'

They drank to success. To each it meant something different. To Da Silva, an end of the elephant worry and a governorship even if only that of a small island. The colony was too much to hope for. To Carew, a final hunt with death and Esther at the end of it. The hope that this was the last road and that there would be no more turnings. To Maniero, success would mean that he would be able to retire to his little farm and live in peace with some reputation and honour. He saw in his mind the full panoply of the forest. The grasses and trees growing to feed the buck and the deer. He saw the carnivores as grass eaters, also, through the intermediate animal. Only a buck stood between a lion and a blade of grass. He thought of Carew's cup of knowledge and the shame that it should die with him, that he could bequeath it to no one. He saw in his mind the garden that was to be. The pawpaws, fat as melons, clinging to the tall stems of the trees. The plants male and female, with their branched, greenish flowers. He saw bananas, their leaves like green flags in serried rows, the red purple ball of their fruits obscenely pendulous. He thought of the rich smell of the turned earth, of the smell of blood and cordite, of wood fires, of native sweat, and cooking meat, of the scent of some beetles, of flowering trees. He thought of Maria Theresa Ferreira.

He thought of the triangle now created, of himself and Carew and the elephants. Two points of a base whose apex was death. He said, 'It is a strange thing that the pawpaw should have male and female trees.' He thought of the triangle created by Maria Theresa's act. The warm pressing of her body against his had released new forces.

'Like breasts,' the Chef de Poste said, his mind on the heavy fruits.

'Like breasts,' Maniero repeated. It was strange the pictures that came into the mind.

'When do we start?' Carew asked. Time looking more important to him than the others.

'To-morrow,' Maniero said, tearing his mind away from his plantation, to which he had forcibly carried it. 'Will that be too soon? Perhaps you should rest, Senhor.'

'I will soon have rest enough,' Carew said.

'More Madeira?' Da Silva asked. This old man with his emphasis on death disturbed him. He wondered what it would be like to be so old. To have death ticking like a watch in your pocket. 'I have never had better Madeira,' Carew said, putting down his glass on the desk.

'It is sent to me by a friend,' Da Silva said. 'He sends me a cask twice a year.' Why had he said cask?

Why must the picture jump to his mind of this old man, curled like a pickled foetus, in his barrel of doctored brandy? Why did everything you say bring you back to the point of departure? What were they doing but celebrating, perhaps prematurely, the death of the elephants that had plagued him for so long? Death. There would be death all right, but whose? These elephants had killed other men. Would their skill and courage save the two who sat before him? They had come to him here. He had called them to this place of assembly. At least he had called Maniero, and to-morrow they would go forth into the unknown. Into the vastness of the dark interior. Into the green womb of Africa, a part of which was in his keeping.

'After dinner,' he said, 'I will show you my collection.'

'Your collection?' Carew said.

'My stamps, Senhor. I am an ardent philatelist. I will show you my triangular Cape of Good Hopes. They are valuable,' he said, 'and beautiful. I love them because they are unpractical. In those days there were no perforations and each stamp was cut from its fellows with scissors. Stamps,' he said, 'are a great mystery. Is it not mysterious that I, here in Querida can send a letter by means of a stamp to the United States of America, to England, to Portugal? I love to think of those who have written the letters. Letters of love, of passion, blackmailing letters. Letters bringing news good and bad. My stamps give me hope, for since there is an international post, are not other international things possible? May it not be possible that one day all men will live in peace and brotherhood? At times like this, when war seems so certain, it is good to look beyond it into the more distant future. Yes, Senhor,' he said, 'in these pretty little pieces of sticky, coloured paper, there is hope.'

Chapter Twenty-three

THE AVENGERS

It was impossible for Maniero to discover when he had made his decision to retire. He had been surprised to hear himself tell Da Silva that this was his last hunt. The words had sprung unbidden to his lips. His ears had heard them.

His mind had said—'Is this me, Maniero, talking?' And now, in the rondavel put at his disposal, he considered the matter.

The farm, of course, was not a new idea. He had always meant to have one some time. But the period had been in the unfixed, distant future, not now, in the present. Of course this was no ordinary hunt. It was a final contest and if he killed the elephants, he would have conquered the greatest beasts of the forest. After that, anything else would be an anticlimax. But there was more in it than that. From his heart, his soul, the depths of his personality, had come the command to stop, the feeling that he had killed enough. As, in his boyhood, the urge to hunt had come upon him, flooding out all other dreams and aspirations, now the command to stop hunting had come from those same inner sources. In life, it seemed to him, there was a time for all things; a time to love and a time to hate, a time to plant and a time to reap. For years now, for all his life almost, he had reaped the harvest of the forest in meat and ivory and skins. Now he must sow. Our factor remained constant. The forest itself. He could live nowhere else. But killing was done with, except for predators that molested him, buck for the pot, and some specimens for the museums that required them. It was a new phase of his existence, a new life. From drifting over the vastness of this inland sea of bush, of trees and marsh and scrub, he would turn to the cultivation of one section of it. His sword he would beat into a ploughshare. He would send down roots. If he could find a woman who would live this life with him, he would marry. Twice a year or so, he would visit his mother and friends in town. In winter, perhaps, his mother would come to visit him.

All that stood between him and this ambition was the lame one. Hatred for this elephant welled up in his heart. Never before had he hated an animal. He knew, suddenly, that he feared the lame one. That he had feared him all his life, that there had been occasions when he might have followed him, but which, seizing some excuse, he had refused to take. I have become infected with the Kaffirs' superstitions, he thought. What was the lame one but another pachyderm? What was his brother but an invention of his own fears? Yet he had seen two spoors, large as tables, worn smooth with a hundred years of marching, sandpapered by the thousands of miles traversed.

He had not even told Carew about it when they had talked together in town. He had not even really thought about it himself till now. Till he had said, in Da Silva's office, 'There are two elephants, brothers. I feel it in my heart.' Before that he had refused to face it. Calling it a lie, a Kaffir invention. But Carew, wise in the ways of men, had accepted his statement as if he knew that before he had lied, or had at least kept back a portion of the truth. And he had kept it back, in the inner recesses of his soul, encysted under layers of later experience. It was like a painful letter from a lover that is neither looked at nor thrown away, but kept in a bottom drawer and never forgotten. One day we feel we will read it again, when the pain is less. But the day never comes. Then the fates had turned things upside down so that that which had been at the bottom now lay on top, and read he must. Read and act. Fear, and anger, which is born of fear, its emotional mate, rose again in his breast and he was suddenly glad of Carew's presence.

At one time, though he did indeed think he could learn something from the old man, he had felt he would be a drag on him in the bush. But now he felt something else. He felt a sense of security in having another of his own craft at his side. A great master of the art, perhaps the greatest now alive.

Theresa he forced into the back of his mind, again astonished at the way words, which appeared casually in conversation, had brought her back to him. Da Silva's speaking of breasts. His own thoughts of the smells of the forest had brought her perfume back into his nostrils. The aphrodisiacal odour of perfume and powder, of sweat and soap, of clean-washed linen—all blended into a scent which his hunter's mind registered as Maria Theresa. He had never even called her Theresa.

His thoughts were interrupted by Carew who came into his room and said, 'Now we will talk to the men of Querida. My old hunters wait—Lunda, Matissa, Siloko, and their people.'

'Ah, the old hunters,' Maniero said. 'There are none like them left.'

'There are no times like the old times either,' Carew said. 'The days when the nyala swarmed, the buffalo ran in great herds, and wildebeeste were found in every flat. No,' he said, 'the world has changed in my lifetime. The game has gone. Even here, there is much less, and men, as I knew them, have gone too. Both white and black—they are less than they were. But come, Maniero, we must convince them that we are still great. Greater than a couple of spook elephants.' He spat out of the screened window. 'See,' he said, 'improvements. No mosquitoes, but a man can't spit any more. My God!' he said, 'women can live here now.'

'Your wife lived and hunted with you.'

'My wife was more than a woman,' Carew said.

'And you were more than a man.'

'I have survived,' Carew said. 'And in man or beast, that is an achievement. It is a strange thing,' he continued, 'that even at my age, I may still survive many boys in their twenties. If there is war, and it seems likely, thousands will be killed in the first week, and I may still be alive. That is a commentary on our times, Maniero. That the old, the sick and the blind, the halt and the lame have a better chance than the young and the strong. That the dwellers in the wilderness, you and I, and the others of our kind, and the indigenous peoples of the forest, may have a better chance than the city dwellers, despite their doctors and hospitals, despite all their comforts. For who would bomb a forest? Do you know the advantage of age, Maniero?' he asked suddenly.

'No.'

'You have a great deal to think about and much time in which to think. By a paradox, because there is so little time, there is so much.'

'I have just reached the age of thought,' Maniero said, 'though I am not yet old. It is like puberty. It comes suddenly, in a flash in the darkness.'

'Some men never attain the age of puberty. Some men and women die as aged infants,' Carew said. This time he opened the screen door to spit. 'Now,' he said, 'let us go. And bring your rifle. In the forest the rifle is power.'

They left together, their rifles over their arms. The rifles, butts and smalls, were dimpled with scars and polished with use. They were weapons, not toys. They were weapons as the tusks of an elephant are weapons.

In the native quarter, round a great fire, the company of old hunters, trackers, their descendants, and the curious were gathered. Matissa was declaiming as they came. He was telling of Carew's greatness. And then, suddenly, slipping through the assembly as though they were ghosts, as though the men were trees and shrubs, as though they were hunting, so silently and quickly did they come, the two white men were beside him. Carew put his hand on the naked, black arm that shone with grease in the firelight.

'We are here, old friend and companion.' Abandoning Maniero as a mere accompaniment, he said—'O! people, I, whom you never thought to see again, am here out of the dead days, out of the past. I have come once again to free you from your thrall.' His voice rose. He pointed a hand at an old, almost naked man squatting by the fire who held a great bow ornamented with strips of skin and charms. 'Do you remember, Obiki, how you stood at my side, a young, strong man, when we recaptured the women the slavers had taken? Do you remember the hunts we had? The spoors you followed? The meat you ate at my fires?'

'Aai, Inkoos, aai, O Chief, O King, I remember.'

'Now I have come again, with him upon whom my mantle is cast. With him who will carry my spirit on when I go to that distant place where so many of our friends await me. Hunters, warriors—men who were great with me.'

'The Lord is still great,' a man shouted.

Carew held up his hand. 'I still cast a great shadow. I can still make one more great hunt. Can still, like wounded buffalo, make one more charge. And because I am great, I would kill one more great thing before I go.'

'Aai,' the men chanted.

'To-morrow I and he,' he pointed to Maniero, 'go to kill the great ones. The lame one and his brother.'

'So you know,' an old man said. 'You know there are two. We thought no white man knew that.'

'All things are known to me,' Carew said. 'And now who goes with us?'

Four old men stood up supporting themselves on long sticks. 'We go, Inkoos. We go carried by our sons. We, the old ones, would also have one more hunt.'

Matissa pushed his cap of wild catskin back on his head. 'They are not far, Lord,' he said. 'No, they are near. It is in my heart and liver that they await us. Death has been long coming to them too. It is in my heart that they are ready.'

'Who will come?' Carew asked. 'Who will come with

us old ones? Who dares?' he shouted. 'Who dares?'

The crowd stood up shouting, 'We will come. All that the Lord needs will come.' Their eyes grew bloodshot in the firelight.

'It is beer that talks,' said Carew, taunting them. 'Even women with milk in their breasts are brave when their bellies are round and shining, replete and filled like drums with beer. To-night you will come. To-night you are lions, but to-morrow you will be jackals when, at the hour of the horns, we go hence to battle.'

'We are men, O Chief,' they said. 'We will come.'

'And you will dare?'

'With you, O Chief, we will dare.'

The two white men left as they had come. One minute they had been there, the next they had gone.

They went over to Da Silva's house. He was still up, sitting reading by a green shaded light. Beside him were the stamp albums he had shown them. 'Well, gentlemen,' he said. 'You have seen the people?'

'We have seen them,' Carew said.

'And?'

'And they will come. Some of them, at least.'

'They would not go with me,' Da Silva said.

'Your Excellency is the Chef de Poste, is an administrator. We are hunters. You, Senhor, they love and fear. You are their father. We, though of a different race, they know. We are their brothers, their colleagues. Brothers of the chase, Senhor. We have the scent of wood fires on our beards and clothes. Our hands, like theirs, are stained with blood.'

'God be with you,' Da Silva said.

He brought out the decanter of Madeira and the glasses. 'And your plans?' he asked.

'We leave to-morrow,' Carew said. 'We will make a forward camp. A base, and then send out our trackers. When we have news, we will hunt. Till then, we will rest.'

'I will pray,' Da Silva said. 'I will pray for the avengers.'

'It is good to pray,' Carew said. 'It gives strength and we shall need it.' He held up his glass to the light and stared at it.

'A friend sends it to me in cask,' Da Silva said. Then apologetically he said—'I spoke without thinking, Senhor. My mind runs on casks.'

'Ah,' Carew said, 'us and our casks. But yours is a small one, your Excellency, and without croton oil and gasoline.' He laughed. 'It does not worry me, Senhor. It only makes me laugh, when I think of my agent extracting me like a baby from a womb of brandy and trying to fit me into a coffin. Or do you think it would be permitted for him to bury the whole cask? Would it be seemly?' he asked. 'It would cause talk, but there has always been talk about me. Mad Carew I was called. Mad, because I loved my life in the wilderness, because Kaffirs and animals were my friends. Mad, because my wife went with me.'

The clearing where Mashupa and his family had met their death was a march of thirty-odd kilometres beyond the last piece of negotiable track. At this point where the road became a game trail, and finally ended, Carew's truck and Maniero's car were parked near a big wild fig tree that screened them from the heat of the sun.

Their tents and goods had been carried from here to the camp by porters and Carew had walked followed by a litter, with his old hunters round him, also followed by litters of a rougher kind. By the miracle of being again in the great forest, these old men had gained new strength. The forked-tailed blue jays sparkling in the sunshine, the lowries, the parrots, the black drongo shrikes, the spoor along their route, the buck that they glimpsed at times, all brought back the past to them, all made this final effort easy. The hum of the insects in the air, the croaking of the frogs at night, the feeling that the world about them was palpitating with unseen life and with death, threatening each creature, excited them. The twin laws of nature, the law of life and increase and the law of death and putrescence, that would lead to more life, never ceasing for an instant, all added to their feelings. The white men knew it and understood it, put it into words. The brown men only felt it.

Before and behind the procession of old men and their litters were the bearers. A long way in front was Maniero with his trackers, hunters, and gun boy. Enclosing them all, encysting them, was the vastness of the forest world, and the great, blue, burning cup of the African sky. In it soared the vultures, the eagles and the kites, the hawks and buzzards. They saw the little caravan creeping slowly through the bush as their ancestors had seen the slavers pass, and other older hunters, and the seekers of gold and precious metals. The traders of gum and ivory and wild beasts.

At the ruins of N'Tembi's kraal, as they called it, Maniero was waiting for Carew.

'It happened here,' he said, and handed him a rough little knife made from the blade of an arrow. 'They missed that,' he said.

Together they went over the ground, over the cold trail, but the giant clues of the elephants' wrath remained, and some other things. A child's drinking cup made of a tiny tortoise shell, a jew's harp that must have belonged to N'Tembi. The terrible saucer where the girl had been moulded, like bloody dough, into the red soil, and naturally, the broken trees, the hut remnants, and other signs of the massacre.

Carew said suddenly, 'It all comes back now. This place is familiar to me.'

'You have been here?' Maniero asked.

Carew did not answer him. Instead, he sat down on a fallen tree with his head sunk in his hands. Then he looked up and said, 'There is a small spring near here and over there,' he pointed north, 'a giant baobab where two old roads meet and, near it, a pan of fever trees?'

Maniero said, 'I think there is a big simao near here, but I will ask the boys.' He came back and said, 'Everything is as you describe it.'

'So that is why it happened,' Carew said. 'The lame one came back.' Then he said, 'I will go on. I will go alone. Give me an hour and then follow me. That will be our forward camp. It is a good camping spot.'

'You have camped there?'

'Yes,' he said, 'sixty years ago.' Then, picking up his rifle, he left them. He followed Mashupa's little path and came to the tree. It had not changed. Not a leaf was different. It had not grown, it seemed no nearer death. The bees were still there as they had always been, tending the giant, hanging combs in its hollow shell. He went up to it and laid his hands upon its bark. 'Esther,' he said, 'Esther, I am back. You have brought me back to where my life began.' For his life had begun with his love, and though he was still alive, had ended with it. He felt Esther's arms about him again. He felt her lips on his. The perfume

184

of her hair was in his nostrils. Yes, there were his initials and hers. Their C. & E. C.—Charles and Esther Carew— surrounded by a carved heart. Sixty years. And he was back at the point of his departure. He sat at its bastioned roots. This was where they had sat. This was where they had lain. This was where they had loved. Always, after that, when they were alone, and came upon such a tree, Esther had called it a 'honey-moon tree.' He stared upwards at the giant, tortured limbs at which they had stared sixty years ago.

And this was where Mashupa had lived, knowing nothing of him or Esther. He found Mashupa's shelter of leaves and branches, and picked up a carved, wooden spoon from the ground. It was almost finished. He saw the cold ashes of his fire, the two cooking stones, his pot of mouti. He smelt it. Elephants, he thought. Elephant dung and clay. So that had been his protection. A good one too, but not good enough. He picked up one of the stones. It was ours, he thought. These are the stones we cooked on and they have lain here ever since. He wondered if Mashupa had ever thought about them, of how they came to be here where there were no stones. He looked at the other marks on the tree and then he heard them coming.

'We'll camp here,' he said to Maniero. Suddenly he had taken the lead. Maniero accepted it. The tent was put up, the stores piled. Wood was collected for the fire. And it was from here, at dawn, that the trackers started their work casting forward, spread in a fan, like hounds, looking for fresh spoor and sign.

They waited three days, living on canned goods, never firing a shot. On the morning of the fourth day, they got the news they wanted. The trackers had found fresh spoor. Two men came in, pale under their dark skins, with wide eyes, to tell them. 'They are here,' they said, 'nearby. Two and a half days' march away, in a piece of forest where there is no life, no water. Where there is nothing but trees as grey as the elephant themselves, where there is no bird. It is a land of the spirits.'

'You know the place?' Carew asked.

'We know of it, but no one has gone there before us and come out alive!'

'You are alive,' Carew said.

'Aai, Lord, we are alive, but that is because they are

waiting for you, the Senhors. It is as Matissa said—they are there waiting to make an end.'

'That too, is our intention,' Carew said. 'To-morrow you will put us on the spoor and wait. We will go alone with two gun bearers, and the old ones who are so near to death, so accustomed to his countenance, that they fear him no longer.' He turned to Maniero. 'Will your gun boy go with you?'

Maniero called his boy. 'Will you go with me, Joaquim?'

'I will go, Lord.'

'Then this is the plan,' Carew said. 'When we are on the spoor, I will lead with Matissa if he can get that far, and his son carrying my second rifle. You, Maniero, will follow me.'

'I should lead,' Maniero said. 'This is my business.'

'You will follow,' Carew said, 'unless they go too far and fast for me. Please remember, Maniero, that though I do not court death, I am ready to go. I have had enough of life—the cup is drained. This is my request, that you let me lead.'

'If you insist,' Maniero said. In his heart he was relieved that it should be so.

'Then to-morrow we start,' he said.

'And I, Lord?' one of the trackers who had brought the information asked.

'You,' Carew said, will put us on the spoor, then Matissa, Lunda, and Siloko and I, who hunted elephants before your father was conceived, will proceed alone.'

That night he told Maniero the story of the tree. He said, 'This is where Pretorius died after he had wounded the lame one. He shot him in the grove of fever trees and the lame one killed him there. That's where he is buried. Among the yellow fever trees. They found him covered with leaves and branches. The lame one must have come back to do it.'

'They do that sometimes,' Maniero said.

'Yes,' Carew said, 'they do sometimes. Just as sometimes they come back to the bones of their dead friends and roll them about, and carry them in their trunks.'

'Yes,' Maniero said, 'I have seen that too. I have seen the great skulls moved.'

'Do you remember what I told you?' Carew said.

'What?'

'That the lame one revisits this spot every so many years. You saw how the trees are damaged?'

'Yes.'

'You saw the remains of older trees that had been broken?'

'I saw them.'

'And still older stumps?'

'Yes.'

'It's what I said. Those elephants come back to destroy the trees because the trees are Pretorius. His juices are in them.'

'Fantastic,' Maniero said. 'Fantastic!'

'What,' Carew asked, looking round, 'is not fantastic here? This tree that stood where it now stands when the Lord Jesus was hanging on the cross. Is not that fantastic? In all the world, Maniero, there are no two men who know more of elephants than you and I, but they remain a mystery. We have killed many hundreds of them, but that is all. We know how they die, but we do not know how they live.' Then he said, 'This tree . . .'

Maniero said, 'The baobab?'

Carew said, 'I brought my wife here sixty years ago. Our marks are on its trunk. This is where I loved her.' His old, grey eyes were innocent as those of a child in the firelight. There was nothing to be modest about. Where was the shame in a man of his age telling his friend where his love had been consummated? It was as if he said, 'This is the church where we were married.' He thought of Mashupa's fire, newly dead, and rain-washed, and his own old fires. And the stones of Mashupa's fire. They were the ones he and Esther had brought and left here. They were the stones of their cooking fire. The altar, as it were, of their love. With the firelight gleaming from between them, they had made love all those years ago. Fire. His own fires and Esther's. The ardours of their dead passion—the embers of it still glowed in his heart as the breeze of memory refreshed them.

Maniero stared at him.

'It was our honeymoon,' Carew said.

How odd it was to think of this old man once being young and ardent, Maniero thought. It was as if a skeleton had suddenly clothed itself with flesh before his eyes. But that was also true. Every skeleton had once been flesh, had once known love. Known it and outgrown it, as the fires within it died, and potency, the cause of the effect, was lost. Old men loved women, but out of habit rather than desire. They loved them as one would love a pretty pet, a charming animal. To an old man, a young woman was a toy. She was not his heart's desire. She was not his life, merely an ornamental addition to it, a buttonhole to be worn.

In these last days, he had thought much of love. He was in the very state he had described. Musth—like a bull elephant. Why had it not happened before? With his race which was precocious, he knew it was strange. Perhaps love had never been offered him before. Never so blatantly. After all, who would want to marry a hunter? And his sudden desire to settle down—was Theresa Ferreira responsible for that too? A new set of circumstances had arisen in his life. New feelings enveloped him, warming his blood, causing his heart to beat faster.

And Carew had known all this. Had known it here where they sat. Carew, a young man with a young woman in his arms, and the tree the same. The tree unchanging. Life unchanging, the pattern just repeating itself. Everything coming back to its beginning, like Carew to his baobab. Ready to end his life where he had begun it as a man.

There was an aura about the place. Carew was certainly not the only one with a tree so ancient. What else had been spilt beneath these gnarled branches, beneath the humming canopy of bees? Here men had died and men had been conceived. These cross-roads in the wilderness were a punctuation mark in Africa. The tree, a giant speculative question mark, underlined with blood and passion. He thought of Theresa and the glimpse she had given him of her body and the promise in her dark eyes. It was hard for him to remember she was married to his friend. That is always a hard thing for a man to remember when a woman gives herself to him with her eyes.

Chapter Twenty-four

THE GREAT HUNT

In a hunt there are two sides, as in a war, two points of view—that of the hunter and that of the hunted. That of the victor and that of the victim. But sometimes these two sides can merge as the battle joins, the hunter being hunted, and the hunted becoming the hunter. This can only happen under certain circumstances with great beasts. The elephant, the buffalo, the whale; or if the beast is a carnivore, a lion or a leopard. Normally, the odds are weighted in the favour of the hunter and they only change when he has struck—till then he moves in safety.

But when a beast has been hunted as the great elephant they called the lame one, and his brother, had been hunted, and when they have reached an age that is incomprehensible to man, and when they find, on their trail, and following it, on several occasions over a period of years, the same smell, that of a white man, the scent finally gets registered in the convolutions of their ancient brains, and produces a peculiar effect—an effect of show-down, of furious resentment against the monotony of a peaceful old age being broken into, pierced by the irritation of interference. So, when the elephants found the man there, on their spoor again, remorselessly attached to them by his will, the intermediate bond between them being his traces in the bush and their footmarks, their dung, the fallen branches they had torn down, the twigs they had chewed, they planned to make an end. The elephants as much as the man. All now were planning, not as they had been before on other occasions, one to follow and the other to escape, but all to kill.

The elephants stood in a vast, dead island of quazine. Waterless, lifeless except for themselves, who though still alive were without the qualities of full life. Who were like rocks endowed with wisdom, and subject to habit. It is impossible to believe that, as the trackers said, they were waiting for an end, that their minds functioned as men's minds might, as a criminal's might. Yet they had laid ambushes before, had tempted hunters to their deaths before. They were still uneasy. The fire had not quite died out of

189

their old eyes. They stood swaying on their forelegs, swinging the vast bulk of their bodies from side to side. They were uneasy still with the smell of blood. Its memory had not yet faded from their minds, and, despite their washings and tramplings and mud-wallows, they still had vestigial traces of it in the interstices of the crinkled hides of their legs, in the crevices that surrounded the horn of their toenails. They had eaten. They had filled their tanks with water. They had left an unmistakable trail. They had come not too far, but just far enough from the avengers whom they knew would follow them. Not so far that the hunters would think they had got clear away and give up, but far enough for the hunt to be stretched to its limit. Everything about them was taut, tightened to the snapping point. The nerves of both the elephants and the hunters. The bow of action was bent, the arrow fitted to the string. The scene of the drama, its next act, all set, latent behind the curtain of silence. The forest seemed to await the final scene. The silence and the heat were unbearable, palpable. Each instant of it poised, each waiting to be shattered by the explosion of a heavy shell, or the screaming trumpet of a charging elephant. But nothing broke it. The elephants waited and the men progressed.

Maniero led with the trackers. Carew followed in a litter. Behind his litter came others—those of his old hunters, carried by their grandsons. It could have been a funeral cortege proceeding through the forest, but the old men who were carried were not dead, only near to death. Behind them again, like mourners, came the carriers, their burdens consisting almost entirely of water in cans and bottles. The food they had with them was simple; biltong, the dried, jerked beef of Africa, boer tusks, which are dehydrated chunks of bread, and mealie meal, divided into small sacks for easy porterage. Maniero had said they need not carry water as they would find pans for the first day at least, and fill up there since there had been rain. He knew this forest, he knew it at least up to the quazine. There he had never hunted. Nothing lived there. But Carew said, 'We will carry water.' And Carew was right because when they reached the pans with the usual fever trees, they found them fouled by the elephants beyond use. They had tramped all over them, leaving their enormous football sign both in the water and on the banks. They had wallowed in it, they had rubbed their backs against the larger trees. Higher than a man could reach with a rifle in his outstretched arm, there was still mud on the bark, dry on the outside, but moist underneath, baked like dough.

'Well, you were right,' Maniero said.

'I was right,' Carew said, 'because I know elephants. Because I am older than you. If you had lived to my age, you would have known too. They are aware of us, Maniero. They did not have to do this. They drank their fill and then spoilt the water.'

The native hunters knew it too. This was the way these elephants trapped men. It was one of their tricks, a strategy of war, and were they not inhabited by the spirits of the great ones, the Zulu kings long dead, but masters of the arts of war and massacre?

Carew calmed them. My children,' he said, 'this was, as you say, a stratagem. But we have water. My wisdom was greater than theirs.'

The next day they came to the edge of the quazine.

'They are here,' the trackers said. 'They are near.'

They found fresh sign, still cool on the outside, but warm within and moist from the heat of the elephants' bowels. There was the stink of elephants disturbed. It was as if fear and anger liberated foul juices into their excrement. Then they heard the elephants. There was a crash of a tree breaking.

'They've gone,' Maniero said.

'Yes,' Carew said, 'but such elephants do not make a noise when they go. Why would they make a noise except to lead us on?'

'I must follow them,' Maniero said. 'I have my orders.'

'His Excellency the Governor-General is now having his cup of coffee in bed, in his palace in the Capital. He is rubbing the sleep from his eyes,' Carew said. 'He has forgotten us.'

'I must follow,' Maniero said. 'What else is there to do?'

'We can wait,' Carew said 'This is a trick. These elephants'—that there were two was now beyond all doubt since they had been at no pains to disguise their spoor —'are angry. They are at war and will come back.'

'I have never heard of such a thing,' Maniero said.

'Nor have I,' Carew answered, 'but this is no place to think of what we know, or have heard. These are not ordinary elephants.'

'I will follow,' Maniero said.

'Then follow. I shall remain here till the water is nearly done. Make camp,' he said to the boys, 'and good luck, Maniero. But be careful and do not go too far!'

'I will be careful,' Maniero said, laughing. Careful, in this situation, was a word that could not apply. All he could count on was his experience, his senses, and the extra sense that all great hunters have. The ability to feel danger before the danger is critical.

The elephants, when they had heard the hunters coming, had moved on, carelessly crashing their way through the small trees, moving through them as a boy would move through a field of wheat. They moved upwind, so did not know whether they were being followed. They marched all day, hardly pausing to eat, only snatching at branches as they passed.

Time pressed upon both hunter and hunted with an urgency that neither understood. The man forced himself forward. The elephants drove themselves on into the dry lands, digging in, as it is called, moving so fast that a little heap of dust was left in the spoor of their forefeet by the swift running pressure of the hind, as it kicked up the sand. They ran, but not in fear. They were not running to escape. They were not even going into the country where their spoor would be lost on the hard outcrops of flat rocks, where there was no water, and where on other occasions, they had suffered the tortures of thirst when pressed, but had waited till the hunt died down before leaving the sanctuary of the desert.

On the contrary, this time, they led their pursuers from water hole to water hole. But they were bad, nearly dried up. And since the man followed them, he took their leavings of water. Water mixed with the mud squeezed up by their great feet, and their urine and defecations. They were forcing the man on, making him follow, but poisoning him and exhausting him. Perhaps they did not know this. It is hard to believe that elephants, as Carew had said, would knowingly foul the water for their pursuers, as men have done in wars, by throwing bodies into the wells. It is more probable that they drank what they could, and then stood cooling themselves, spraying the muddy water over their backs with their trunks. Perhaps lying in the pan for a bath, cooling their tired feet in the ooze, and since they stood there, the natural functions of their body took place in the water which the white hunter, who pursued them, must perforce use. This is what seems more likely, but to Maniero, the elephants had become the devil, were all evil, were deliberately soiling everything and passing on. All that he had heard of these elephants came back to him exaggerated by his explanation. One elephant, two elephants, two in one. Elephants inhabited by spirits. A man could not live as he had done in the forest among natives and have his unconscious mind remain completely immune to their superstitions.

Each drove the other, for the faster the man pursued, the faster the elephants had to go to evade them. On they went, the beasts and the man from pan to pan, from water hole to water hole. But this time Maniero was prepared. He carried only biltong and water. They, he and Joaquim, his tracker, could live on that for days. Biltong and a reserve of water in four canteens, that they had not touched yet, a blanket each and the 10.75 and ammunition. That was all.

At last the elephants marched into an area of bush and sandveld, where, no matter how much rain fell, none stayed, every drop being drunk in by the ever thirsty ground. That night they fed, there was some succulent growth here, though there was no water, and then, as if they had consulted each other, they swung north, and then east towards the sea, and then south again, moving fast till they came on to their own spoor once more, and that of the hunter superimposed upon it. Spoor that stank to them, that brought the heat of their ancient blood back, pumping through their great arteries and veins, reddening their eyes with anger. The stink of the white man, the enemy, the aphrodisiac of war.

When the elephants reached the sandveld, Maniero turned back. What a fool he'd been to come so far. It was hopeless to follow elephants when they knew they were pursued and started digging in. Once they began moving in a straight line, only a fool would follow them. Yet he had gone on like a man possessed. Possessed, that was the word, some madness had got into him which cancelled out all previous experience and forced him on. He was tired, but not exhausted—and he still had water. For, despite what the elephants had done to the water, he had drunk it, filtering it through his handkerchief. The taste of elephant and buffalo urine was in his mouth, but his precious water was safe, it would get him back. It would get him back to Carew. Carew would know what to do. There was something here he could not fathom. Perhaps it was the age of his adversaries which only the age of Carew could parallel. Magic was out of the question. His sanity was returning.

While Maniero was away, Carew waited. It was not unpleasant to wait, here in the bush and the silence. This was what he had wanted. The last hunt, he thought. Well, Maniero was doing the hunting. He had boasted in vain about leading. He was too old. He sent boys back for more water. They returned with it and food as well—sour, curdled milk, cassavas, monkey nuts, and other things. Some of the porters made traps and set snares and got fresh meat. He would not allow a shot to be fired.

The old men sat with him and they gossiped about the great days of the past. Esther was all that was missing. And he felt her near him. How she had loved the bush, the silence, the smell of the wood fires. At night a hyena walked round their camp for several hours. He enjoyed hearing its moaning cry that was something between the low of a cow and the scream of a woman. There was more life at night. Once he heard a lion in the distance, an owl hooted from a nearby tree. There were doves, so there must be a little water left somewhere nearby. The time passed very pleasantly for him. It was much nicer here than in town. He was in his element among the people he understood, the old-fashioned Kaffirs who had not been spoilt by learning the worst of the white man's ways, and forgetting the best of their own. They told tales, remembered old legends, smoked and spat as old men do, and the sun that was so hot for the young only served to warm their blood.

And all the time as he waited, he watched and listened. In this stillness, the sound of a shot from a 10.75 would carry a long way. In his heart, he was sure the shot would come from nearby. Sure that the elephants would return. He did not know why, only that if he had been an old elephant, it was what what he would have done. It was what himself had done. Come back to the beginning to make an end. It seemed nearer to him that way, somehow. Those elephants must be about ready to die, he thought. Perhaps they, like himself, wanted one more hunt, wanted to kill one more white man before they went off to die. There was no great elephant graveyard. That was just a story. But elephants did tend to return to the privacy of the swamps where they were born, and die there. Men did that too. It was not sentiment alone that took men back to the scenes of their youth when they felt the end was near. A thousand things called to them. Diet, food, the food that they had been weaned on, and memory, for as the present faded, the past grew stronger, grew irresistible, so that sixty years ago was nearer than yesterday. So that Esther was nearer than Maniero. And all the time he listened and watched, for the hunter in him was never at rest.

When the elephants came to their spoor and Maniero's, they did not cross it. They stood back from the track and fingered it with their trunk tips, savouring their anger, building it up. Then moving parallel to the spoor, they went into a thick patch of bush that overhung the trail. Here the tuskless elephant waited at right angles to the track while the lame one stepped into it, leaving a clear spoor. Fifty yards further down, he too, went into the forest and stood beside the path. They were now in position.

Maniero was tired, but he still hunted. His eyes were everywhere. On the spoor, and in the forest on each side of it. Every few minutes he halted to watch and listen. He might see a tickbird, he might hear the rumble of a giant stomach. He might hear the flap of an ear, or the gentle crack of a branch. He did not miss the spoor of the lame one when he came on to it. So he had come back and was ahead of him again. Carew had been right. He had said they would come back. Maniero stopped. Unseen by him, the trunk of the tuskless elephant was directly over his head. The elephant waited. Perhaps he wanted to take Maniero from behind, to chase him. At any rate, he waited, and Maniero went on with his tracker behind him. The wind was in his favour. He tested it, picking up a little dry dust in the path and letting it run from between his fingers. How near was the lame one? He was not travelling fast now.

Then he saw him. At least he saw a dark patch in the bush that might be an elephant, if it was not an anthill. He moved nearer; at thirty yards he was certain. He saw the elephant's head. He saw the brown tusks, like great, curved limbs of a tree. The head became clearer. Clear enough for a brain shot above the eye. He raised his rifle. In his mind he was thinking how dark the tusks of some of these bulls were, and then, just as he squeezed the trigger, the elephant moved his lower jaw. There, at the root of the tusk, was a clean spot, a section of ivory white. Where had he seen that before? An elephant's tusk—a woman's thigh. Maria Theresa's thigh. He saw her as she had stood with upraised skirt, as his finger completed its pressure on the trigger. But the thought of the woman had been enough. The whole trinity, the total force of mind and body, of personality, the projection of the hunter's will, in conjunction with the rifle and the shell exploding in the chamber of the barrel, was out of key. When, above all other times, the attention and the will should have been a hundred per cent on death, it was only ninety-nine per cent. The bullet went low and right. It crashed into the skull where the brain was protected by the vast honeycombs of bone that surrounded it. His failure surprised him so much that he was slow in reloading. He was tired too. He tried, even in action, to alibi himself, to rationalise his failure. *Tired, Theresa, the flash of her thigh*—the bolt went home. He was ready, but the wounded elephant was on him, charging. There was still time for a frontal-brain shot. Through the roof of the mouth. He got it. The elephant staggered and fell, landing on his knees, his body supported by the great prong of his tusks. As he reloaded again, the tuskless elephant, who had come up from behind him, struck. For an instant, as he died, he wondered how he had forgotten that there were two elephants. How had a lifetime of experience, a lifetime of hunting, slipped from him?

The tuskless elephant struck only once with the great hawser of his trunk, then stepped on Maniero's body, popping it like a grape. Then he seized Joaquim by the waist and threw him against the trunk of a tree. The body bounced away from it as a rag doll might, and lay sprawling at its roots. He went back to Maniero. Setting a foot upon his belly, he put his trunk about his waist and pulled him in two. Pulled him as a child pulls a Christmas cracker.

The elephant then went to his fallen brother. He pushed at him with raised trunk, trying with tuskless gums, to raise him. He caressed him and blew on him. Then he gave vent to his fury in wild blasts of his trumpet. He went back to Maniero and mashed him, trampling him, kneeling on him, throwing the empty sacks of his remains this way and that. Holding them with his hind legs while he stretched them with his trunk. He went to the gun bearer and did the same. Then he went back to his brother as if to tell him that he was avenged, as if to apologise for his own mistake in not killing Maniero sooner. He trumpeted again and went off to water, to the muddy pan the hunters had left behind them when they made their forward camp.

When Carew heard the shots—they were not more than three miles away—he got up. So Maniero had made contact with the enemy. Two shots—he might have got them both! He picked up his six hundred, slipped some spare shells into his pocket, and walked up the path. Matissa, Lunda, and Siloko, assegais in hand, followed him. Like frail leaves, three brown and one white, they drifted down on the wind of destiny.

But none had lost his skill. Old as they were, they moved fast and silently, almost invisible in their old khaki, and their nakedness. Of the forest, a part of it, as much as the elephants themselves. Then, suddenly, Carew stopped, raised his rifle and fired. The two shots rang out, like shots from a cannon, shattering the shimmering stillness of the afternoon. There was an elephant's scream and a crash as the tuskless one fell, breaking off the small trees like twigs beneath him.

'Maniero!' Carew shouted, 'Maniero!' as he reloaded. There was no answer, there was only a silence that seemed more profound since he had shattered it. 'Wait there,' he said. 'I am going on.'

'Where the Lord goes, we go,' they said, 'for a shadow cannot be separated from its principal.'

They went on till their path was blocked by the great bulk of the fallen, tuskless elephant. They went round him and to make certain, Carew gave him a shot into the root of the tail. It was like shooting into an anthill. 'He's dead,' he said. Then he shouted, 'Maniero! Maniero!' There was no answer. Carew went on followed by the trackers. They moved cautiously. Nothing stirred and then they came on to the tusked elephant broadside on. He had fallen on his knees and was propped up in a position of prayer. He was dead all right—no doubt about that! Carew shouted. The only answer was a vulture that flew with heavy wings from a tree. How quickly they came. 'Maniero!' Carew shouted again, 'Maniero!' Maniero was dead. He must be. They spread out and went round the elephant. There they found part of Maniero. The rest they found further away among the smashed and uprooted trees. A battle ground. At the foot of a big marula, they found most of the remains of Joaquim.

'I will remain here,' Carew said. 'Bring the men and the gear, Matissa. Send back for more men. Your spooks are dead and the great hunter, on whom my mantle was to have fallen, has preceded me into the land of death. Moselekatse and T'Chaka are no more. Maniero is no more.'

'Aai,' Lunda said, 'he is dead. Very dead.'

Carew took off his sweaty hat. 'While you go,' he said, 'we will collect what is left and make a fire. Go fast, old one. There is much to do.' He sat on the ground and stared at the vast bulk before him, at the great tusks that were like the bowsprits of a schooner. So the elephants were dead. Both of them . . . Their long marches were over. They were at rest. And Maniero's little farm remained a dead man's dream.

Once again he had survived. He wondered why, when you were so tired, it was so hard to die. Maniero, poor Maniero, who had laughed with him about his barrel of brandy. Well, who would be pickled in it now? He got up and began to collect what he could of his friend. It was hot, they'd have to hurry to get him back to the truck and the brandy. Two days. If they hurried they could do it in two days, but by to-morrow even, putrefaction would have begun.

The body had been torn in two. The head, arms, and torso in one part, and the legs still joined together on the crushed pelvis in the other. Carew covered them with branches. The boys would bring blankets and gear. He would camp beside the body.

He reconstructed the disaster in his mind as he went over the spoor. He saw where the tuskless elephant had stood. Why had he not struck when Maniero passed him? And why, when Maniero had killed the tusked elephant, had he not been ready for the other one? There was an un-exploded cartridge in the breech of the broken 10.75.

When the boys came, he put Maniero's remains in a blanket, salted them, and folded the blanket over the body, making it into a kind of parcel which he lashed with riems. That was the best he could do now. As night fell, the boys chopped out the tusks by the light of an immense fire.

In the roof of the tusked elephant's mouth, they found the blade of an assegai. It had not been there long. It must have been flung by the dead boy, Mashupa. In the left thigh, they cut out the great four-ounce bullet that Pretorius had fired into him all those years ago.

But even before the tusks were out, crowds of natives had drifted in, like ghosts, from every track in the wilderness. The news of meat had been told. The news that the giants that had haunted the forest were dead had gone with it. Here was sacred meat, mouti, on an unprecedented scale. To eat this meat was to drink the very blood of T'Chaka.

They came marching through the night with flaming torches. They surrounded the recumbent giants. They built great fires. They disappeared into the vast caverns from which the viscera had been withdrawn, and reappeared, plastered with blood and mucus, into the firelight. They climbed the bodies. Their assegais and knives carved great strips of meat from it. Platters of hide were flayed and piled with meat so that the skin which had once covered the meat of the elephants, was now covered by the meat.

Witch doctors came in their panoply of rattles, bones, skins, and charms, and frightened the earlier comers into giving them the fragments they coveted—the white, stubby tails, the eyelashes, the trunk tips, the hearts and livers, the very toe-nails.

The vast, scarlet bulks grew smaller in the firelight. By dawn, only the mountainous guts remained to become fly-blown with the earliest light. For with the light would come the blue and green metallic flies to lay their white lozenge eggs in the pink mass of bowels, on the bursting bellies where fermented leaves and branches, some of which only yesterday had been growing on the trees, spilled out on to the ground. Starving dogs licked at the blood. They ate the smaller, broken pieces of Maniero, indistinguishable to them from the fragments of elephant flesh.

The smell of roasting meat, mixed with the stink of offal, of sweating Negro bodies, of wood smoke and the excrement of the despoilers, filled the air. Like ants, men and women poured into the arena, paused to stare, to butcher, to feast, and finally to leave in a long string, chanting as they marched. The women, laden with their spoils, the blood dripping from the meat on their heads, dripping on to their shoulders, running down between their naked breasts. The men, bloodied from their butchery, assegais in hand, marched with them. At their heels followed the prick-eared dogs still thin, but for once bloated. The devil-god elephants were dead. The old hunter, Carew, whom they had called 'the killer,' was back among them. A story that they had heard since childhood come to life—material-ised in their midst. There would be songs made of this!

Carew had poles cut and the tusks were lashed to them. Two men carried each tusk holding the poles on their shoulders. The parcel, that was Maniero, was put into Carew's litter. He walked beside it. Death. By God! he was further from death than he had been before he started. The hunt had put life into him, had stirred the very centres of his being. Death—death to all but him. I am alone again, he thought.

Joaquim, Maniero's gun boy, they had buried where he fell. Perhaps Maniero should have lain beside him, but it seemed better that he should go back. They would give him a fine funeral—with soldiers and flags and a gun-carriage—for he had died like a soldier in action. This would console his mother and make his dead name famous. So that, dead, he would live in the minds of men more fully than he had alive. Alive, he had only been known to hunters, but now he would be known to all—a hero.

By God, Carew thought, a pickled hero. Pickled in my brandy! Maniero would see Esther first. He would tell her of the forest, tell her about himself. Carew's idea of heaven was that of a big hotel. He thought of the names of the dead being entered in a book. Like a great visitors' book, but in this case, the visitors were permanent. He had pic-tured Esther coming over a great green carpet to meet him in the lobby. Why green? he wondered. Perhaps because the forest was green. He saw himself walking towards her, his double-barrelled rifle over the crook of his arm. His old hat pushed back over his head as he wiped the sweat from his forehead.

They got back to the old camp. They rested and went on. When they got to the lorry, he broached the cask. Broke out its head, and put Maniero in. There were bubbles of air from the parcel as it sank. He forced the top back into position. They lashed the barrel making it fast with riems. They lashed the tusks. Their great, curved ends projecting far beyond the truck's tail made it look like a strange, distorted elephant itself—an elephant running backwards over the forest track.

Querida, and Da Silva. That was the next thing. Carew felt ashamed at being alive. It's me that should have died, he thought.

'There is little to say,' Da Silva said. 'One can only wonder at the inscrutable laws of fate, at chance, at accident, at Providence.'

'You wonder, Senhor,' Carew said, 'that it was Maniero and not me.'

'I do,' Da Silva said. 'Not that I should not have regretted your demise, Senhor. It was only that . . .'

'Only that it would have been more natural.'

'Exactly. You see, Senhor, I was prepared for your death. The barrel . . .' he said.

'Yes, the barrel, and now Maniero's in it. But it was a hunter's death. You remember what he said when he sat there?' Carew looked at the chair where Maniero had sat as if he saw him in it. 'When you spoke of the tragedy, when he said, "it's just another forest tragedy, only this time it is not a weaver bird's nest torn down by a hawk, but the hut of two human beings." A matter of degree,' he said. 'And now this.'

'Now this,' Da Silva said.

'And I, who was in haste, must wait, Senhor,' he said. 'It is a terrible thing that a strong man should take so long to die.'

'And now?' Da Silva asked.

'Now I shall take him back. You must see that he has honours. A brave man, Senhor, a fine hunter and a good friend.'

'He shall have them. At least I will do my best. And you, Senhor?'

'Me? I? The dream is past, Senhor. The dream that I had of death in the forest that I have loved so long. I shall go back. But now I shall die like a woman, in a bed. In Esther's bed.'

'Esther?'

'Esther, my wife who left me twenty years ago. It is a lonely bed, Senhor. But for an old man, everything is lonely when only life is left. Death. Has the Senhor thought much of life and death? Of birth? Of how all men are born in the same fashion, from between their mother's thighs, and of the vast variety there is in the manner of their dying? There is illness and war, murder. There is fire and water. All these can claim a man. And age, if the others miss, if, by chance, he survives them all. But a man can survive too long, Senhor. He can outlive his time.'

'Perhaps it will not be too long, Senhor,' Da Silva said.

'Pray for me,' Carew said. 'Pray that it will not be long.'

Chapter Twenty-five

THE TESTAMENT

Raimundo da Silva had written his report. It had left the Poste by runner at dawn, for once again the poles were down, but more than this, he felt, was necessary. The report was too cold, too stylised, too official. The circumstances warranted, nay, demanded, more than this. He was a Portuguese, a man of imagination, of heart, of soul, an artist like all his race and he had been touched to the profoundest depth of his being.

'The garden,' he said to himself. 'In the garden it will come to me. More must be done, but what more?' That was the question. Soothed by the flowers, by the sunbirds' flashing, jewelled wings, by the spirit of his Octavia, it would come to him as he sat there on the seat she had constructed under two flamboyants. 'Raimundo,' she had said when she planted them, 'one day we will sit under these trees side by side. We will prune them so that they grow into an arbour.' They had been little trees then, only fifty centimetres high and it had seemed inconceivable to him that they would ever become an arbour. But the arbour was there now. And the woman who had planned it was dead. Only her concept lived on, grew on, so that, as her bones mouldered, her spirit, which was the spirit of the growing trees and of all things that she had planted, waxed and grew greater year by year.

On the seat in the arbour, looking over the vast panorama of the coastal plane, it came to him. He thought, I will write to His Excellency the Governor-General. I will write personally, as one man to another. He smoked one more cigarette, and went into his office.

With great care he chose a piece of paper and picked up his pen. This was not a letter to be typed. It must be written by hand. Why this was so he did not know, but that was the way it had to be. He wrote 'Your Excellency' in a pointed, copper-plate hand. After Excellency he put a colon, making the two spots with great deliberation. Then he continued—

I am taking the liberty of writing your Excellency a personal letter about the events which I reported on officially this morning. I do this out of the emotional full-ness of my heart, trusting that your Excellency will under-stand my motive. This is a lonely life and events assume a magnitude which is, perhaps, out of proportion to their true value, yet the impact of such events upon such a man as I, demands relief, demands explanation, and in my opinion, deserves something more than the official record in the files of the Colony. Again, feeling that your Excellency has always been sympathetic with my aims, the aims of my administration, and remembering your kindness to me when my first wife died, and your Excellency was Chief Administrator and Acting Governor, I, with all respect, submit this letter hoping that it will interest you, as one of the phenomena which make life in the Colony interesting and even fantastic.

On the face of it, as per my report, what is there of the remarkable? A native killed, his wife and child killed. A famous hunter killed. One who will be a great loss to the Colony. And the death of the two greatest elephants of our time, which we thought, till this happened, to be but one elephant, and this elephant the 'political elephant' that both amused and infuriated your Excellency. That, at least, is finished now. There will be no repercussions of this nature, and the spirit of the great black kings is now forever laid by the bullets of the late Senhor Maniero and the old English hunter, Carew, of whom your Excellency must have knowledge, though he only returned to end his days in the Colony.

I have added to my collection of trophies the tragic remains of this disaster. A tiny tortoise shell that must have been used by the child as a cup. A rude knife made from the point of an arrow. An assegai head that was taken from the roof of the mouth of the lame one. A wooden spoon beautifully conceived, but still unfinished. And, finally, the bullet weighing a hundred grams that lamed the tusked elephant, and was fired, it is believed, by Manie Pretorius, the Boer hunter, whom he killed a century ago—all of which were brought to me by the old hunter, Senhor Carew.

Yet, there is more than this. There is a certain spiritual factor, an element of justice in the death of the hunter Maniero. For many years he reaped the harvest of the forest, only in the end to fall its victim, impaled on the tusks of the great beasts he hunted. Always, your Excellency, I have warned the hunters, the reapers of the forest, that the wind begets the whirlwind, and that the reapers must beware of his harvest. Maniero always laughed at me as your Excellency did, as they did in Lisbon with my 'political elephant,' but God is not lightly mocked, and those who live by the sword must face the risk of perishing by the sword.

Even the simple peasant cultivator, should he scratch himself with one of the tools of his trade, may die of tetanus, owing to the very fertility of the soil that he has nurtured. All this is the will of God, and part of God's pattern, something to be accepted by men without question. But here, in Maniero's death, is great drama. The tetanus bacillus is replaced by a leviathan of the forest; the hospital in which the hunter died is the forest. His bed, the soil that is our mother; his attendants, instead of being good sisters of mercy, are naked savages, brother hunters. His mourners are the tribes for whom, over a period of many years, he hunted food. The bells that toll for him are the trumpeting of elephants, the wild cry of the eagle, the bark of the baboons, and the lions' roar. This is the difference between the dramatic and the banal. Other hunters have been killed in the district of Querida, but they were not Maniero, the famous Nimrod, and the elephant that killed them was not the lame one or his tuskless companion.

There is, too, the strange paradox that Carew, who wished to die—even paying the Colony the compliment of returning for that purpose, and surely there is no greater compliment than this—should live and that Maniero, in the full strength of his manhood, should be dead. Maniero leaves a widowed mother without support, and I have the hope that your Excellency will obtain a small pension for her from the Central Government in Lisbon. Maniero has been of inestimable service to the Colony in general, and to my administration in particular, killing many dangerous elephants and hunting meat for the people in my charge in times of scarcity at my request. Hunger, as your Excellency well knows, is both the mother and father of discontent. Perhaps this idea of obtaining a pension for my poor friend's mother is the motive, or at least one of the motives, for this letter to your Excellency. A man does not even know his own motives, so varied are they, so hidden. God, alone, can know them, and I feel that God, removing his protection from Maniero, will, in guise of your Excellency's generosity, allow the soft rain of his charity to fall upon the man's mother.

I have given Senhor Carew a letter to your Excellency and hope that your Excellency will give him audience, for he is a remarkable man. Though nearly ninety years of age, he killed the last of these two terrible monsters with a single shot, as if it were a partridge. I can vouch for this performance. I may add that nothing would have induced me to accompany Senhor Carew who, perhaps, because he courts death, has eliminated fear from his soul. I, on the other hand, as your Excellency knows, am a man of some timidity, being more intellectual than active in my approach to life. When Maniero was killed, Senhor Carew said, 'I was afraid of this—the boy was too impetuous. It was the hot Portuguese blood that boiled in his veins.' He lacked the calmness of the north. This calmness Senhor Carew certainly possesses. This old man with the macabre humour of his nation, arrived with an immense barrel of cheap brandy in which his boys were to pickle him should he meet his end in the forest, and into this barrel went not old Senhor Carew, but poor Maniero. So that he, who drank no alcohol, will return to Lourenço Marques completely impregnated by the raw spirit. The tusks, which are immense, measuring respectively three metres and two metres eighty centimetres, and weighing one hundred and ninety-four kilos, Senhor Carew wishes to present to Maniero's mother. That is to say, they are to be sold, and the proceeds given to her. It appears, from what Maniero told me that he had been commissioned to get a very large tusk by an Indian dealer with which to make a special crucifix that is to be donated to the Holy Father in Rome. It is an order, I understand, from the Spanish Chargé d'Affairs in the Colony. And here, once more, we encounter the strange paradox of circumstance: that this great beast that was all but a god or a devil, or a blend between the two in the native mind, should have the teeth, that were his ornament, carved into a representation of our Saviour suffering in agony upon the cross in Calvary, and hung in Rome itself. So, perhaps, after all, Maniero did not die in vain, but died for the purposes of God. To serve Him, and that something of his spirit will enter those who look upon this cross. The second tusk, I would suggest, should be bought by the Government as a natural curiosity and hung, suitably mounted, either in your Excellency's official residence, or in the Museum of Natural History.

But a further paradox, the tails, whose stumpy hairs were white, the eyelashes, and many other parts of these great beasts were removed by the natives at once, and are, I understand, already in the hands of the witch doctor, Tembula, who is to blame, from what I can make out, for the first of these tragedies—the death of the native, Mashupa, his wife, N'Tembi, and their child. Since it was he who told the young man that to expiate his crime of marrying within the elephant totem he must live among them.

All this passes the comprehension of the ordinary man, like myself, and I am left only with a contrite heart and a soul filled with wonder at the strangeness of life and the wonderful ways in which the Almighty directs the destinies of men. God did not wish Senhor Carew to die, so he was saved. But Maniero He took to His bosom. Maniero, my friend, the reaper of the forest. Perhaps, as I am told the

American Indians believe, there is a happy hunting ground in the future. Perhaps Maniero, the lover and protector of all wild things, still hunts in celestial regions, for it is hard to imagine him out of the wilds. Perhaps, even in heaven, there are wildernesses and forests, a separate heaven for the wild animals and those men who are only happy among them.

I now close this letter with a renewed apology for the liberty I have taken in writing it, and trust that the exceptional circumstances which caused me to write will be justification enough to cause your Excellency to pardon me, and to repeat once more my plea that something substantial be done for Maniero's mother who cannot have many more years to live.

I remain your Excellency's obedient servant,

RAIMUNDO DA SILVA,

Administrator of the District of Querida

Outside, in the burning sunshine, the murderers were weeding the garden that Senhora da Silva had constructed. One of them squatted with a chain attached to a great cannon ball to his ankle. He was no worse a murderer than the others. His only crime had been to strike his mother-in-law too hard, with too big a stick, so that she died. The cannon ball was the penalty of an escape from the Poste. It anchored him, and before he could move along the bed he was weeding, he had to move the ball with his two hands. His colleagues laughed at him because he had been so foolish as to walk off instead of remaining contentedly till the time of punishment was done, and obtaining his discharge like a sensible man. He was, in fact, a stupid murderer.

In the kraals in the district forest, the people were happy because their bellies were full of elephant meat, that was more than mere meat, that possessed the special significance of the lame one and his brother who had been inhabited by the spirits of the departed kings, conferring, by homœopathic means, great courage and long life upon those who had consumed it. This was the same belief, in another form, that led men to eat lion's flesh for bravery, and certain parts of the bull for potency. The same which caused the Chinese to partake of rhinoceros horn as an aphrodisiac, a potion which, whether it helped them or not, had led to the near-extermination of the horn-bearers both in the far East and Africa where the white rhinoceros, the easiest to kill, now only exists under protection.

Beyond the kraals and villages, gorged vultures sat on trees or flapped down heavily to the ground to feast on the guts that still festered in the sunshine. Hyenas slept heavily in the ant-bear holes, jackals curled themselves up, nose to tail, under bushes in somnolence induced by satiety. Little was now left of the elephants except the skulls bereft of tusks, the great leg bones, shoulder-blades, and vertebrae. Soon there would be nothing left for any of the denizens of the forest to consume, except the insects, who would find food here for many days. Already armies of ants had penetrated the honeycomb of the skulls and were coming and going in long, soldier columns through its dark corridors.

So the bodies of the great elephants were dissipated like smoke, carried into the air on the wings of the vultures and kites, spread over the veld in the bodies of the scavenging hyenas and jackals, carried from kraal to kraal by the men, women and children and dogs that had partaken of them. The tickbirds that had fed upon the great ones found other hosts, and when the rains came, the last remnant of the leviathans would find its way down into the soil, be fed upon by the roots, and go up into the tree tips again where they had originated. So they joined the bodies of those they had slain. All were absorbed by the forest.

The great baobab, which had been the vegetal centre of these events, remained unchanged. Events were nothing to it.

Nor could it be said that the earth was lightened, for though the inaudible tread of the giants' footsteps was taken from its green skin, the great weight which had been concentrated into the two giant pachyderms was still there, only now distributed into a thousand bodies, its presence everlasting and indestructible.

So ended a myth that was a fact. So was a fact turned into a new myth, cause following effect and effect becoming new cause in the never-ending chain of life, be it that of men, or elephants or trees. For, in life there is no beginning or no end. The end of one thing being the beginning of another. So that life is, indeed, eternal; all living things being brothers in life, and all made of earth, of dust. Being born of it and returning to it—indestructible.

All this was in Da Silva's mind as he put his letter to the Governor-General in the leather Poste bag. All this and Carew's last words to him: 'A man can survive too long . . . Pray for me, Senhor.'

APPENDIX

In the writing of this book a great deal of information was turned up which was irrelevant to the book itself but of interest to nature lovers. The elephant, like the whale, the lion, and the tiger, is one of those animals that somehow has a special appeal to men due to their size, ferocity, or the age to which they live, the intelligence they show, and the references that occur about them in ancient books.

Of them all the elephant is perhaps the most interesting, having almost human intelligence, and being the greatest of those animals which we have the audacity to describe as the servants of man.

Elephants resemble man in their ability to reason, and of this faculty man has taken advantage, taming them to serve his purposes not only in India but in Africa too. To-day in the Congo and yesterday—the yesterday of two thousand years ago—when they served in war, and offered amusement to the blood-hungry audiences of the amphitheatres of Rome in combat with the other wild beasts, lions, tigers, bears, and leopards—competitors for attention in the arena with fights between gladiators and the martyrdom of Christians.

African elephants (the ancestors, perhaps, of the two great beasts in the story) were used in the First Punic War. In the Second Punic War, 218 B.C., thirty-seven elephants were trained to act as a living rampart to hold back the current of the rivers so that the troops could get across. Hannibal defeated the Roman army on the banks of the Rhone by ferrying his troops over the river on rafts drawn by elephants. It was with African elephants that he crossed the Alps, losing half their number, and again in 216 B.C. he put the Roman cavalry to flight by using elephants against them. But when the Romans, having won the war, made a treaty of peace in 201 B.C., one of the clauses of the treaty was that all trained elephants were to be handed over and no more to be broken in for use in battle.

During these wars Hannibal sent to Carthage, where there was stabling for six hundred, for more elephants, and these were sent to him at once from the reserve held there. Some idea of the fertility of this area in those days can be deduced from the fact that an elephant consumes from 900 to 1100 pounds of food a day. These African war elephants were ridden by Nubians, but when in the struggle for Syria they came into contact with the Indian elephants they proved inferior to them, as they did when pitted against them in the Roman games.

In the Indian wars their main purpose was to batter down defences and in 'the Wars of the Princes' from A.D. 1024 on, elephants are mentioned in trains of thousands.

It has been suggested that the elephants used by the Carthaginians were of Indian variety. The Carthaginians were a seafaring people and it would have been possible to import them by sea from India to Iraq and to march them overland to Tyre for trans-shipment to Carthage. On the other hand it is unlikely that the Carthaginians would have sent to the east at a vast expenditure of time and treasure for animals which existed in great numbers at their back door. Appian states 'that the Carthaginians, fearing an invasion by Scipio, collected and trained numbers of elephants in a short time,' which would have been impossible if they had had to send to India for them.

After the Fall of Rome, the secret of taming the African elephant was lost for twelve hundred years and has only recently been revived by the Belgians.

The Indian method of capture and taming are not applicable to the African elephant. The keddah or great kraal is useless, and African elephants must be captured young by driving off or killing their mother and roping them. They must be weaned because they are difficult to raise by hand, being subject to diarrhoea and intestinal troubles, and if cut by the ropes when caught are liable to fatal infections, the elephant's skin, contrary to the popular concept, being very easily damaged. Much more nervous and high-strung than the Indian, the African elephant can only be trained by kindness and never forgives a reprimand or an unjust injury. Some die from this cause, and others from sunstroke, and of a broken heart. Mahouts were first brought from India to train them but were unsuccessful in everything but in teaching the Azande natives the songs and talk that calm and soothe elephants of all kinds—the language of the elephants.

It is probable that modern man has lost many of the old techniques of animal training which were possessed by the ancient civilisations of Assyria, Babylon, Rome, and Egypt.

The Egyptians not only tamed but trained to the chase such animals as wild cats, cheetahs (still in use in India), leopards, striped hyenas, wild dogs (Lycaon), and lions. Lions were used in war and accompanied their masters to battle.

Up to the time of the Roman occupation of Egypt, anyone who could afford to keep lions were allowed to have them. The Assyrian lions were shaved and it is thought that the shaving of poodles may be derivative of this practice. These beasts were allowed the freedom of both palaces and temples. In the temple of the goddess Anahita, the Persian lions were so tame that they caressed the visitors in a friendly manner, and behaved 'with modesty and decency,' or in other words were house-trained.

The Belgian station for the domestication of elephants is at Aru in the North East Congo. Indian elephants were imported in 1910, but died, and the mahouts returned home. But before going they succeeded in teaching some of their techniques to the Azande people.

The best age to catch young elephants has been found to be between twelve and fourteen, and the method used is to stampede the herd by firing shots in the air and then to catch the youngsters with ropes and nets. Should a mother charge to protect her offspring, she is shot.

The training is a very slow process and music is used to charm them. The Carnacs, as the mahouts in Africa are called, approach the elephants that are tethered to trees, waving branches, and chanting a monotonous incantation. As they approach, the elephant closes its eyes and rocks from one foot to the other. According to the director of the station, elephants can be put into a hypnotic trance by songs, and even a stampede can be stopped. It is usually a year before the young animal can be mounted, and ten or more years before it can be put to hard work. Its value then, when fully trained, is about five thousand dollars.

Before the use of gunpowder the elephants were hunted with spears and arrows by the natives. Some were killed by being hamstrung with swords as they slept, or pierced from above, with weighted javelins, by men hidden in the trees, or taken in great pits skilfully covered with branches set in their paths. Sometimes whole herds were exterminated by being ringed in by fire and burnt.

Sometimes they were killed by poisoned darts, or slain in great numbers as they crossed rivers—walking on the bottom with trunks upraised into the air above—where men in canoes severed their trunks and drove spears into them which were attached to floats. The elephants then drowned, for they could not come up, having weighted themselves down like submarines with their bellies full of water. Elephants swim well but seldom need to, as few rivers in Africa are more than fifteen feet deep. But the calves swim beside their mothers, holding on to their ears with tiny trunks.

The trade in ivory is old. Ivory was used three thousand years ago by the Egyptians; and in 445 B.C. Phidias built a great statue of ivory and gold, making it not out of carved ivory but of ivory flattened and processed in a manner unknown to-day, the art having been lost in antiquity, some such statues being as much as forty feet in height. The Romans demanded ivory to ornament their women, the wives and daughters of the patricians; and the prostitutes and slave concubines required it of their masters and lovers, and to this end more elephants died. They demanded until the elephants of Africa, except for the smallest tuskers, were finished off and it had to be sought among the lesser animals of the East, in India, Siam, and Ceylon; and it was not until Rome fell that the elephants were at peace again, since the commerce between Africa and Europe ended with their empire, the Roman loss being the elephants' gain for a thousand years or more.

The natives continued to hunt them sporadically in a planless manner for meat, and because they destroyed their gardens. The ivory, now useless in commerce, was used for door-posts and planted in serried rows as palisades for their mashambas and cattle kraals. An Englishman in the seventeenth century reports having seen piles of tusks in Angola used as bases for the pyramids of human skulls that commemorated the victories of one tribe over another. Then once again the trade began with the slavers, the traders in ivory, both black and white. And the tusks moved in a new direction westwards, in swift wind-driven ships across the Atlantic, sometimes as ballast to a too light cargo of living human flesh. First went the accumulated hoards, the palisades and door-posts transmuted by the alchemy of trade into brass, baubles, rum, and guns. And the hunts began once more and have continued to this day, to this hour.

The ears of elephants are also articles of commerce; the leather from them, being of a singular grain and texture, is suitable for the fine luggage that ladies like. It is stripped in thin sheets from the cartilage, and network of veins, that separates one side from the other, and which, according to some, serves the purpose of a cooling system to the blood as the elephant flaps its extended ears in the heat of the summer sun.

There are innumerable myths and near-myths about elephants and innumerable facts which are so strange that they would appear to be myths. There is, for instance, a great deal of doubt about elephants helping each other when wounded, though a wounded beast may at times be supported by its companions accidentally in the press of a stampede. I have, however, used this incident because it is picturesque and many hunters believe it to be true. But there is no doubt about the fact that elephants sometimes cover their victims with leaves and branches as the birds of the air covered the babes in the wood. Nor can the fact that they tend to visit the place where their companions have been killed and move the bones about, doing this not once only but whenever they are in the vicinity, be questioned. As to the age to which they live, authorities can in no way agree. Almost all the museum people put the age at seventy, approximately that of man. But almost all the hunters put it much higher, some even hazarding 400 years. It would seem probable that 70 is old, as it is for a man, but the 100 is definitely possible, and might easily be exceeded in particular cases.

When I wrote and told Colonel Charles Pitman, the famous Uganda warden, that I was going to make my elephants 200 years old, he said it was too much, and considered such an age utterly impossible. He thought even 120 years was stretching a point, but might get by without provoking undue criticism.

Mr John Tee-Van, in a letter to Mr Fairfield Osborn, of the New York Zoological Society, stated that there were a number of estimated ages running up to 98 years, but that they always gave the maximum age as 70.

In 1891 W. T. Blanford wrote that an elephant is fully grown but not fully maturing till it is 25 years of age and individuals have been known to live to over 150 years in captivity. Major Flower, however, in his paper, *The Duration of Life in Vertebrate Animals*, questions the remark and much regrets not being able at present to agree with his statement.

Mr T. C. S. Morrison-Scott of the British Museum of Natural History states that elephants lose their last teeth long before they could possibly reach the age of 200, and says that the greatest well-authenticated age any elephant, Indian or African, has attained is 67.

Dr G. J. Broekhuysen of the University of Cape Town agrees with the others that elephants do not live more than 70 years.

The late Dr F. C. Simpson, R.V.S., Veterinary Surgeon to the Pretoria Zoo, however, states that in freedom elephants have been known to live 100 to 150 years, possibly 200, but in captivity their allotted span is much the same as in a human being, threescore and ten, but that probably 40 or 50 is nearer the mark. This refers to the Indian and Burmese elephants, but the African, owing to the climate, environment, and its general hardihood, will often exceed these figures by perhaps 20 or 30 years. When in freedom, he may attain 150 to 200 years. At least one case of a Burmese elephant is on record in which the animal served with the Dutch government for 143 years, from 1656 to 1799. Burmans consider that elephants live from 80 to 150 years.

John Taylor, the American ivory hunter, after a lifetime's experience in all parts of the continent, believes that elephants may live to 200 years, and even 250 or 300 in exceptional cases.

Major P. J. Pretorius—possibly the greatest elephant hunter of our times—judging from experiments made with elephants he had captured, found that elephants' ivory grows at the rate of from ¾ of a lb. to 1 lb. (in each tusk) each year, so that the age of an elephant whose tusks weigh 250 lb. each must be very great, possibly almost 300 years old.

The reader can now, having the evidence, decide for himself. But it would appear to me that in freedom and on a natural diet 150 years should not be impossible, though

70 years is probably the maximum age of a working elephant on a restricted diet. There is no reason to imagine that work and a poor diet does not age both elephants and men. And if men can live to well over a hundred, as they are believed to do in the Balkans, on a diet of whole grain and sour mare's milk, it is not impossbile that wild elephants should equal them in age. (It should be noted that there are some 2000 centenarians in the United States to-day.)

As far as dentition is concerned, there is further controversy: one authority stating that elephants lose their teeth with age, and would therefore die of starvation, and another, Dr Simpson, veterinarian to the Pretoria Zoo, giving a detailed description of their teeth and asserting that as their molars wear out they are replaced.

In a letter to me he states:

Dentition: Besides the tusks—which start as shown in males at birth—growing from the pre-maxillary bone, elephants possess massive, molar, grinding teeth, only four of which are present in their mouth at a time. One on either side of the upper jaw and one on either side of the lower jaw. Only the fully developed molars or a portion of an oncoming molar come into wear at the same time. This applies to both the Indian and African elephant.

1st	set (milk teeth)		1st year
2nd	” permanent teeth		2nd year
3rd	”	”	”	2nd to 6th year
4th	”	”	”	6th to 10th year
5th	”	”	”	10th to 14th year
6th	”	”	”	14th to 19th year
7th	”	”	”	19th to 25th year

After which the molars continue to be shed and replaced at increasing intervals during the rest of life. Only the shells of the molars are shed, owing to the grinding surface being gradually worn away and the fangs or solid lower portion of the teeth being absorbed by the continuous pressure from the advancing new set.

As to the tusks, here we are on firm ground, all authorities being in agreement.

The world's record tusks are in the American Heads and Horns Museum. The left tusk of one pair is 11 ft. 5½ in., and the right, 11 ft. long. (Unless they have been damaged by accident, tusks are usually approximately the same length and seldom differ more than 5 lb. in weight. This difference is due to the elephant's being right- or left-tusked—handed—and therefore using one more than the other for digging.) The circumference of the larger of these tusks is 15½ in., and the net weight of the pair is 293 lb. Another pair of tusks in the American Museum measures 10 ft. 4 in. and weighs 336 lb., their maximum circumferences being 19½ in.

Tusks vary in colour from the traditional ivory white, through various shades of brown and sepia, to almost black. The colour depends on the age of the elephant, its habits, and the area which it inhabits. Most tusks that come on the market have been scraped to enhance their appearance. Tuskless elephants are not uncommon and multiple-tusked elephants occur. These animals appear to be venerated by the others of their kind. There are also elephants which have only one tusk.

Breeding may start with the Indian elephant as early as the twelfth year, and from the eighteenth to the twentieth year with the African elephant.

Gestation is about 20 months, but believed to be slightly longer if the calf is a bull. The average period between births is 2½ years, and cows may become pregnant before the calf at foot is weaned. The young elephant begins to feed itself at about 6 months and is more or less independent, as far as food is concerned, at 6, resembling human children in this respect.

Among Indian elephants, 7 is the average number of calves born to a cow. Twins occur and calves of different ages are often seen following their mother. For the first month, a cow can pick up her calf, wrapping it in her trunk.

Milk: Elephants have proved very hard to raise by hand, being very susceptible to diarrhoea, though Major Pretorius had the milk analysed and it was found to contain 100 times more albumen than cow's milk. He then evolved a formula with which he raised several. It consisted of 1 gallon of cow's milk, ½ pint of cream, the whites of 24 eggs, and 4 lb. of boiled rice.

Very young elephants become tame almost at once when their mother is killed and will follow a man like a dog within a few hours,

In Burma, when the mother of a sacred white elephant died, it was suckled by twenty young Burmese women and successfully raised.

The mating of elephants resembles that of the other large herbivorous animals, the bull mounting the cow. He remains in position for three or four minutes with his legs along her back, and as the act is consummated he stands almost upright with his feet on her hindquarters. Elephants appear to fall in love, and meet each other away from the herd in a courtship which is remarkable among animals for its gentleness. Fights, often to the death, occur between bulls when a second bull appears on the scene.

Musth begins between the ages of 20 and 40, during the hot months which are the breeding season. After 45, the fury of musth decreases. Most elephants will mate when not in musth. The exact cause of musth is not known, but it is accompanied by mental disturbances and fury. No elephant is trustworthy at this time and nothing can satisfy it. It has been suggested that the discharge rubbed against foliage indicates the presence of a bull in this condition and attracts the cows to him. The brown, evil-smelling matter runs down the elephant's face into his mouth, and its taste appears to exasperate him.

Height of African elephants— 8 to 11 ft.
Weight   "   "   — 3000 to 7000 lb.

An elephant drinks 20 to 30 gallons a day, but can go without water for several days.

An elephant requires up to 1100 lb. of forage per day.

Elephants need very little sleep, 3 to 5 hours being enough. They usually sleep standing, shifting their weight from one foreleg to the other. But upon occasion they lie down, sometimes even using a large antheap as a pillow.

SOME REMARKS ON OTHER ANIMALS AND THE TREES OF THE LOW COUNTRY

BABOONS: Baboons are not afraid of women whether they are white or coloured, and will rob lands and gardens when they are present, quite fearlessly.

There is, however, no record of a baboon ever attacking a woman sexually. But there is reason to believe that they have carried off and raised small children, and there is at least one case on record (Major P. J. Pretorius) of a man-eating baboon. This baboon would attack natives as they came down the path and tear open their stomachs. It would then break their skulls and eat the brains. In Zululand, baboons have been known (Captain Potter) to surround young bush buck, tear them to pieces and eat them. And farmers suffer from their depredations among lambs and kids which they kill for the milk in their bellies. The near extermination of leopards has led to a vast increase of baboons, and the burning of the mountains has deprived them of much of their natural food which consisted of fruit and berry-bearing bushes and edible roots. So once again man is paying for his disturbance of the balance of nature.

HYENAS: Are not known to have killed a man, but they will attack sleeping men and bite off a heel, or even take off the whole mask of the face with a single bite.

The low veld is remarkable for the beauty and variety of its bush and trees. Here are notes on some of the more interesting.

The Baobab or Cream of Tartar Tree—*Adansonia Digitata:* Deciduous. Height: up to 175 ft. with a diameter of 100 ft. Flowers: large, white, and showy. Fruit: 5 to 6 in. long. 3 in. wide, but may be much larger. The hard seeds are embedded in a white pulp which, when mixed with water, gives a refreshing, acid drink. The largest trees are probably thousands of years old. Often hollow, and may contain water. Sometimes used as dwellings or to store grain by natives. Can be raised from seed.

Hardekool—*Combretum imberbe:* Deciduous hardwood tree reaching 70 ft., with a diameter of 4 ft. The wood is ant-proof and very hard. It was used for hoes before iron could be obtained by the natives.

Jakkalsbessie—*Diospyros mespiliformis:* A large tree, evergreen. Height: 60 ft., with a diameter of 3 ft. Because of its fruit, it is seldom cut down by the natives.

Sausage Tree—*Kigelia pinnata:* Evergreen. Height: 30 ft.,

with a diameter of 3 ft. Large, leathery leaves and dark red flowers. Fruit: cucumber-shaped, up to 2 ft. long and 2 in. wide. Heavy, hard, not edible.

Marula—*Sclerocaraya caffra:* Deciduous. Height: up to 30 ft., and 3 ft. in diameter. Has male and female flowers. Fruits like small plums, much relished by natives for making beer, and eaten by wild animals including elephants. Each fruit contains an edible seed or nut.

Tamboti—*Spirostachys africana:* Deciduous hardwood. Foliage turns red in fall. Height: 40 ft., and 18 in. in diameter. Sap is milky and dangerous to the eyes. Timber: very handsome golden yellow with black heartwood. Fragrant.

Fontana African Novels

My Mercedes is Bigger Than Yours
Nkem Nwankwo

A hilarious, but also very serious, story of life in modern Nigeria by the author of *Danda*. 'Gentle, finely-judged satire . . . he speaks eloquently of his deeper concerns without ceasing to be lively and entertaining.' *Sunday Times*. 'A tragedy comparable with Dreiser's *American Tragedy*.' *West Africa*

Many Thing You No Understand   Adaora Lily Ulasi
Nigerians *versus* white officials – a comic confrontation set in the colonial Africa of the 1930s. 'Mercilessly funny.' *Sunday Times*

Many Thing Begin for Change   Adaora Lily Ulasi
The riotous sequel to *Many Thing You No Understand*. 'Pleasantly hilarious confrontations between white officials and black tribesmen – the Nigerian pidgin is uncouthly comical.' *Daily Telegraph*

Emperor of the Sea   Obi B. Egbuna
Five strikingly original stories of Nigeria past and present, by one of her most talented young writers.

The Minister's Daughter   Obi B. Egbuna
Young love clashes with the greed of a power-hungry politician in this brilliant satire on life in modern Nigeria.

The African Child   Camara Laye
The story of the author's childhood among the Malinke tribe. 'A remarkable book. Camara Laye is an artist and has written a book which is a work of art.' *Times Literary Supplement*

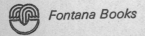 *Fontana Books*

Fontana African Novels

Sunset at Dawn Chukwuemeka Ike

A satire and a love story as well as a story of battle and refugee camps, *Sunset at Dawn* is the definitive novel of the tragic Biafran war. 'Mr Ike tells a human story with skill and humour.' *Sunday Times*

The Potter's Wheel Chukwuemeka Ike

'A sympathetic eye for details of family life and local customs make this a memorable book.' *Daily Telegraph*. '*The Potter's Wheel* is utterly delicious.' *The Times*

The Naked Gods Chukwuemeka Ike

'Brilliant . . . funnily entertaining . . . conflicts in a university campus, with sex, juju and witchcraft thrown in for good measure.' *Birmingham Post*

Toads for Supper Chukwuemeka Ike

'Scores a bulls-eye for Nigerian writing.' *Guardian*. 'Charmingly funny, touching yet sad . . . executed with vivacity and deftness.' *Sunday Telegraph*

Modern African Stories
                              Edited by Charles R. Larson
More Modern African Stories
                              Edited by Charles R. Larson

Two collections that cover the spectrum of African story-telling, from folk tales masterfully retold to sophisticated and caustic stories of protest and culture clash.

Voices of Africa *Edited by Barbara Nolen*
More Voices of Africa *Edited by Barbara Nolen*

Stories, poetry and drama from yesterday and today—by some of modern Africa's most famous authors.

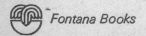 *Fontana Books*

Eric Ambler

A world of espionage and counter-espionage, of sudden violence and treacherous calm; of blackmailers, murderers, gun-runners—and none too virtuous heroes. This is the world of Eric Ambler. 'Unquestionably our best thriller writer.' *Graham Greene*. 'He is incapable of writing a dull paragraph.' *Sunday Times*. 'Eric Ambler is a master of his craft.' *Sunday Telegraph*

Doctor Frigo

The Dark Frontier

Judgement on Deltchev

The Levanter

The Light of Day

The Mask of Dimitrios

Dirty Story

A Kind of Anger

The Night-Comers

The Intercom Conspiracy

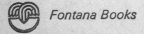 *Fontana Books*

Fontana Books

Fontana is a leading paperback publisher of fiction and non-fiction, with authors ranging from Alistair MacLean, Agatha Christie and Desmond Bagley to Solzhenitsyn and Pasternak, from Gerald Durrell and Joy Adamson to the famous Modern Masters series.

In addition to a wide-ranging collection of internationally popular writers of fiction, Fontana also has an outstanding reputation for history, natural history, military history, psychology, psychiatry, politics, economics, religion and the social sciences.

All Fontana books are available at your bookshop or newsagent; or can be ordered direct. Just fill in the form and list the titles you want.